RICK PARTLOW

DROP TROOPER BOOK EIGHT

RELEASE POINT

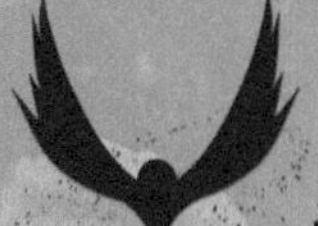

www.aethonbooks.com

RELEASE POINT
©2021 RICK PARTLOW

Aethon Books
www.aethonbooks.com

Print and eBook formatting by Steve Beaulieu.

Published by Aethon Books LLC.

Aethon Books is not responsible for websites (or their content) that are not owned by the publisher.

CONTACT FRONT
KINETIC STRIKE
DANGER CLOSE
DIRECT FIRE
HOME FRONT
FIRE BASE
SHOCK ACTION
RELEASE POINT
KILL BOX

[1]

I squinted my resentment at the afternoon glare. Tahn-Skyyiah was too close to its star for my taste and we were lucky enough to catch Tahn-Khandranda in mid-summer. We weren't even off the ramp from the shuttle and I was already sweating.

"I don't remember it being this hot the last time I was here," I murmured as an aside to Vicky.

Vicky Sandoval looked much more at home in her Marine uniform than I felt, and she definitely seemed more likely to be wearing captain's bars than I was. She'd even cut her hair to make the 'face jacks in her temples more prominent. I liked her with short hair. I liked her with long hair too, of course.

"Last time you were here," she reminded me, "you were in a battlesuit."

"I wish I was in one now."

"You and me both, bud," Wade Cunningham said from over my right shoulder, and I realized I'd spoken too loudly.

If the discomfort I felt had been illustrated in a dictionary, Wade's face would have been the picture they used. He wasn't a handsome man at the best of times and the heat reflecting off the fusion-form pavement of the Tahn-Khandranda spaceport had turned his face beet-red.

"That's *Captain* Bud," I reminded him, smirking.

"Oh, you can shove that, *sir*," he said, tugging at the collar of his fatigue top. "I've been working for Colonel Hachette a lot longer than you have, and just because they didn't have time to send me to OCS doesn't mean I'm suddenly going to be fetching you your Goddamned slippers and coffee in the morning."

"You can do that for me, then, Wade." Vicky smacked him on the arm. "Get into character; our ride's coming."

I followed her gesture to the road heading up from the city. It took me a second to see the groundcar because I couldn't look away from the buildings. Everything looked so neat and clean now. Twisting towers clawed their way to the auburn sky, obelisks that might have made their home in ancient Egypt if the Egyptians had achieved starflight. It all had a surreal haze over it, as if I'd stepped back into the past.

The last time I'd seen it, it had been on fire, in ruins, littered with dead bodies. Ours and theirs. We'd assumed the Tahni would stick their civilians in the underground shelters the way they had on others of their worlds, but not here. Here, they'd put their anti-aircraft missiles on the tops of apartment buildings full of noncombatants, sent their fighters on strafing runs through their own neighborhoods. They hadn't given a shit. This had been it for them, the last stand.

They'd lost, and they'd probably figured that was it, that we'd wipe them out to the last male, female, and child, because that was what they would have done to us. But we hadn't, of course. Not because we were better than them, but because you can't make money off dead aliens, and the Corporate Council never passed up a chance to make money. I hadn't really known during the war just how deep their hooks ran into the Commonwealth government, but I'd learned quickly after I'd taken up Wade's offer to work for the Corporate Security Force.

That had been a cover, of course. He'd already been working for Hachette, and he'd recruited us into the CSF to bring us into the task force. I hadn't had the chance to ask him, but I wondered if he resented the fact that Vicky and I had horned in on the whole operation.

The car grew from a black dot at the edge of my vision to something oblong, boxy, and ugly in its practicality. It had to be human, I thought. Not that the Tahni were incapable of ugliness, far from it, but with them, I always got the impression it was from the differences between us. This was intentional ugliness, something that had to be a product of a government contract. Only the military could buy a car this ugly on purpose.

It skidded to a stop in front of us and we made no move toward it. Every step meant more sweat and we'd all be sweating enough before this was done. The side door slid open, the motors grinding from the ravages of sand and disrepair, to reveal a woman in a black uniform, her hair pulled back into a severe bun that matched her features. I thought less of her presence than I did of the blast of cold air coming from the vehicle and I surged toward it instinctively.

"You Alvarez?" the Intelligence officer asked me.

"Yeah." I nodded toward her. "You're Geiger?"

Vicky slid into the seat beside me and Wade squeezed in past us with an impatient grunt, yanking the door closed.

"Thank God," he hissed, sinking into the cheap, plastic chair, pulling the safety harness across his chest.

"I am," the woman confirmed, turning back to the controls. No autonomous vehicles in the military. Supposedly because we didn't trust AI, but mostly to give all those privates jobs.

"Don't captains rate a driver in this posting?" I asked her, frowning as she pulled away from the shuttle.

Marine battlesuits stood at the edge of the landing field, silent sentinels, unmoved by the glaring wrath of the primary star, uncaring of the millions of potential enemies to their front. I watched them through the windshield until they slid off to the side, almost forgetting the question I'd asked Geiger.

"I was told this was compartmentalized," Captain Geiger told me, shooting me a glance, her eyebrow cocked upward. "You want some enlisted puke talking about your visit over a few beers?"

"It *is* compartmentalized," Vicky said. "Are you in the compartment, Captain?"

Geiger laughed. It wasn't an unpleasant sound, though somehow, I'd imagined it would be, given the harshness of her expression.

"It's all need to know. And all I need to know is where I'm supposed to take you."

"How long have you been stationed here?" I asked her.

"Since the end of the war. Every Goddamned minute of it."

"Jesus," Wade hissed. "Don't they even give you leave or something?"

"I'm saving it all for terminal leave," Geiger told him, and if I couldn't see her smile, I could hear it. "In six months, I'm out of here and out of the Space Fleet and heading for Eden with enough credit in my account to buy a house in the mountains."

"Are we going straight there?"

I was trying to drag the conversation, kicking and screaming if need be, back to the task at hand. Not that I was suddenly such a straight-arrow, hard-charging Marine just because I'd made captain, but there was a time pressure. Somewhere, Zan-Thint was sitting on that last Skrela seed pod, and I couldn't think of a single good reason for him to refrain from setting that nightmare loose on the Commonwealth. Except sanity, and I was pretty sure he didn't suffer from that particular malady.

Geiger laughed sharply.

"No, we're not going there in this piece of shit. Not unless you want our informant to get stoned to death by his neighbors. We have to sneak in at night in the back of a cargo truck."

I very carefully did *not* snap at her, not just because we were the same rank and it would have been a shitty thing to do, but mostly because we were going to need her help, and pissing her off minutes after we met her didn't seem like a good plan.

"I don't mean to be insensitive," I told her. "But this is a priority assignment. I don't want to get anybody killed, but I'm also not crazy about the idea of waiting around several hours to talk to this guy."

"Nothing to be done about it," she said, shrugging far too casually. "It's too late to reschedule. Don't worry; you guys can hang out in our offices until then."

"Oh, wonderful." Vicky rolled her eyes, then leaned into my shoulder. "Hachette's going to shit a brick."

I remembered his mission briefing and didn't disagree.

"We need intelligence on Firbolg," he'd said, seeming even more stern than usual, if that was possible, although looking stern in free-fall must have been one of those senior-officer things I hadn't learned yet. "I'd love nothing more than to go tearing in there, guns blazing, and turn that Tahni bastard into incandescent gas, but we don't have the whole Fleet behind us, just this task force, and I need to know what we're walking into."

"Why Tahn-Skyyiah?" I'd asked him. "Do we have any reason to believe he's been operational there since all this started?"

Top had answered for him, and I really needed to stop calling her that, since she'd been promoted to sergeant-major, but I couldn't break the habit.

"He hasn't been back to the Tahni homeworld," Sgt.-Major Ellen Campbell told us, boots attached to the deck of the

Orion's conference room by sticky plates in the soles, her hands clasped behind her back. "It would be too risky. But he has to recruit somewhere, and we've got chatter from sources on Tahn-Skyyiah that he had people onplanet recruiting fresh troops up until a few weeks ago. If you can locate one of them, we can find out the sort of numbers we're facing."

"And why us?" Vicky had asked, a lot more direct than I would have been while talking to Hachette. "No disrespect, sir, but neither of us is a spy and, given our last two outings, we're not that great at it. You got anything you want blown up, we're your best bet, but this sounds more like a job for someone with training with the Tahni culture."

"Of course, it is," Top had agreed, the corner of her mouth twisting in the closest she came to a smile. "But you're what we've got and the only other choice is a bunch of Intell geeks who've never heard a shot fired in anger...or a couple of my Marines who've never done any field work."

"Or you," I'd suggested, half-kidding and half-hoping she'd actually come along.

"Oh, sonny," she'd snorted, "when you get to be my age, you know what your strengths and weaknesses are. And subtlety is *not* one of those strengths."

"And anyway, it's an order," Hachette had added, and that had been the end of that.

———

It sucks to lose a war. I don't think I'd ever realized it as much as I did while driving to the Fleet Intelligence headquarters in Tahn-Khandranda that summer afternoon. And it also sucked to have occupation duty. Drop-Troopers in Vigilante suits were at every major intersection, watching like the bogey-man and being watched in return by dark, sunken eyes. I couldn't read

Tahni body language, but I knew resentment even in an alien face, and it was everywhere.

"How would you feel," Vicky whispered next to my ear as if she were reading my mind, "if *we'd* lost and they were on every street corner in Trans Angeles?"

"I'd be dead," I assured her. "And so would you. Because that's the only way they'd get to Earth, over our dead bodies."

The civilian traffic thinned out as we left the lines of Tahni rowhouses behind and rolled into the one section of the city that hadn't been rebuilt in the alien image, the section of ugly, squared-off office buildings and squat, buildfoam warehouses, a canker in the heart of their city reminding them that things would never be the same again.

Roadblocks parted for our vehicle, or for the IFF transponder in it, and the only pedestrians were humans in Fleet and Marine uniforms. The duty troops walked with their heads down, as if they couldn't keep up their focus on their purpose if they looked around them, and the ones off-duty moved with a listless shuffle like the Tahni civilians I'd seen, as if they'd been beaten into submission by the heat and the boredom and the endless, sullen hatred.

"We should've just fusion-bombed this place to ashes," Wade opined, not even trying to keep his voice down.

"I tell myself that same thing every day," Geiger agreed, pulling the van up to the curb beside a one-story, eggshell-white building decorated only by the Commonwealth flag and a small, stenciled sign advertising that this was *Headquarters, 120th Space Fleet Intelligence Brigade, Third Battalion.* "But the brass is smart enough to keep the launch controls out of my hands." She hit a control and the side door slid open. "Last stop. Everybody out."

"I hope to God there's air-conditioning inside," Wade said,

his face already getting red from the brief exposure to the mind-numbing heat.

There was, though I was so conscious of the disdain in the looks Geiger was giving Wade that I did my best not to sigh with relief when the door shut behind us. Tahn-Khandranda in summer wasn't *quite* as bad as the Fleet headquarters on Inferno, but it was a close second, made worse because I'd been spending so much of my time in more temperate climates.

There wasn't a front desk inside the Fleet Intelligence headquarters building, probably because this wasn't a place where people wandered in not knowing what they wanted. Offices were separated by thin partitions, most of them looking as if a stiff breeze would have blown them over, and the functionaries working inside them looked about as happy to be there as I was. Everyone wore Intelligence blacks except for the Marine guards at the front. Not Drop-Troopers, these, not indoors. Force Recon in light body armor, the visors up on their helmets for comfort, their Gauss rifles slung low across their chests.

"Captain?"

Geiger looked around at the voice and so did I. A lieutenant shuffled up to her without enthusiasm, motioning back at one of the few rooms with sturdy walls and a solid, metal door.

"What's up, Jonesy?"

"We got another priest here complaining about the temple," the lieutenant told her, sounding as if he'd rather endure physical torture than talk to the Tahni for one more second. "I tried to pawn him off on Civil Affairs, but they insist that he's a security threat and we have to talk to him before they can clear him to leave."

Geiger sighed, miming ripping out her hair, a theatrical gesture since it was too short to really get a grip on. She eyed us sidelong.

"You wanna come see why I'm retiring early, Alvarez?" she wondered.

I glanced at Vicky and she chuckled, pushing at my shoulder.

"You go ahead," she told me. "I'm going to go to the little girls' room while I have gravity."

Wade didn't even offer, apparently counting on his NCO status to keep him out of it. He didn't announce where he was going, but if I knew him, it was to find some food.

"Sure," I told her, shrugging. Maybe hearing about her troubles with the Tahni would make me forget my own.

The secure room was, I thought, an interrogation center. Nothing else made sense. The table and chairs were bolted to the concrete floor and if I couldn't see the cameras and sensors, I could still feel their presence. The Tahni who sat at the heavy metal table was dressed in flowing robes of strips connected to each other in some mysterious way I'd never been able to figure out. He was somewhere in middle age for one of them, which looked pretty damned old to me, older than anyone I'd seen since Tijuana, with deep lines around his dark, sunken eyes and grey woven through his wiry hair.

He started to rise as Geiger and I came through the door, but the Force Recon guard put a restraining hand on his shoulder and kept him on the chair. The old Tahni glared at the Marine, and I wondered what the priest's attitude to being manhandled was. He gabbled something in their language and a translation system built into the room rendered it in English through my 'link to my ear bud.

"I will not be treated as a common laborer! I am a priest of the Spirit Emperor!"

"No, you're not," Geiger reminded him, leaning against the table with exaggerated casualness, in what would have been an insult to a human, though I wasn't sure that the Tahni would be able to read it. "The worship of the Emperor died with him, with the destruction of your temples to him. You're a priest of the Tahni religion and damned if I know what it is or what it believes in, but it no longer includes any emperor. Now what do you want from me?"

"The worship you've left us is a travesty," the priest growled, "and I am a traitor for agreeing to it, but it remains my duty to tend to the needs of the people, and I will continue to do so until my last breath."

"Glad to hear it," Geiger interrupted. "Now that we've settled that, what the hell do you *want* from me?"

I chuckled, appreciating the Intelligence officer's bluntness if not her diplomatic skills. The Tahni shot me a look that might have been confusion or outrage, but I couldn't tell the difference. I ignored it, resting my shoulder against the wall, arms crossed as if I was watching a soccer game.

"We were promised a new temple," the priest said, smacking a palm against the table with a hollow bang. "If you infidels are going to force us into your unholy sham of a religion, you could at least provide us with a place to meet."

Geiger's jaw worked as if she were chewing up the words before she spat them out.

"You *know* you're supposed to speak to Civil Affairs about this kind of thing, Jon-Fel Non Rog. You've been through this before. I am not in charge of building temples and I can't tell the engineers what to do or when to do it."

"I *did* speak to your Civil Affairs!" the priest said, pushing himself to his feet, ignoring the attempt by the Force Recon guard to keep him in his seat. "They tell me the same lies, that they're busy, that they don't have the time to hear my complaints! That the engineers are occupied with rebuilding the city and the temple is not a priority!"

"And why do you think that's a lie?" Geiger's voice was taut with strained patience. "Do you think we should build your temple before we make sure all your people have a place to live, before we make sure you can build your own houses and factories?"

"Do you think my people *care* about houses or jobs more than they care about their very souls?" The Tahni was screaming now, and it was incredibly odd to hear the bellowing echo off the walls in another language before it was repeated in my ear. "You are devils! You've destroyed us all!"

Geiger's lips skinned back from her teeth, her eyes flaring with anger at the Tahni, and she planted herself only centimeters from his face.

"Maybe you should have fucking thought of that before you went to war with us, then."

There was no translation this time, just a scream of incoherent rage as he reached into a fold of his robes and produced the knife. Time froze.

My brain was disconnected from my body, seeming to have all the time in the world to think that the knife had to be ceramic, built to evade detection, and that someone had been careless. Maybe the Civil Affairs people hadn't searched him, or maybe the Marines who'd escorted him to Geiger's office hadn't, or maybe the Marine guards here had assumed someone else had searched him, but the bottom line was, someone had fucked up.

The Force Recon guard didn't see it, the blade concealed by the priest's voluminous robes, and I wasn't sure if Geiger had seen it either. But I had.

The expansion of time was an illusion. So was the extended debate inside my head. All of it had happened in the seconds afterward, shifted backwards in my mind by a trick of perception, the illusion that I was acting out of reasoned debate. In fact, I was acting on instinct, training, habits, things ingrained years ago, and any choices I'd made were in the long past.

The move was basic, learned in unarmed combat training during Boot Camp, reinforced in Armor School and practiced again and again on board the *Iwo Jima*, because there wasn't anything else to do sitting in Transition space. I lunged at him, both hands going to his forearm, catching him above the wrist and leaning my weight into it.

He was damned strong for an old guy, but that had a lot to do with the fact that his tendons and ligaments were attached differently than ours...and maybe that I'd spent too much of the last few months cooped up in a starship. But I didn't have to overpower him and I didn't have to hold on forever, just long enough for Geiger to act.

She was armed. I hadn't noticed it before, because I was so used to everyone around me being armed, but she had a pulse pistol holstered at her side. I didn't care for them, myself. They were big and bulky, built around a focus crystal almost as big as my palm, and they weren't much more effective than a Gyroc sidearm. But they did make quite a mess.

The burst of laser pulses was invisible, but the heat of it turned the air to plasma in a thin, lightning-bolt line between the emitter and the old priest's chest. It was as much of an illusion as my free will. The real damage came from the pressure pulses, and by the time the ionized gas lit the priest's robes afire, the heat from the laser had already turned his blood to steam and blown a hole straight through his torso.

The heat burned my right arm even through the fire-resistant sleeve of my fatigues and I jumped back, cursing and patting at the smoking fabric, thinking she'd shot me as well. The Recon Marine was swinging around his Gauss rifle as if he was going to put another round into the dead body for good measure, but the priest was already sinking to the floor, blood bubbling from his mouth as his life slipped away.

His blood had sprayed across my fatigue shirt, drops of it hitting the side of my neck, scalding it like boiling water, and I wiped at it, the liquid smeared black on my fingers, still hot. I hadn't panicked because it wasn't in my nature, but now the shakes hit me, my heart about to pound out of chest, bile rising in my throat. Geiger flicked the safety back on and shoved the pulse pistol into its holster. She shook her head and offered me an apologetic look.

"Welcome to Tahn-Skyyiah."

[2]

"Are you all right?" Vicky asked, her hand on my shoulder.

I didn't speak. I sat hunched over on the uncomfortable bare metal bed of the cargo truck and held my right arm as if it still hurt, taking comfort in the regular, rhythmic *thump-thump-thump* of the truck's wheels on a rough road never built for individual vehicles. It was easy to lose myself in the swaying and jouncing of the wheels, the baking, stifling oven that was the enclosed cargo compartment. It was easier not to think.

When I thought, I kept reliving the death of the old priest. I didn't know why. I'd seen so many people die, humans and Tahni alike, killed so many of them myself. Why did this one death keep replaying itself in my mind? I hadn't known him. I hadn't liked what I *had* known of him. He surely hadn't meant more to me than my mother, my father, my brother, or all the friends and fellow Marines I'd lost over the years.

The question that kept bugging me, that kept boring into my depths and making this so much worse than it could have been, was whether this was going to be how it was from now on. Because I was as sure as I was of anything in my life, I was certain that the old priest wouldn't be the last person I saw die.

"I'm not what I'd call all right," I told Vicky, "but I'll get through it."

At least Geiger had found me a new shirt.

I wiped sweat out of my eyes and glanced around at the others in the back of the cargo container. It was dark in there, shaded by the canvas covering from what light there was in the city at night, and there wasn't much. The Tahni didn't have much in the way of personal vehicles, and thus, had never seen the need for extensive street lighting. But I could see Captain Geiger's outline against the front of the cargo compartment, a pulse carbine balanced between her knees, steadied loosely in her hands. She was so cool about everything, as if she hadn't just blown a hole through an old priest who was trying to stab her to death.

She'd brought the same Recon Marine along who'd been in the interrogation room with her, though I wasn't sure why. He hadn't done much good against the priest. He was wearing light body armor and carrying a Gauss rifle and I couldn't remember his name for the life of me. His helmet visor was up, but his face was shrouded in shadow and I couldn't tell if he was as unbothered by everything as she was pretending to be.

And that left Wade Cunningham, sitting on the other side of me from Vicky, knees drawn up, pulse carbine cradled across his chest like the son he never had. He hadn't been anywhere near the shooting, but his hands were shaking. I could see it even in the low light. His mouth was a hard line and he clutched his weapon against his chest so hard, it must have left indentations in his skin.

"Wade," I said, nudging him with my shoulder. His eyes darted toward me, a prey animal watching for hunters. "You okay, man?"

"Yeah." He said the word too fast, too automatic. "Yeah, it's just...this place, you know? It's been a long time."

"Oh, yeah, I know," I told him. A thought struck me and I leaned closer, speaking low enough that not even Vicky could hear me. "Does it ever get to you?" He looked a question. "The war. It gets to me, sometimes. I drank pretty hard for a while, when we first got to Hausos."

He shrugged, didn't say a word for a few seconds, and I thought he wasn't going to.

"A little," he finally said. Then he laughed a sharp, humorless snort. "A *lot* at first. It hit me pretty hard when I first got out. Alcohol at first, then drugs for a while. Until I got back in. I *needed* to get back in. Things were a lot better when I got back in."

"What do you think it is?" I asked him. The words were spilling out of their own accord. But I had to say them. I'd held them back too long from myself and it had almost killed me. "What about it gets to you? Because for me, I always thought it was just the people who died. But now, I know it's not. It's the fact I *didn't*."

Wade's eyes were wide.

"That's crazy." But there was no conviction in his protest. "I mean, people die, other people live. It's just like...chance, man. Nothing you can do about it." His voice broke, just a quaver, but I heard it. "It's not my fault."

"No," I agreed, "it's not. But it *feels* like it is. It always feels like it is, doesn't it? Like if we hadn't survived, maybe one of them would have?"

"Maybe. Maybe I just...I felt more like all the times I cheated it, like when I fell in my suit that time on Brigantia. I should've died. Maybe when I cheated, I took someone else's luck."

"But you didn't. And neither did I. And we have to know that, right? We can't go on blaming ourselves."

"Yeah." And maybe that was just as noncommittal as his

denial, but I had to say something, just so he'd know he wasn't the only one.

"We're almost there," Geiger said. I wasn't sure how she'd know back here in the truck bed with us, but I assumed she either had an ear bud or an implant transceiver and was getting a signal from the driver, or maybe even a drone. "Two minutes." She pushed herself to her feet using the buttstock of the carbine and steadied herself against the side of the cargo box as she made her way to the back door. "When we get there, keep quiet and follow me close. No one should be out, but you never know."

Vicky grabbed my shoulder as I was about to stand.

"What were you and Cunningham talking about?"

"He's nervous."

"Shit, so am I," she said, using my arm as leverage to get to her feet. "We're on Tahn-Skyyiah, for God's sake."

The truck was old and beat-up and so were its brakes, and they squealed in protest as the driver pulled to the side. What did Geiger think the Tahni civilians would believe the truck was doing here this time of night? Did this dude get night deliveries at his shop? Did *anyone* in this city? I would have asked, but I'd already established I didn't care. Not to sound speciesist or anything, but there hadn't been one Tahni who'd ever done anything but try to kill me.

Geiger threw the door open and jumped out with Vicky so close, she nearly landed on top of the Intelligence officer. The streets were nearly as dark as the back of the truck, the light of the planet's moon almost perpetually hidden behind a low bank of clouds.

"You could have given us night-vision glasses," I told Geiger, hopping down beside her and Vicky, slinging the carbine over my neck and then double-checking to make sure the safety was on.

"I could have," she agreed, "if I had any. Sgt. Biko here will be our Polish mine detector." She gestured at the Force Recon NCO, who acknowledged the mention with an offhanded salute, then went ahead of us.

This section of the city was the original construction, not the rebuilt people-boxes the Corps of Engineers had popped up to house displaced civilians. The Tahni males generally lived in what might be called townhouses, except their living quarters were on the upper floors while the ground floor was taken up by various sorts of workshops. Some used modern fabricators, some more traditional forges, kilns, and spinning wheels, and when I'd read the briefing on it before the invasion, I'd thought it sounded quaint and kind of nice. In practice, it was ugly and utilitarian, turning every house into a factory instead of every factory into a home.

The first floor of all the buildings bulged outward in a swelling, windowless tumor, sloping upward into straighter lines as they climbed to their full height, which wasn't at all uniform. Some of the buildings were two stories, some four, some as tall as ten, and there didn't seem to be any rhyme or reason to it. The rooftops were jagged, like broken teeth, and gave the city a feral, predatory look even without the battalions of armored Tahni troops hunting through the streets for humans.

Actually, the streets were ghost-town empty and I had to admit that maybe Geiger wasn't stupid after all, and night had been the best time to come. Biko led the way, with Geiger behind him, then Vicky, me and Wade bringing up the rear, walking backwards half the time.

"How far did you say this was?" I asked Geiger after we'd walked what felt like half a kilometer but was probably more like a hundred meters, pushing up closer to her so I wouldn't have to speak too loudly.

"Through this alley," she said, and Biko immediately turned

into a gap between buildings that I hadn't even noticed until she mentioned it. "Keep quiet."

Another hundred meters and I was about to annoy her by asking if we couldn't have parked the truck closer, but then Biko stopped outside something that I knew from experience was the Tahni equivalent of a door. It didn't look too much like a door in Tijuana and nothing at all like one in Trans-Angeles. Tahni doors were curved where ours were straight, angular in weird places, and had their catch down at the bottom, at the same place as what they called a kick-plate, which was a combined door-knocker and knob, somehow. I didn't quite understand the etiquette behind it.

Geiger did, apparently, because she hauled off and kicked it. The sound was hollow, echoing on the other side of the door. Biko held his rifle at low port, watching the door as if he expected a squad of Shock-Troopers to barge through it, but what came instead was the scrawniest, shortest adult Tahni males I'd ever seen. He wasn't old, or at least I didn't think so on first blush, but his face seemed hollow and wizened, and his queue of hair was definitely not wrapped around his neck in the way of a blooded Tahni warrior.

His eyes darted between us, his steam-shovel jaw working nervously.

"Why are there so many of you?" he demanded in heavily-accented English, making motions with his hands and shoulders that no human could have replicated. "By the blood of the Emperor, do you wish to make a public announcement out in the central square and tell the entire city that I am your agent?"

"If you're that worried, Ven-Wan," she snapped back, "then let us inside so we can close the damned door."

The Tahni looked as if he wanted to argue, but he made a sound like a cat about to puke up a hairball and motioned for us all to come inside.

I had never entered a Tahni house by invitation, and never without a Vigilante battlesuit to make the entrance more dramatic. Walking in armed with nothing but a pulse carbine, no armor, no jets, no way to get out of there except the same way I came in, was enough to make the hair on the back of my neck stand up. Or maybe it was the smell that did that.

I was raised on a chicken farm and I spent my formative years living on the streets of the Underground, and that was even before I'd enlisted in the Marine Corps, so my tolerance for stench was pretty high. But there was an otherness to this smell that was worse than the pure strength of it. In all those other places, if I'd been asked to describe the particular scent, I would have been able to give Earthly analogies. Wet dog mixed with nitrogen-based fertilizer. Rat and cockroach shit stirred into a puree with diesel fuel.

Not this. The smell inside the workshop was something organic mixed with something metal mixed with something chemical, and then heated up just to make it even more penetrating, but beyond that, I couldn't have identified it. Nor could I have given an adequate explanation for the machinery stacked on top of what looked like cargo pallets on either side of the central walkway. It used metal slugs for raw materials, and put out a finished product that looked something like the undercarriage for a hand-pulled cart.

"There a big market for wheelbarrows here?" I asked, but this Ven-Wan stared at me, uncomprehending. I guess his cut-rate English classes didn't include the word.

He took us through the workshop into some kind of sitting room or, shit, I don't know, maybe their version of a home office. Anyway, there were the stuffed bean bags they used as chairs and mushroom-shaped tables built into the surface of the tiled floor, and it smelled like food. The lights were burning bright in the corners, the bulbs tubular and a meter long, so bright I flinched away from them when I accidentally looked directly at one. Must have been something about the difference between Tahni and human eyes, and the way theirs were engineered to endure the brighter light from their star.

"You're here," Ven-Wan snapped, making another of those oddly fluid gestures. "You're inside. What do you want, Captain Geiger?"

"Ten-Lenon-Zan-Karan-Thint, the Emperor's Own Hand Over the Souls of 128 Octuples," I broke in, deciding I'd had enough of this asshole's whining. If he made his living as a rat against his own people, I didn't care if he sweated a little. "Or, for the too-long-didn't-read crowd, Colonel Zan-Thint."

Ven-Wan stared at me in silence for a moment, and even though I was no expert in Tahni body language, I was fairly sure I sensed fear in the way he tried to back up into the shadows.

"I know the name," he said, his accent getting stronger, giving the words a sing-song quality. "He hasn't been on the homeworld in years now. Since well before the end of the war."

"Don't waste our time," Geiger said, taking a step toward him, the muzzle of her carbine not raising, but the gun seeming more menacing just the same. "We know he's been recruiting fighters here in Tahn-Khandranda for his rebellion against the Commonwealth. We've picked some of his low-level people before, with your help. What we need is to find someone who actually knows something. The guy who hires the guys we've picked up."

"If I had someone like that," Ven-Wan protested, "don't you think I'd have sold them out to you by now? Look at me!" He tapped a long, multi-jointed finger against his sunken chest. "I'm no warrior! No recruiter looking for rebels is going to come trying to get me to sign up with them."

"Don't give me that shit." Geiger let her carbine fall to her side and grabbed the Tahni male by the front of his tunic, jerking him out of the corner and out of the shadows. "Nothing happens in this city without you hearing about it. You either know who's been doing the recruiting or you know someone they've contacted." Her demeanor changed and I blinked, caught off-guard by her doing both the good cop *and* the bad cop all on her own. She smoothed down the section of his shirt she'd ruffled, her palm resting against his chest. "We've given you a good life here, Ven-Wan, but I *know* what you really want."

"You know nothing of me, human," the Tahni insisted, but it was a weak protest.

"You want power," Geiger went on, making it sound like the most reasonable thing in the world. "You want influence. You want what we humans call *face,* and most of all, you want to mate. You want children of your own, but no female is interested because you bring nothing to the table. Your genes are bad, your business is only mildly successful and most of that is due to the money you get from us, and you never served in the military. You aren't even a priest, which seems to be the last refuge of the truly desperate in your society."

Ven-Wan was a small male, not someone I could even imagine trying something violent, but I kept a close eye on him even so, because those words would have set off even the most passive human I knew. But the Tahni, as I knew but somehow couldn't yet accept, were not human, and Ven-Wan said nothing, staring at Geiger as if waiting for her to finish.

"And I am prepared to offer you that power and influence," she told him. "We control the civilian government, and if we tell them to make you, for instance, the legal magistrate for this section of the city, well...they don't have much choice but to do it. And once you have that position, you can use it to strongarm the Tahni you don't like, or who don't like you, into accepting you...and that's sure to catch the attention of one of the more desirable females, isn't it?"

"Damn, I'm impressed," Vicky admitted, murmuring the words close to my ear.

"By how corrupt the whole setup is?" I asked her. "Or by how good she is at selling it?"

"Bit of both."

"You have this sort of authority?" Ven-Wan asked, never once questioning the morality or ethics of it all, which was not the least bit surprising.

"Of course." Geiger let her hand slide off his chest and took a step back, arms crossed. "You get us in touch with someone close to Zan-Thint, someone who can give us details, and you'll have everything you want. Everything you've *ever* wanted."

"I need to call someone," the Tahni told her. "Excuse me for a moment." Ven-Wan left us in the room and I glanced quickly at Geiger as the Tahni swept through the beaded curtain between rooms.

"Shouldn't one of us go with him?" I hissed, hoping my voice wouldn't carry, or at least that the Tahni's command of English wouldn't be enough to understand a whisper.

"What's he gonna do, run away?" Geiger waved the worry aside. "I know this guy. He's got nowhere else to go."

"I kind of feel bad for him," Wade said, testing the give of one of the bean-bag chairs before falling into it. "He was dealt a pretty bad hand."

"*I* don't feel bad for him," Vicky said, casting a baleful glare after the alien. "Imagine if the situations were reversed. How would you feel about a human who sold us out to the Tahni?"

"They're not humans." I didn't know if I was reminding her or myself. "That's why they're so dangerous. We just *think* we know them."

"I dunno," Wade said, not even trying to keep quiet. "They

seem pretty fuckin' human to me. They grab more than they can hold, they buy in to a kooky religion that tells them they're the chosen ones and anyone who doesn't believe like they do needs to be killed, they stab each other in the back when times get rough." He was staring at the wall, or at something far past it, something long ago maybe. "They start wars that don't make any sense and they'll sell their soul to get power." He laughed, though there was a not stitch of humor in it. "Sounds pretty human."

"Jeez," Biko sighed, leaning against the wall beside something that might have been a candle. "You lot are sure a bunch of cheerful bastards." He had an accent I couldn't place, something between British and Australian, and a face white and bland enough to have been from anywhere in Europe or Oceania. "Is that what happens when you start working for the spooks?"

"It's what happens when you understand what's really going on," Geiger said, sounding no less cynical than Wade. And given what I'd found out since all this started, I wasn't ready to argue with either of them.

I frowned, checking the time on my 'link.

"How long has he been gone?" I asked. Geiger scowled and pushed aside the bead curtain, sticking her head through and looking around.

"Ven-Wan?" she called, then paused a few seconds before repeating it. Then she cursed softly and waved Biko forward.

The Force Recon NCO slapped down his visor and plowed ahead of her, his rifle catching on a string of the beads and pulling them down, trailing behind him like the train on a bridal gown. I followed him, ignoring Geiger's outraged squawk that she should be ahead of me, and found out that the Tahni didn't really do stairs. Instead, a twisting ramp went up to the second level of the townhouse, the walls undecorated and unfinished, bare aggregate. The walls were close and Biko let his rifle drop to an automatic retention position at his side while he drew his sidearm. It wasn't a pulse pistol—it was the same service pistol I'd used in the Corps, though I couldn't remember if I had actually ever fired it during the war. *Zwischenwelt Waffen Herstellung* was the name of the orbital factory where it was made. The ZWH-110 10mm fired a slug on a burst of inert coldgas before the round's internal rocket engine took over. It wasn't a Gyroc weapon, though. The rocket could be guided by the shooter's eye if they were wearing a visor like Biko's or a set of enhanced-optics glasses, which I wish I had. It wasn't much against armor, but Ven-Wan hadn't been wearing any.

The ramp came out into a kitchen, connected to one of those funky Tahni dining rooms that also served as a worship center, with the tables sunken into the floor so they had to bow down in order to get a bite. It was empty, and at the side across from the counter where he'd been prepping a meal, there was a small hatch hanging open, heading out onto a balcony.

I didn't wait for Biko, scrambling out through the little door, the muzzle of my carbine shoved ahead of me. A ladder led down from the balcony, into the alleyway below, and though I couldn't see anything moving, I knew exactly where our Tahni informant had gone.

"Shit," I sighed, pulling back into the kitchen.

"That runty little bastard," Biko added, then snapped something even stronger and smashed the buttstock of his Gauss rifle into the ceramic serving bowl where Ven-Wan had been making his evening meal. The receptacle shattered into a dozen pieces, sending shards of ceramic and sloshing bits of something green and purple flying across the room, and I stepped to the side to avoid getting hit by it.

That's why I saw the movement in the alley.

"There's someone down there," I announced. Biko perked up, but Geiger more so, edging past me to get a better look.

"Is it that low-life piece of shit Ven-Wan?"

"No." I motioned at the shadowy figures, at least a dozen of them. "I think it's the help he called." For the first time since I met her, Captain Geiger seemed at a loss for words.

"Oh, shit."

[3]

"Delta Three, this is Gamma November Actual requesting priority support!"

Geiger was yelling into her 'link despite the fact that it was totally unnecessary, particularly if she had an implant mic. She'd lost her informant and now she was losing her cool, clomping down the ramp to the ground floor even ahead of Sgt. Biko. She hesitated between one step and the next and the Force Recon NCO swore and squeezed around her, running for the door. Not out of it, but to set up security.

"Well, dammit, twenty minutes is *not* good enough!" Geiger snapped at some unlucky junior officer. "We have an immediate threat at this location and we need an air asset out here immediately!"

I tried to move past her, but she slashed her hand in an expansive gesture and nearly smacked me in the face.

"What the hell do you mean the reaction force shuttle is down for maintenance? Don't we have a standing patrol? Where the hell are they?" I made another attempt and her fist slammed into the wall as she swore in frustration. "Twenty minutes out. Right, I should have known. Well, get me a ground patrol out here, then! I know the Vigilantes can get here by then and we at least need them to know we have support coming!"

I grabbed her arm and she speared me with a glare, but I moved past and made sure Vicky and Wade could as well.

"We should make a break for it," Biko suggested, pulling the door open to peek out into the alley. "We could make the truck before they..."

The door was five centimeters thick and constructed of some sort of local wood filler wrapped with fastenings of metal, and the burst of tantalum needles didn't *quite* penetrate all the way through it, but they chewed the shit out of it and splinters of metal and wood spanged off of Biko's helmet, sending him and us stumbling backwards.

"Fuck!" I wasn't sure if he'd shouted it or I had, but the sentiment was universal.

"Get upstairs!" I yelled, waving the others back toward the ramp. "We can't hold down here if they have KE guns!"

"How the fuck did they get them?" Geiger yelled, as if any of us knew or as if her headquarters would understand what she was talking about. "Even the fucking Tahni cops aren't allowed to have lethal weapons!"

"I'm sure breaking the law is foremost in their Goddamned minds right now," Vicky snapped. "Can you get the fuck upstairs before we get stuck down here with the whole bunch of them in our lap?"

Geiger might have replied to that, but I couldn't hear it because another burst of gunfire smacked into the door, this time a half a dozen rounds chopping through it and on through the wall behind it. Biko swore again and stuck his Gauss rifle out the door, firing two rounds in return before he ducked back through and ran up the ramp behind the rest of us.

"You hit anything?" I asked him.

"I think I did," he told me. "At least one of the fuckers went down. But there are about twenty or twenty-five more out there, if the thermal analysis in my helmet's right. We ain't gonna be going out that fucking door!" Another, longer burst and a meter-long chunk of the door split away. "Hell, there ain't gonna be a fucking door in a second!"

Geiger made it to the second floor and was at least quick enough on the uptake to head for the hatch to the balcony, the only other way out that we knew of. She didn't, however, have the tactical sense or the brains to wait for the rest of us and scope the exit out before she tried to climb through it.

"Wait!" I yelled, just a half-second too late.

She was there, and then, the next heartbeat, she was gone, ripped to pieces by a long burst of KE-gun fire, disappearing in an explosion of blood that splattered across the room.

"Goddammit!" I swore, feeling something hot and wet hit me in the face. "Fucking assholes!"

I don't know whether I was pissed more about Geiger dying or about being hit with someone's blood twice in one day, but I knew I was pissed, and I was ready to do something stupid, because everything smart involved us staying in this fucking house and getting killed. I didn't remember picking up her pulse carbine, but it was in my left hand, my own in my right, and I sailed through the hatch to the balcony, hitting on my shoulder and rolling to a crouch.

The Tahni were coming up the ladder. I couldn't see them well just by the light filtering out from the kitchen, but I could make out their silhouettes, the cylindrical cooling jackets of their KE rifles. I didn't aim, not really. Not this close. I just pointed and pulled the triggers, both of them. If the pulse pistol had been a violent flash of contained lightning in the interrogation room, the two carbines fired at once were a thunderstorm seen from a high mountainside, ripping apart the atmosphere and reality itself, turning the night to brief, incandescent day.

I saw the Tahni then, for the space of a second, the duration of the multi-round burst of laserfire. They looked a lot like any other Tahni male, though these were all of military age and had their queues wrapped around their necks in the style of a blooded warrior. They wore black and grey to blend into the night, but no armor, and the plasma sheath set their clothes on fire like a funeral pyre as their corpses rained back down to the street in a haze of steaming blood heated to the boiling point.

With the climbers gone, I straightened and leaned over the balcony, emptying both magazines at the shadowy figures scurrying on the street, scattering them like cockroaches from the light. Both weapons were empty and I tossed Geiger's aside, swapping out the spent magazine from my own and replacing it with a spare from the tactical harness Geiger had given us back at Intelligence headquarters.

"This way!" I yelled, and didn't wait to see if anyone followed.

I had bought us time, a few seconds at least until the enemy regrouped on the ground, and if we wanted to survive, we had to get out of this damned building. I grabbed the ladder and swung out from the balcony, holding on with my left hand, my right pointing the carbine below me, ready to blast anything that moved. Someone had followed me over the edge of the roof, and from the size and the agility, it was Vicky. I hoped Wade and Biko would be smart enough to do the same, but if I was being honest in front of God and everyone, she was the only one I cared about enough to stop if she hadn't come with me.

We were only on the second floor, and I didn't climb the whole way, jumping off about two meters up and landing in a crouch, a twinge hitting my knees from the impact but not enough to slow me down. And then I froze for just a second, realizing I had no idea which way the truck was from here. It wasn't long, but it was time enough for the others to reach the ground beside me.

"This way," Biko grunted, pointing ahead of us. If he was broken up over Geiger's death, he was doing a good job of hiding it, but then, he was a combat vet who'd been working for Intelligence since the end of the war and I figured he'd developed a fair callousness for such things.

Biko had moved out front and I let him, feeling exposed and vulnerable on foot with nothing except a fatigue top between me and a rain of hypersonic metal. It had been a stupid idea to come out here on the down-low, a stupid idea to trust this Ven-Wan, and a Goddamned stupid idea not to have backup hiding just around the corner. And as annoyed as I was at all that stupidity piled on top of each other, I was even more annoyed that the one to blame for it was dead and I couldn't even yell at her.

We hadn't quite made it out of the alley when the Tahni came back in force. I'd figured the ones I chased away wouldn't stay gone long, but they'd beaten my estimations through the virtue of running headlong at us, firing as they went. But so were we.

Biko's Gauss rifle was a slow-firing weapon, built to penetrate armor, firing a round every second, but Wade and Vicky and I took up the slack. The pulse carbines had the weakness of absurdly high energy signatures and a thermal bloom that pointed right back at the shooter like a neon sign, but the enemy already knew we were here, so that part wasn't a worry. There were six or seven of them in the group that came around the corner, and they went down in the blink of an eye, before they could even adjust their aim to take advantage of the streams of plasma marking our positions.

And then everything was silence. I swapped out magazines again, the motions rote, the clatter of the empty on the pavement deafening, and waited for the spots in front of my vision to clear. That was the gun's other weakness. It blinded the shooter just as effectively as it did the shootee.

Biko didn't have that problem and he loped around the corner like he thought his Force Recon body armor was a Get Out of Jail Free card against Tahni KE guns, which I knew for a fact it was not. And he was the one who had the key code for the truck.

"Damn it," I murmured, jogging after him.

Around the corner was a vehicle. Individual vehicles had been rare on Tahn-Skyyiah before the war, but apparently, they were gaining popularity, because these assholes had themselves a passenger van. It was ugly, slapped together from fabricated parts, but it was as roomy as the one that had brought us in from the spaceport and at least eight Tahni were piling into it, planning, I supposed, on a quick escape since their attack had gone sideways on them.

Biko had alternate plans. He took a knee and began firing his Gauss rifle into the front of the van. I didn't know if it was alcohol-fueled or if it ran on batteries or fuel cells, but apparently, whatever it ran on was in the front, because smoke began pouring out of the engine compartment after the third round from Biko's rifle.

Only six of the Tahni exited the vehicle, which I thought meant that the hypersonic tungsten slugs Biko had fired penetrated right through the engine compartment and into the Tahni behind it.

The smart thing to do, the pragmatic thing to do at that point, would have been to hang back and pick off as many of them as we could before they faded back into the darkness, but we hadn't come all this way just to get shot at.

I could have stayed home if I just wanted to get shot at.

"Aim low!" I yelled at the others, then took off running.

The Tahni were stunned, not expecting a counterattack and *definitely* not expecting an idiot, jackhead Drop-Trooper to run at them like a maniac. I swept my carbine's muzzle from left to right and fired it at the pavement at their feet before they could run. Hot tar and molten gravel splashed up at their legs and one of them screamed as he tumbled forward, an eerie, ululating sound like the cry of a banshee. The others started to turn, and it was their last mistake.

More night blindness, more afterimages, and I made up my mind that I was never setting foot on a planet again without some kind of night vision. If the damned military wouldn't pay for enhanced optics glasses, I'd buy a pair of my own. I squeezed my eyes shut and ran the last few steps, opening them in time to see the Tahni who'd gone down crawling toward his KE rifle, the fabric of his lower legs smoking and smoldering.

I kicked the rifle away, then stomped down on his right hand, feeling bones break under the sole of my boot. He screamed again, and while I was not a sadistic person, not prone to hurt people for the sake of it, I didn't mind hearing him scream because he'd killed Geiger right in front of me. Or one of them had and he was the only convenient target.

"Get some flex cuffs on this asshole," I told Biko. "He's coming with us."

The shuttles and the Drop-Troopers and the medics all came too late, of course. The other Tahni had scattered, Ven-Wan was long gone, and Captain Geiger was dead. We'd made it back to the truck about the same time as the shuttle landed at the intersection, and then had to waste another half hour explaining what had happened to the Marine lieutenant in charge of the reaction force. At least the medics stabilized the Tahni, though I don't know if I'd call that a positive. I needed him alive, but I didn't necessarily need him unbroken.

"I need some sleep," Wade moaned, falling into a chair outside the interrogation room, burying his face in his hands. "Or some food. Or some food *and* some sleep."

I didn't reply, intent on searching the cabinets in the office's small kitchen for a cleaning cloth. I finally found one in a drawer and soaked it in water from the sink before using it to scrub my face and hair.

"I could use some sleep," I agreed, "but after watching Geiger get blown apart, I think I can live without eating anytime soon."

There was blood on the cloth and I looked over to Vicky. She was sitting on someone's desk, though I doubted the Intelligence officer would object since it was past midnight and none of them would be in for hours. A stranger looking at her wouldn't have been able to tell that she was in the middle of a pretty good post-adrenaline shake, but I could see it.

"Did I get it all?" I asked her, gesturing at my face.

She nodded, and I thought maybe she didn't trust herself to speak. I slipped an arm around her shoulders and gave her a squeeze and she returned it.

"So much for our milk run," she said quietly. "I hate to say it, but maybe Colonel Hachette was right, maybe we *were* the ones to send out on this operation."

"No, who he *should* have sent was a platoon of Force Recon." That came out sounding more bitter than I'd intended, and I sighed out resentment I hadn't realized I was holding on to. "Which would have meant sending someone who didn't know what the hell was going on and didn't have any experience with Zan-Thint. So yeah, maybe he was right."

"Hey." I looked over at the interrogation room and saw Sgt. Biko standing in the doorway, motioning for us. "He's ready."

The Tahni was strapped into a heavy, padded chair, secured at the wrists, ankles, waist and forehead, the whole setup bolted against the far wall. It didn't look very comfortable and he was already gabbling a long, involved protest that called down the spirit of the Emperor to curse us and the line of our descendants for eight generations, or at least that was how the translator in my 'link interpreted it. I wished there was a way to turn him down the way I could turn down the translation feed in my ear.

"He doesn't sound very cooperative," Vicky observed, crossing her arms as she regarded the Tahni like a researcher watching a lab experiment.

"That's why Bergh is here," Biko said, nodding toward the medical technician standing off to the side, adjusting the settings on some sort of drug pump, plastic tubes from the device running to a patch on the side of the Tahni's neck. "I'm just an NCO and we're fresh out of Intelligence officers, but I figured you'd want me to call in someone to handle the chemical interrogation."

"I appreciate the initiative, Sergeant," I assured him. "Bergh, do your thing."

"We'll start off with a mild sedative," the man decided, waiting until the captive had paused in his never-ending diatribe to take a breath.

It took a few minutes before the sedative took effect, but it was obvious when it did. The steam ran out of the Tahni's screed and his head sagged the quarter of a centimeter or so it could before it came up short against the restraint strap. His eyes were partially hidden under his brow ridges, but they seemed to glaze over and his mouth dropped open a few centimeters, a low moan coming out of his throat.

"That's a *mild* sedative?" Vicky wondered, cocking an eyebrow at Bergh. "Reminds me of when the docs on the *Iwo Jima* used to tell me I might experience some *mild discomfort*."

"Well, it's a little harder to be exact when you're working with the Tahni," Bergh said, shrugging. "He'll talk, though, once I give him the cocktail of barbiturates and hallucinogenics." He traced a line across a menu screen. "There you go. He'll be very suggestible in another couple minutes." Bergh chuckled. "You know, if he were human, this would be so fucking illegal." He shrugged. "Honestly, I'm not one hundred percent sure it's legal even now, but no one's taken it to court yet, so we should be good for now."

"Comforting," I told him, though I was mostly being sarcastic. Among the many worries I had, some overzealous JAG attorney bringing me up on charges ranked pretty low on the list.

The Tahni began babbling, his voice barely above a whisper, his face slack.

"What's your name?" Biko asked him, and speakers in the room repeated the question in Tahni, sounding as if they were coming from all around us, a haunting effect that I guessed was meant to freak him out even more than the drugs.

"Tren-Din Kit Vin." The words came out slurred and I didn't catch them until my translator reiterated them in my ear, amplifying the volume and the clarity. "Commander of three octuples in the High Guard."

Which translated to platoon leader. As I'd assumed, a combat veteran. Not leg infantry, though, which was probably why he was a prisoner and I was alive, since we shared a general lack of experience running around with nothing but a rifle.

Biko turned to me, motioning in invitation toward Kit Vin. I wondered if I should ease into the questions or just jump headfirst. As Vicky and I had reminded the colonel, neither of us was a spy. And Geiger wasn't around to correct my mistakes. I decided to just jump in and hope for the best.

"Why were you at Ven-Wan's house?"

He didn't say anything at first and I waited for a moment before repeating the question, louder this time.

"He called us. He said we needed to kill the infidels who had come to his home, that they could not find out about the General."

"General Zan-Thint?" Vicky interjected.

"He is the right hand of the Spirit Emperor," Kit Vin insisted, straightening as much as his restraints would allow. "He will bring justice to the infidel." He shouted the word like a battle cry...or a chant at a soccer game.

"Did you help to recruit warriors for the General's army?" I asked.

"It was my honor! The only shame is to ignore our duty when the Spirit Emperor calls us."

"Jesus Christ," Wade said, standing in the doorway, staring at the ranting Tahni. "He sounds like a street preacher."

"Close enough," Biko agreed. His helmet was off and I noticed, for the first time, how young he was. I'd imagined him as some hardened veteran, but there was no way he was even thirty yet. "You get used to it, here. Most of 'em are beaten down like they'll never have a happy day again and the rest are like this, Bible thumpers or Muslim fundamentalists, except their god is a bit more material."

I glared at the two of them. Maybe the Tahni couldn't comprehend what they were saying, but maybe he could, and I wanted him in the mood to answer questions, not argue religion.

"Were you going to join the General once you were finished recruiting warriors?" I asked, trying to steer things back to the subject. "Were you going to join him on Firbolg for the last battle?"

"Firbolg?" The Tahni's face screwed up in confusion and I cursed my own stupidity. That was *our* name for the planet. I was searching my memory when Vicky came to my rescue.

"Venlann-Skan," she supplied. "Were you going to join the General on Venlann-Skan before the end?"

"Venlann-Skan." Kit Vin repeated the word again, but this time, it wasn't a question, it was an affirmation. "Venlann-Skan will be the forge where the future of the Tahni is shaped in fire. And I will be at the General's side, bathed in the blood of our enemies!"

I hadn't been aware that Tahni could spit when they talked if they got worked up enough. It might have been a strictly human thing for all I knew, our own particular curse as a species. It was not. One less thing that made us unique, I suppose, because Kit Vin was spraying spittle like it was gunfire and he was trying to kill us all.

"What sort of defenses does the General have on Venlann-Skan?" This was the key, the question we needed answered, but it was also where we might hit a wall. The Tahni was doped up, but he wasn't stupid. Everything we'd asked him so far, he might have discussed with his fellow veterans...in fact, he was probably imagining he *was* discussing it with his fellow veterans. But this was something secret, not something he would tell just anyone.

"The General will slaughter the hunting dogs of the Commonwealth!" He could only have sounded more like a political ideologue spouting his belief system in front of a bar full of college students if he were waving a half-full mug of cheap beer around. "They will walk into his trap and be savaged like the prey they are!"

I sighed. This was going to be harder than I thought.

"Kit Vin!" Vicky snapped, smacking him lightly in the cheek. "Kit Vin!"

The Tahni's eyes seemed to clear and focus on her.

"Kit Vin, the humans have found the fortress at Venlann-

Skan! All is lost! They have a dozen ships and hundreds of troops! What shall we do, my brother?"

Kit Vin's expression wasn't anything near human, but I thought it was an attempt to exude confidence.

"Be not afraid, my friend. He has thousands of troops at his base, High Guard, Shock Troops, the elite. And his fleet will destroy theirs, though it is not as large as it might have been. And once they're gone, the General will unleash the wrath of the gods on the infidel!"

"Does the General keep the faith of our ancestors?" Vicky asked. "Does he still hold that no life shall be taken except by the living hand of a Tahni warrior?"

I raised an eyebrow at my wife in awe and appreciation. Not only did she manage to phrase it in the stilted sort of English that the translators always seemed to assign to the Tahni, she even managed to ask whether or not we'd be facing mines and automated weapons platforms without asking it outright.

"Of course, the General holds with the old ways!" Kit Vin said, the tone the translator gave his words one of outrage. "He would never betray our heritage!"

I nodded to Vicky. Just one more question.

"When, Kit Vin?" I asked. "When will you join the General at Venlann-Skan for the final battle?"

"The time is short." He whispered this part, as if finally coming to something he thought should be kept secret. "He knows the infidels are coming. He calls his warriors to him even now. My place is reserved on one of the human shuttles, concealed in a cargo container. It will not be more than a few days and our time will come."

I shot a look at Biko.

"You might want to check that out," I told him.

"I'll be sure to bring it up with Captain Geiger's boss when I call him." He shrugged. "I assumed you wouldn't want me to do that before we got your information, since you were pretty clear how urgent that was." Biko sighed, as if the death of the officer was just hitting him. "Was it worth it?"

"It's what we needed," I told him. "Whether it's worth it...."

"If you're still alive in a month," Vicky said, "then you'll know it was worth it."

[4]

The *Orion* wasn't much to look at. She had an air of slapdash to her, bits and pieces of other ships jammed together—the massive drive bell and armored fuel storage spheres could have come off a Fleet cruiser, while the habitation drum would have been more at home on a research vessel dedicated to spending long stretches of time floating free in realspace where gravity couldn't be generated by the Transition drive. And the weapons emplacements...well, they weren't anything I had ever seen before on a Fleet ship. Gatling lasers were crammed into every free nook and cranny of the ship, as if some rogue Fleet supply clerk had found a warehouse of the things somewhere and decided it would be simpler to just slap them all onto the same ship to save on the record-keeping. It lacked missile launchers, but it made up for their absence with a laser emitter powerful enough to rival the weapons on Tahni destroyers, and with one other weapon, something I had never seen on any Commonwealth or Tahni military ship.

There was a reason neither we nor the Tahni used railguns as primary weapons. If you're fighting for possession of a star system, you expect to eventually take control of it, to exploit its resources. So, sending tungsten slugs the size of a groundcar sailing out into the shipping lanes at thousands of meters per second, just roaming in orbit around the primary star until they hit something, was bad business. At least it was when fleets were fighting each other, when hundreds of ships were filling space with thousands of missiles. But when a ship was on her own, on a mission as far-ranging as the *Orion*'s, she needed an edge. And the railgun running all along the dorsal spine of the ship was definitely an edge.

I found myself staring at it as the shuttle passed around the ship toward the hangar bay. I'd never seen it fire, but I had the feeling I would before this was over.

"You know," Wade said, snapping me out of my deep thoughts, "she was kind of an asshole."

"What?" I blurted, twisting around in my acceleration couch to look at him.

Wade was staring at the back of Vicky's seat, but he could have been looking at the next galaxy.

"Captain Geiger," he amended. "She was kind of an asshole."

"She was," Vicky agreed. I turned the other way to look at her, all sorts of confused now. She shrugged as if in apology. "She was bad at her job, careless, reckless, and she panicked when the shit hit the fan."

"Okay," I acknowledged, unable to honestly disagree with any of that. "So?"

"She was an asshole," Wade repeated, then squeezed his eyes shut. "But she didn't deserve to go out like that."

Oh. I got it now. We were in microgravity, only the occasional bursts from the shuttle's maneuvering thrusters shoving us one way or the other, yet I felt as if the weight of a world was pressing me into my seat.

"No one deserves it, Wade."

"You know, I volunteered for this," he said, his expression bleak. "I wanted it. I wanted to be back in because I couldn't handle being out. But sometimes, I think this fucking war is never going to end."

I didn't know how to answer that, at least not any way that would make him feel better, so I said nothing. The hangar bay swallowed us up, shutting out the harsh light of the star, a comforting shadow. Another series of loud bangs and hard jolts from the steering jets and a solid thump, and we weren't moving anymore.

"Last stop," Kyler Dunstan called back from the cockpit. "Make sure to take small children by the hand and check the overhead storage for any luggage you might have brought aboard."

"Was that *ever* funny?" Vicky asked him, yanking loose the quick-release for her safety straps.

"Oh, come on," Dunstan said, floating down toward the airlock. "It's *always* been funny." He came up short against the inner lock, pushing the control to cycle the inner and outer doors, since both sides were under pressure. "By the way, Hachette and the sergeant-major want to see you on the bridge."

"Me too?" Wade asked.

"No, just the officers." Dunstan grinned. "Well, the *responsible* officers, not a flaky pilot like me."

"You're just upset because Hachette made you cut your hair," Vicky said, squeezing past him to be the first out of the hatch.

"It's a dirty shame." Dunstan ran a hand over his regulation cut, centimeters shorter than it had been when he'd been a mercenary working for the Corporate Security Force. "All the girls in all the bars between here and the Pirate Worlds who'll cry bitter tears when they see me with this haircut..."

"I don't know if they cover complicated biological processes like this in Flight School," I said, following Vicky through into the hangar bay, "but hair grows back. If you really want to look like a civilian, well...you know, I don't think Hachette would turn you down if you asked for a discharge."

"Oh, hell no, man!" Dunstan said, sounding outraged, his voice echoing through the docking umbilical. "This is the coolest shit I've had the chance to do in years! I mean, getting laid is fine and all, but man cannot live by bread alone, you get where I'm coming from?"

"I don't even think we're speaking the same language, Dunstan," Vicky told him.

"I'll see you guys after," Wade said, waving as he headed down toward the crew quarters while Vicky and I turned toward the bridge. "I'm gonna get some sleep."

And I envied him that, because I had a feeling it was going to be a while before I got the chance.

Hachette and Top were waiting for us on the bridge, and so was Karen Fargo, carrying an issue folding tablet and a stylus. I hadn't expected to see her there, first of all because she wasn't bridge crew, she was an enlisted Marine whose job it was to kill people and break shit, but second because she annoyed the hell out of Top.

"Hey, Cam, Vicky," Fargo said, smiling broadly. Then she blinked as if coming awake. "Sorry, I meant, hello, Captain Alvarez, Captain Sandoval." She giggled. "It's taking a little time for me to get used to being back on active duty." She motioned with the tablet. "Sgt.-Major Campbell has me working as her personal assistant. Isn't that cool?"

"It was either that or try to make her a squad leader," Top said, as close to a whine as I had ever heard coming from the woman.

Ellen Campbell had served in the old United States Marine Corps during the Sino-Russian War and the subsequent Collapse, enlisted in the Commonwealth Marines during the First War with the Tahni and stayed in through the Pirate Wars and the Second War, seen countless battles, unimaginable death and destruction. But all it had taken was a few weeks' exposure to Karen Fargo to bring her to despair.

"I blame this on you, Alvarez," Top informed me, arching an eyebrow. "And I *will* cut you, promotion or no."

She was kidding. I hoped.

"That didn't go as smoothly as I'd hoped," Hachette told us, hands on his hips.

The man was a walking recruiting poster, square-jawed and clear-eyed, filling out his uniform jacket's shoulders and chest through hours in the gym, and I didn't know when the hell he found the time because I'd never seen him doing anything but work.

"I'd say it went as well as it was going to, given that our contact had no clue what was going on in the city and her informant was double-crossing us," Vicky said, staring the tall man down without a hint of fear. "She got herself killed, but we got the intell you wanted."

Fargo's eyes went wide, though I wasn't sure if it was because she'd found out someone had died or because she couldn't believe Vicky would talk to Colonel Hachette that way. It might have been the latter because I thought I saw a few sideways glances from the bridge crew.

"Maybe," I amended. At Vicky's raised eyebrow, I shrugged. "We don't know that this guy Ven-Wan was clued in to Zan-Thint's plans. He was a street recruiter. He thought he was going to be in on the big apocalyptic battle when the Tahni saints come marching in, but that doesn't mean he *actually* knew anything."

"Well, aren't you just the font of sunshine and happiness,

Captain Alvarez?" Top sighed. She looked back to Hachette. "Unfortunately, he's right. We can't be sure."

"Who can be sure of anything?" Hachette asked, staring at the star map with Fomor highlighted in red.

I resisted an urge to laugh. *That* was the military intelligence I recalled from the war.

"We don't have any choice," Top mused. "If we wait any longer, he could set that Goddamned pod thing loose and we'll be chasing alien monsters all around the fucking Cluster. I don't know how we even got this far without him doing it." She didn't quite scowl at Hachette, but I could tell she was having a hard time controlling herself. "I was against this little detour from the get-go, if you remember. Sir."

"Oh, I'm sure you'll never let me forget it, Sergeant-Major," Hachette told her, rolling his eyes. He raised his hands in surrender, and I guess I shouldn't have been surprised that even a full bird colonel in charge of a super-top-secret task force was cowed by Top. The only person I'd known who wasn't had been Captain Covington. "Okay, perhaps you were right. But right now, we have a decision to make, and we can't wait for better intelligence." He looked to Vicky and me. "You two know Zan-Thint better than anyone. You've talked to him. If we run hot right into Fomor, go in guns blazing, is he going to stand and fight or retreat and try to preserve his military force?"

Oh, wonderful. Put that ball right in our court, a couple of newly-minted captains. I suppose that isn't really fair. He was asking our opinion, not foisting the decision off on us, and I guess that was better than making the call unilaterally without asking for any advice.

"He's ready to die for his cause, that's for certain," Vicky said, rescuing me from having to make the first assessment. "But it's not his first choice. He's willing to sacrifice his people if he has to, but I think it's always the mission first with him. And if he doesn't throw his own life away, it's because he thinks he's the best one to accomplish that mission."

I tried to build on her thinking, sounding it out as I spoke.

"Yeah, he had the chance to stand and fight on Bathala, but he took off and kept himself in play. He's not looking to be a martyr; he's looking to be the HMFIC at the end of all this."

"HMFIC?" Fargo repeated, squinting at me with obvious incomprehension.

"Head Mother-Fucker In Charge," Vicky explained to her.

"This guy Ven-Wan thought Zan-Thint wanted a last stand," I went on. "But I think he'll only fight if he thinks he can take us."

"What would you recommend, then?" Hachette wanted to know.

I considered that for a second, hoping Vicky might jump in again to give me more time to think, but this time, she stared at me and shook her head.

"Your SOP would be to jump into the outer system, right?" I asked. "Take a look around before we commit?"

"Of course," Hachette agreed.

"He's going to have early warning out there. If you want my opinion, we should jump in as close as we can and start orbital bombardment before we even launch troop transports. You keep his ships engaged, the assault shuttles and missile cutters keep his landers trapped, and we lead the ground assault and try to trap him on the planet."

Vicky was nodding.

"It's simple," she said. "But I think that's the best bet unless you're ready to bring the rest of the Fleet into this."

"Not an option," Hachette declared. "Even if I'd been given the clearance to call in support from the Fleet by General Murdock, there's no time to organize it. Sgt.-Major Campbell is correct, we really couldn't even afford this detour." He sighed.

"I suppose you can blame it on an Intelligence officer's instinct not to proceed without more data."

"The time for talking is over, sir," Top said, respectful but unyielding. "We need to go end this."

"Captain Nance," Hachette said, addressing the ship's master, who I don't believe I'd said two words to the entire time we'd been a part of the task force. The ship's flight crew seemed to regard those of us assigned to the Intelligence end of things as off-limits, like we might tell them some secret by accident and have to kill them. Nance was a doughy, shapeless sort, with a face that looked like wet clay ready for molding.

"Colonel?" Nance responded, looking up from the display at his command station, acting as if he hadn't overheard any of the conversation and had no idea why Hachette would be asking for him.

"Take us out of orbit. One-gravity burn to the nearest Transition node, and have your navigator lay in a course for Firbolg in the Fomor system."

"Aye, sir." Nance touched a control on his command station, and when he spoke again, his voice echoed through the ship and over the earbud of my 'link. "Attention *Orion*, this is the captain. Secure rotational drum for immediate departure. All hands to their stations. One gravity acceleration in five minutes. Repeat, one gravity acceleration in five minutes."

An alarm klaxon began to sound, adding to the urgency. On one of the small sections of the main screen that showed an exterior view of the ship from somewhere on the drive bell, the armored swell that was the rotational drum began to grind to a slow but inevitable halt. The crew inside would already be abandoning the area, heading for duty stations aligned vertically with the drive, ready for the blast of fusion energy to make aft down. Once we were in Transition Space, the field generators that kept us enclosed in a bubble of realspace inside that other reality would also serve to generate a gravity field. On smaller craft, like Dunstan's cutter, it was more efficient to arrange it horizontally, to make the eventual down perpendicular to the fusion drive since the crew was small and no one would be moving around the ship when it was under acceleration. Not on a vessel of this size, and not on the troop transports Vicky and I had ridden during the war. Down was always in the direction of the fusion drive, whether it was lit or not.

When five minutes had counted down and the orders were repeated between Nance and his Helm officer, the entire super-structure of the ship rumbled like distant thunder, vibrating for a long moment before the shaking disappeared and the ship settled into the rhythm of the fusion drive. The sticky plates in my ship boots that had been holding me to the deckplates became suddenly superfluous and my sinuses went back to the business of smelling and breathing again.

Everyone looked relieved once we were out of free-fall, from the biggest landlubber to the most hardened spacer. If there was anyone who actually liked spending significant time in free-fall, I hadn't met them yet.

"We have a week in Transit to Firbolg," Hachette reminded us. "Get with Captain Solano and get yourself integrated into our Drop-Trooper companies. And if Solano tries to pull time in grade, tell him to come talk to me." He smiled thinly. "Or Sgt.-Major Campbell, if I'm feeling particularly ungenerous."

"What about her?" Vicky asked, motioning toward Fargo.

"What about me?" the younger woman repeated.

"You don't need a Goddamned personal assistant, Top," Vicky scoffed. "But Cam and I might need someone we can count on watching out backs out there. Let her come with us."

"You don't have to twist my arm," Top said. "And I wouldn't recommend it on general principles anyway. Fargo," she gestured at the junior NCO, making a motion, that half a

Catholic cross sign and half a wave goodbye, "I manumit your service to me and sell your debt to these two lunatics."

"You've been reading historical romances again, haven't you, Top?" Vicky asked, laughing softly.

"I am verily certain that I doth not know what you snapes prattle on about," Top affected, waving a pretend handkerchief at her face as if she might faint. "Though if you haven't read it yet, *Honor and Compromise* by Delia St. Clair is excellent."

I stared at Top with horror growing inside my chest, the sort of unreality where everything you thought you'd know about the universe was suddenly proven wrong.

"You *read*?" I asked Top. "*Romance?*"

"Victorian mostly." She seemed not the least bit ashamed of it. "Though Regency will do in a pinch." She tapped a finger against her 'link. "I have enough stored on my private account that I'll never live long enough to finish them all." Her stare was challenging. "What, you don't read? Because I rank people who don't read somewhere on the level of Hell just above child molesters and serial murderers."

"Oh, I read," I assured her. "Captain Covington wouldn't have let me get away with not reading once I'd graduated OCS. Von Clausewitz, Sun Tzu, Stephen Ambrose, John Keegan, Miles Chen.... All the military theorists and historians."

Top snorted and shook her head.

"Son, that ain't reading, it's work." She speared an accusatory finger at me. "You need to let your brain have some fun, something that lets your imagination run wild. Read some damned fiction, boy."

Vicky was staring at me archly, one of those knowing looks I hated, because she'd said the same thing more than once.

"Okay," I acceded. "But I'm not reading Victorian romances."

"Your loss," Top said with a shrug.

"If you ask me," Hachette said, arms crossed, looking down his nose at the thought of historical romances, "you need to check out Robert Heinlein."

I shrugged as I followed Vicky and Fargo off the bridge.

"Never heard of him."

[5]

"What the hell use is it being a captain," I wondered, "if the only thing we're in charge of is the damned Headquarters Platoon?"

"And Fargo," Vicky reminded me. "Don't forget Fargo."

I wanted to glare at her, but it wasn't much use when we were both encased in our Vigilante armor. Though it was probably safer.

"How could I forget Fargo?" I agreed. Particularly when she wouldn't ever shut up and *let* me forget her.

"You know, sir, ma'am," she said, prattling on as if she hadn't heard our private conversation—because she hadn't, "I was thinking, the Fleet has like, new missile cutters, like the ones that Dunstan...I mean, *Lieutenant* Dunstan is flying now. They replaced the old ones and sold them off for surplus. I was wondering why they didn't ever upgrade the Vigilante. I mean, not that it's a bad design or anything. It got the job done and I think it's better than the Tahni version—well, *obviously* it's better than the Tahni version because we kicked their asses in the war. But I mean, why haven't we got a new one by now? It's been like, three years now?"

"Fargo," I interrupted. It didn't take.

"I always thought," she went on as if I hadn't said anything, "that they should do *something* with the interface jacks. I mean, we have them implanted and they let us walk and move in these things without falling over like an idiot, but why can't they hook things up so we can use the interface to fire the weapons? It wouldn't be that hard, you know?"

"*Karen*," I said, raising my voice enough to cut through the chatter.

"Oh, yes, sir?"

"They didn't let us use our interface jacks to fire the weapons because someone would start daydreaming and blow away half their squad," I informed her, "or the side of their dropship. They want us to have to physically pull the trigger to make sure we don't do it by accident."

"Oh, yeah, I can see that," she said brightly, and I sensed another burst of non-stop talking was coming, so I jumped on it.

"As for the reason why they haven't replaced the Vigilante, well...tell me something, who are we going to run into with a better setup that we have to worry about? We're fighting the Tahni right now, *again*, but who else is there? The Pirate World cabals aren't going to be running R&D shops building the Vigilante 2.0. Pretty much the only enemy we'd face who could develop a more advanced battlesuit is the Corporate Council, and they're not going to beat us with their Security Force; they're going to beat us by bribing our own people."

"Oh, wow, I hadn't thought of that."

"Fargo," Vicky put in gently, "you do know we're Transitioning in just a few minutes and then we're going to be dropping onto Firbolg, right?"

"Oh, sure, ma'am! I'm psyched we finally get to take down that asshole Zan-Thint!"

"You've only fought his people once," I reminded her, not so gently. "Why are you so psyched to take him out?"

"Well, it might have only been once, sir, but it sure as heck was enough to make me remember how much I didn't like the Tahni!"

"Fargo, you're going to be attached to us in Headquarters Platoon," I said. "When we hit the ground, Lt. McReady is going to be controlling the Boomers, and you'll be with us."

"If the lieutenant is controlling the Boomers," she asked, "then what are *we* doing?"

Jack and shit. But I couldn't say that. Not that I *wanted* to run the Boomers. They were impressive artillery, basically a heavy coil-gun mounted on a modified Vigilante, but at the cost of mobility and agility. They couldn't run and they couldn't hide and being attached at the hip to a bunch of walking targets wasn't my ideal assignment. McReady could have them.

"The four of us," I told her, trying to make it sound more important than it was, "you, Wade Cunningham, and Vicky and I, are going to be a kind of reaction force. If it looks like one of the platoons is in trouble, we'll jump in and reinforce them."

"But you guys are great in the suits and great leaders!" she protested. "Why wouldn't they make you company commanders?"

"Because there's only one reinforced company of Drop-Troopers," Vicky said flatly, "and they already have a company commander, Captain Solano. And we haven't had the time to train with any of them, so it wouldn't be fair to stick us in the command structure this late."

I wasn't sure if she was trying to convince Fargo or me. Because I wasn't very happy about being stuck off on our own in what was basically a fire team. I'd led a company in the war and it wasn't as if I'd forgotten everything I'd learned.

"We're going to get a chance to fight," I declared, half to

myself. "And that's enough. Just stick close to us and do whatever Wade does." And I never thought I'd be recommending *that* to anyone. I kicked over the comm net to include him, realizing he hadn't said anything since we'd sealed up in the suits and locked into the drop gantries on the shuttle.

"Hey, Wade," I called, nudging his channel. "You awake?"

"Hmm?" he grunted. "Yeah, barely."

I didn't try to find his suit. I knew he'd settled into a gantry across the drop bay from us in the shuttle, but that had mostly been because he'd come in after the rest of the HQ platoon and that was the only space left. And all I could see of any of the Vigilantes was shadowy grey metal, motionless, terracotta warriors waiting for their leader to come and bring them back to life.

"You doing okay, man?"

"Oh, fuck yeah. I'm ready for this, Cam. Ready to get this shit over with, you know?"

"What're you gonna do once we beat him?" It was a presumptuous question, tempting bad luck, but one I thought he needed to hear. "Stay in?"

"What else am I gonna do?" I couldn't see his shrug, but I could hear it. "This is the only thing I've ever been good at."

I didn't laugh, but I wanted to. I'd said those same words to Vicky not that long ago.

"You're gonna live a long time, Wade. There's plenty of chances to learn something else, if that's what you want. Maybe something you like better."

Now, he laughed, and seemed to make no effort to restrain the scorn in it.

"Dude, you sound like my Separation Counselor when I outprocessed. What do you think? Am I gonna do what you did, try to be a farmer? Look how that worked out for you."

"There are other things besides farming," I reminded him,

then tried to rack my brain to figure out what else there *was*, because I hadn't been able to come up with anything when it had been me. "Maybe the Patrol? Or you could work for a planetary constabulary. You have the experience. You'd just need some law enforcement training, and they'd probably give it to you."

"Me? A cop?" He laughed again, not with scorn this time but in appreciation, I thought. "That would be a kick in the head, wouldn't it? After I spent so much time running from them. I guess that would be good experience right there, huh?"

"And if you can get in with the Patrol," I pointed out, trying to sound enthusiastic, "you could travel a lot, if that's what you want. Get to see a lot of the Commonwealth instead of being stuck out in the Pirate Worlds or the Periphery with the dregs of humanity."

"Yeah, that would be pretty cool. And I hear when you get to be an Inspector, the Patrol gives you your own ship. I wouldn't mind jumping around wherever I wanted to go."

I didn't think it would be quite that easy, but I didn't want to discourage him, so I didn't object.

"And I bet you could get a good recommendation from Colonel Hachette. You've done good work for him. He owes you one."

"I don't know if Hachette even knows I'm alive," Wade told me. "Captain Solano sure doesn't. Didn't even keep a spot open for me in the company while I was undercover. But maybe Top would put in a good word."

"Transition in ten seconds." The crew chief's voice was gruff and impatient, as if we should have already known it and he was being bothered to have to tell us.

He didn't bother with a countdown, but I didn't need one. I linked my suit's HUD with the Tactical display from the *Orion* and was rewarded with the last few numbers before the grey blankness exploded into reality. We were in the Fomor system, or whatever the Tahni had called it before we'd taken everything they had and let them keep their home, if not their government or their religion.

And yeah, I guess I was feeling a bit cynical about everything since our visit to Tahn-Skyyiah, and if Zan-Thint was undeniably insane and genocidal, he still had a reason for his anger. We'd fought the Tahni before, in a war where they'd been the aggressors, motivated by religious zeal and a conviction that they alone deserved the worlds the Predecessors had left behind, a war we'd won, or would have won if the Corporate Council hadn't strong-armed the President into a truce.

Maybe the truce wouldn't have lasted, maybe they would have broken it eventually, but they hadn't. We had, or rather, wildcat settlers had. Back when the only way between the stars had been the wormhole jumpgates the Predecessors had apparently left in place for us, at least if you believed Zan-Thint, it had been easy to control interstellar travel. No one went through a gate unless a Commonwealth laser was holding it open and every colonist was cleared and recorded and numbered.

About then, a couple of researchers for Commonwealth Transport named Teller and Fox had developed the warp field generator, a way to access Transition Space from anywhere, not just from one of the jumpgates. The government had wanted to keep a lid on it, but *someone* had leaked the design. The scandal sheets had all said it was the Corporate Council, trying to drum up business for their brand-new development, but pretty soon, Transition Drive ships were everywhere.

And since all the other colonies were so tightly controlled, it only made sense that people who wanted to get away from that sort of control started up their own...in the Tahni neutral zone, the area where the truce dictated neither of us would settle. The

Tahni had done what they had every right to do and fusion-bombed them to atoms. And of course, President Gregory Jameson couldn't let that stand, not if he wanted to get reelected. So, he'd ordered surgical strikes against Tahni outposts, something innocuous and harmless...he'd thought.

The Tahni had other ideas. We'd broken the treaty and then we'd attacked them and they hadn't like that *at all*. And this time, when they'd attacked our shipyards in Martian orbit, there'd been every justification for them to do it. Not that it made a difference. At that point, we were at war and it didn't matter who was at fault. And if humans had caused the war to reignite, then we should have wiped the Tahni out at the end of the first war and it didn't really matter.

It mattered now. Now, we were reaping the fucking whirl-wind with a Tahni who had the capability to end all life not just in the Commonwealth but in his own people's worlds. All as a result of an unjustified war, all from a justified war we hadn't started and hadn't finished. Sometimes, Vicky wondered why I still believed in God, and this was why. Nothing this ridiculous and ironic could have happened by chance. The question wasn't whether there was a God. The question was, had He created us for the amusement of watching us fuck up.

Fomor was bright, and hot, and had turned Firbolg into a charred cinder. I wondered why I'd ever thought it was habit-able. No one had said it was, no one had even implied it was, but I had assumed Zan-Thint wouldn't build his bolt hole some-place that didn't have air. It was a bad assumption. I didn't even have to look at the sensor readout to see that the planet was dead. Not one speck of green, not one hint of blue or white graced its pockmarked surface.

The only signs of life were in orbit, the Tahni fleet. Not as large as it could have been if we hadn't destroyed his shipyard at Khepera...one capital ship in watchful guard over the dead world, gleaming in the light of the harsh, unforgiving star, surrounded by smaller corvettes like remoras clinging to a shark. They sailed on, computer-generated icons because, even this close, we couldn't have seen them with optical telescopes, oblivious for long moments to our presence.

I was in free-fall, the gravity field the warp unit generated in Transition Space gone in a puff of Einsteinian physics, and then I wasn't. I gasped involuntarily, muscles clenching as I was pressed into the back of my armor by the unbridled fury of the *Orion*'s fusion drive.

"Jesus!" Wade exclaimed, still connected via comms to my suit. "How many gravities is that?" The words came out in a pained grunt, and I realized it had to have been a while since Wade had made a combat drop in a suit.

"Four," I told him, reading the details off the ship's display in my HUD. "And I wish it was more."

"The faster we boost," Vicky said, sounding less strained by the high-G acceleration than either of us, "the less time they have to intercept us before we get to orbit."

And as if the words had been a curse called down on our heads, the Tahni ships lurched into motion, flares of fusion energy roaring out of their drive bells. The corvettes moved first, less mass and less momentum required to set them into motion, but the destroyer nosed up slowly behind them, a behemoth rising above the ocean for a breath. I held my own, knowing what was coming next.

"Launch, launch, launch!" The announcement came from the bridge of the *Orion* and the cockpit of the drop-ship at once, an echo in my headphones.

If four gravities of boost behind us had been uncomfortable, then the lateral G's from the launch were unbearable, like my insides were trying to force their way out through my spine, and if I didn't scream, it wasn't for lack of trying.

And then it was gone, along with the *Orion*'s acceleration, and we were out. The link from the *Orion* faded as we emerged from her hangar bay, the drop-ship's drive the only force being exerted on us now. It was bad enough, worse than the *Orion*'s, six gravities this time and Wade didn't even have the breath to complain, nor Vicky the composure to contradict him. And I barely had the mental focus to read the display from the drop-ship.

Maybe I would have been better off not knowing. The corvettes were closing in, heading right for us, and the *Orion* was going to be tied up with the destroyer. But we weren't alone. The missile cutters were blue deltas on the screen, rocketing out from the hangar bay just behind us, faster even than our six gravities, and leading them was Kyler Dunstan in the ship he'd christened the *Angelica* after his first girlfriend, much to the chagrin of the copilot and crew chief he'd been assigned.

Proton blasts glared white on the thermal sensors and were answered by lasers and then the battle was past and the forward screens were full of the black world in the dark of night. Now I could finally make out the assault shuttles flying escort for us, dagger-shaped spacecraft, deadly just to look at. I'd known they were there, launched before us, but I hadn't seen them on the sensors until now. They were our escort down to the planet, but we couldn't count on them for air support. It seemed like we never could, because the enemy always had their own assault birds trying to shoot us down before we could get there.

I'd once suggested that we should come up with an agreement for neither side to have the damned things, then we could all save the money from producing them and at least half the lives of the pilots and crew. Captain Covington hadn't found the idea as amusing as I had, and had declined to pass it up the chain to the high command.

"Target is on the terminator, thirty minutes till drop,"

Captain Solano announced. He was on this bird with Head-quarters Platoon and First, while the other platoons were split between the Bravo and Charlie drop-ships. There were five in all plus Headquarters, a platoon heavy for a Drop-Trooper company, and I hoped they'd be enough. "Target is a hardened, underground facility, according to the orbital scans. There are three entrances, designators Alpha, Bravo, and Charlie on your HUD map overlays, and we're going to hit all of them at once."

Even as he spoke, the alphabetical designators flashed to life in the map in my helmet, though it was difficult to give any real direction to them when everything on the planet was not much more than an ash-heap. He'd told us the target was at the termi-nator to give it some sort of perspective for us, give us a place on the line between light and dark to look, but by the time the red glow began floating over it, it had already turned a few degrees to the east, progressing slowly into the raw glare of the primary star. It was going to be hot down there.

"The drop-ships will launch missiles to take out the entrances and we'll jump right through them. I'll be taking First and Second to Alpha, Sgt.-Major Campbell will be leading Third and Fourth to Bravo, and Lt. McReady will be taking Headquarters and Fifth to Charlie. That includes your team, Captain Alvarez."

Which hadn't been the plan, but I wasn't going to argue with him now. We hadn't had a handle on what we'd be facing until we'd jumped in, and Op Orders always had frag-o's. Vicky didn't say a word, but I could feel her anger bristling like a disturbance in the air.

"There *are* no non-combatants down there," Solano stressed. "Everyone down there who's not one of us is a target and you will not hesitate. I don't know if we'll have reliable comms once we're inside, but if any of you find anything resem-bling the Skrela seed pod you've been briefed about, try to report it immediately. If you can't, get outside and call in an orbital strike on it. There is *nothing* more important than finding and destroying that thing. You copy?"

"Ooh-rah, sir!" That was everyone, all the IFF transponders on our drop-ship lighting up in the Comm display like a Christmas tree. Ours too, because if there was one thing that never changed about Marines, no matter how old or cynical they got, it was the absolute necessity of saying *ooh-rah* when a superior officer asked if you understood what they were saying.

"All right then, Marines. This is what we've been training and waiting for. There are Tahni High Guard down there waiting for us to give them a fight. Don't let me down."

And more shouts and battle cries.

"Solano gives a good speech," I told Vicky.

"You could have done better." She paused and I thought she wasn't going to comment further. "I won't forgive you if you get yourself killed down there."

"Wouldn't dream of it," I assured her. "You watch my back, I'll watch yours."

"And we'll meet for drinks in the O-club after."

There was no atmosphere to buffet the drop-ship this time, no sign of the approaching drop except a countdown I tried to ignore until it reached zero.

"Drop! Drop! Drop!"

I hit the control and the deck fell away beneath me...and I plummeted into hell.

[6]

I guess it wasn't fair to call it hell, though I couldn't imagine hell being any worse.

I'd seen the layout of the place in my HUD, but it hadn't prepared me for the harsh light of a nightmare day. The lines of the mountains were jagged, unworn, unweathered, glittering lava knives brandished at us by a hostile world. And set in the midst of them, in a valley between ranges that would have dwarfed the Rockies, was the dome.

It was huge, bigger than I'd thought at nearly two kilometers around, white and sterile, glowing with a reflection that would have blinded anyone stupid enough to look at it with the naked eye. It had to be reflective, I supposed, to keep the interior temperature survivable in the daytime, with no atmosphere to attenuate the light of the star. And it glowed red-hot in three spots around the base of the dome, separated by a few hundred meters each. No smoke rose from the wreckage of the airlock entrances, not on an airless ball of rock, but the missiles had flown true.

Now I just had to live long enough to see if they'd done their job.

The Vigilante vibrated and rumbled, the sound of the jump-jets muted, confined to the interior of the suit, where there was air and metal and me to conduct it. But they weren't sucking in atmosphere to run through the isotope reactor on my back, to superheat it and spit it out as a plasma. On this airless, naked rock, we had to carry our own reaction mass, squeezed at massive pressures into drop-away tanks affixed to the sides of the packs sticking out from the back of our suits' torsos like a hunch.

I'd dropped in a vacuum before and didn't care for it. The fall was steep and arrow-straight, no atmosphere, no winds to carry me laterally, break up my trajectory. If anyone was aiming upward at me, the targeting pattern would have been damned basic. And maybe that was another reason why Zan-Thint had chosen a lifeless world. I'd make sure to ask him right before I stomped his skull to mush.

The fight raged above my head, visible at the edges of my helmet display as I dropped, but I tried to ignore it. Whether my drop-ship survived, whether the assault shuttles made it through the gauntlet, all of that was beyond my control. I watched the IFF transponders around me, waiting for them to start winking out, for the ground defenses to take them, but none did. Maybe the drop-ships had nailed those as well, whatever coil-gun or missile emplacements the Tahni had prepared for us, but something about it nagged at me.

Stop looking gift horses in the mouth.

And a mouth was exactly what I was looking at, a gaping maw staring up at me and the rest of the two platoons, what had once been a yawning airlock, meant not just to allow dismounts or even vehicles through it, but shuttles and cargo carriers. The outer doors hadn't been that thick and the missiles had shredded them, leaving gaps dozens of meters across, the metal still glowing white hot. Light filtered up through the breaches, and with it, the swirling dust devil of the internal atmosphere escaping out the opening.

Below me, tiny figures were tossed back and forth like puppets on a string, battered by the gusts of artificial wind as the whole facility evacuated through the three airlocks. The updraft hit me as I descended through the largest gap and the Vigilante bobbed as if it had sunk into rough water, and I gave the jump-jets more juice, hoping there was enough reaction mass to correct for the turbulence without leaving me at bingo fuel fifty meters up. My descent steadied just in time, the soles of my boots slamming into the metal grating of the landing platform just seconds later.

And I was just as quickly under fire.

"Contact, left!"

"Contact, right!"

"Contact, front!"

The reports came in from every side, and if there was no contact to the rear, it was only because the external wall was behind us. Data crashed over me in waves and instincts honed in years of combat picked out the bits of it that were vital to me staying alive for the next few seconds. Only one platoon was on the ground, but the rest were coming, and the last to make it down would be the Boomers. They were carrying more weight with the heavy coil guns and they'd been outfitted with expend-able, detachable retro-rockets to get them down safely. We hadn't used those in the war, simply landing them with the drop-ships, but despite what Fargo had implied, there had been *some* advances since the conquest of the Tahni homeworld.

That left the rest of us on the ground, surrounded by enemy troops. Not High Guard suits, though. If there had been battle-suits waiting for us at the bottom, we would have lost a squad before we could have even tried to return fire. These were Shock-Troopers, rushing out of corridors leading deeper into the facility, their stride long and awkward, like toddlers wobbling their first steps. Their heavy KE guns were hosing us down with streams of tantalum darts, the hypersonic rounds digging craters out of my armor, dull, metallic thuds like someone was knocking on my chest plate, trying to get in.

Individually, they were no match for us, but they were a swarm of bees and it was impossible to target them all...and while those darts couldn't penetrate our armor, they could ablate it, and enough of them would eventually wear it away and they'd nibble us to death like the insects they were. So, I applied a little insecticide.

The missiles weren't meant for anything this close, nor anything this small, but they were also self-programming and did as they were told. I launched two of them the second I hit the ground, and I wasn't the only one. Vicky had the same instincts as me, honed as an enlisted Marine under the same leadership, and I knew she was doing the same thing. I wasn't sure who else had fired, but at least four pairs of smoke trails arched upwards, almost to the gaps in the roof, before they reached their perigee and streaked down into the rear of the oncoming horde of Shock-Troopers.

The air-burst explosions were carefully calculated by the computers in the warheads to spread the spears of incandescent plasma wide among the designated targets, and even the armor the Tahni powered exoskeletons could haul around wasn't thick enough to resist the pencil-thin lances of ionized gas. Wedges were cut through the enemy ranks like wildfire spreading through fields of prairie grass, and as if the warhead blasts were a cue, plasma bursts ignited from two dozen emitters, a platoon and a half of volley fire, and the charge was broken.

There were three corridors running out of the landing platform like sunbursts, and the charred and battered remnants of what had to be a full company of Shock-Troopers was straggling back along them, chased by more plasma blasts. I'd fired my own gun twice and didn't remember the second time, though my HUD assured me I'd actually done it.

I sucked in a breath and paused for a beat, checking my IFF board and sensors. All of HQ and First was down, as was Captain Solano, and there were no more enemy in sight. The landing platform was empty of Tahni shuttles and was only occupied now by the wreckage of the airlock.

"McReady," Solano ordered, putting it out over the general net because that was how he did things, making sure every one of his Marines knew all the orders so any one of them could take over in an emergency, "keep the Boomers here and secure this platform for our extraction. I'm taking First and our special guests with me through the central corridor." He pointed with the maw of his plasma gun to the middle of the three concourses leading out of the landing platform, the broadest one, obviously meant to haul cargo through the facility. It curved downward out of sight, hiding the troops that had retreated down it and God alone knew what else.

"Alvarez," Solano said, and I noted that, this time, he'd pared the transmission down to just the two of us, "how would you feel about your team taking point?"

I didn't laugh, though I wanted to. I had the sense that Solano didn't too much care for Vicky and Wade and me playing secret agent, nor did he especially care for Fargo being foisted upon him, and having a captain walk point was probably his way of putting us in our place. I could have said no. I'd been informed in no uncertain terms by Colonel Hachette that I could use my own best judgment when on the ground. But in all honesty, I felt most at home up front.

"Not a problem," I assured him. I wished I could look him in the eye. "But if I'm up front, I'll be making the calls as to which way we go."

He hesitated just a beat, just long enough for me to know he'd understood.

"Sure, no problem."

And I could believe that as much as I wanted to. I switched to our team net and shut Solano out.

"We're up front," I told them. "I'm on point."

"The fuck?" Vicky exclaimed. "You're a captain! Solano does remember that, right?"

"I think it slipped his mind. I'll remind him later, but right now, we've got work to do. Follow me."

———

The walls were too far apart. It had been a long time since I'd felt agoraphobic, and I'd never had the fear inside a Vigilante, but this corridor...the walls felt kilometers wide to my gut, though I knew in my head they were only about thirty meters apart. Big enough for cargo loaders, though I didn't know what they'd be bringing into this place. Weapons? But why? Why would they bring heavy weapons into this base when they'd be using them from their ships? Food? Supplies? This place would have been big enough for thousands of Tahni and we knew he didn't have that many soldiers.

It shouldn't have mattered, but it did. It nagged at me when I should have been concentrating on what was down at the bottom of the ramp. This place was supposed to be his bolt hole, his last stand, but why did Zan-Thint *need* a last stand? I stopped thinking about it abruptly when the ramp downward ended in a massive set of doors...well, what passed for doors among the Tahni. This had been built by them and the cargo portal was three-lobed, coming together in the middle like an iris.

"This thing looks pretty thick," I told Solano, knowing he'd be observing ahead through the feed from my helmet, even though he was still a hundred meters behind me. "I'm gonna go out on a limb and say my plasma gun isn't going to burn through this."

"We have a couple shaped breaching charges," he said. "I'm sending them up."

Chartres was the Marine he sent up with the charge. I didn't know her well, but Vicky and I had run into her on the *Orion*, and she struck me as someone who loved her job.

"Hey, Lt. Alvarez," she said, lumbering up, the footfalls of her Vigilante eerily silent in the vacuum, though I felt a hint of a vibration through the soles of my boots. She hadn't, I figured, been briefed about our recent promotions. "Need a couple of door-knockers up here?"

"It'll have to be a hell of a set of knockers, Chartres," Wade told her. I couldn't *actually* smack myself in the forehead, not while I was in the armor, but I wanted to.

"Oh, Jesus," Vicky groaned. "You've been waiting to use that one, haven't you?"

"Don't worry, Lt. Sandoval." The Marine swung her plasma gun up out of the way, using both hands of the suit to pull the charge packs off her back. "These are the only knockers I plan to show Sgt. Cunningham, barring a galactic apocalypse that leaves us the only two humans left to propagate the species."

"So," Wade interjected, and I could hear his broad smile in the words, "you're saying there's a chance?"

Chartres laughed and kept on setting the charges. I wanted to believe the joking around meant Wade was back to normal, but I realized I didn't know what normal was for him anymore.

"Everybody back!" Chartres warned us, toddling backwards in armor not really meant for it. "This shit isn't *supposed* to have any backblast, but that depends on how thick this fucking door is!"

"Back how far?" Wade demanded. "There ain't exactly any cover in here!"

"Hundred meters maybe?" Chartres suggested. "Hell, I don't know! I've never done this shit in a vacuum before. You can stick your damned dick against the door for all I care, Cunningham."

I don't know if it was a hundred meters, but I stopped when we were far enough back up the ramp that I could see the rest of the company waiting, just up the curve from the door.

"Hit it, Chartres," I told her.

"Fire in the hole!" she called.

I couldn't *hear* the blast, of course, but the vibrations rang through the floor and the walls like a gong, strong enough to rattle my teeth. There was no concussion, no blast of heat, no shock wave, because there was no atmosphere to conduct it. I took off the second I felt the vibration, counting on the others to follow without me having to tell them.

There was smoke from the explosion, but it didn't rise, just clung to the floor like a fog for a few seconds before it dispersed into diffuse vapor and faded as if it had never been there. The door had been thick, but not thick enough to resist two shaped charges with ten kilos of HyperExplosives each. What was left of them was twisted metal, glowing red and white in the darkness of the tunnel. There'd been lights before, built into the walls, but they were gone, smashed by fragments from the blast, and I was glad we'd backed up. The armor *might* have protected us, but I would rather not have found out the hard way.

What was on the other side of the doors was just as dark, too shrouded in shadow for me to see, even with the infrared filters in my helmet optics. No light reached here from the surface and I wasn't ready to use the suit's infrared illuminators. That would be too much like shining a spotlight and yelling, "Please shoot me!" Not that whoever was down here hadn't already realized we'd arrived after we'd blown the door, but knowing the enemy was coming and knowing exactly where to shoot were different things.

What there hadn't been when we'd blown the doors was a flush of air. Whatever was on the other side, they'd already had it in a vacuum before we attacked. That worried me. It meant they'd had time to prepare, which was exactly what we'd been hoping to avoid. That absence bothered me, but what concerned me more was the other absence...of everything. The chamber on the other side of the door was empty.

"What the fuck is going on in here?" Vicky demanded.

"There's nothing here, Cam," Wade reported. "I'm up against the far wall."

I was about to tell them to keep moving when I found... another door.

"Solano," I called immediately. "Hold up where you are. Something's happening here. We got another door. I think this whole chamber is some kind of cargo airlock."

"You want me to send up more breaching charges?"

I opened my mouth to tell him yes, but something drowned out my transmission. It wasn't on our comm net, of course—that would have been impossible. But it was on a general net, broad-waved with enough power behind it to reach every single Marine in the company. And definitely enough to echo inside my helmet.

"Lt. Alvarez, how nice to see you again."

The voice was a Tahni speaking English. There was no mistaking the indescribable accent of vocal cords not evolved to speak any human language trying to pronounce one of the hardest, most complicated languages in human history. Once heard, it wasn't easily forgotten. And this particular voice was familiar. Hackles rose on the back of my neck, and my breath caught in my chest.

I switched to the general net with numb fingers, still staring at the bare metal of the wall. I should be backing out. I knew it, knew there was no way this wasn't a trap, but that was my job as point man...to spring traps. And I just had to know.

"General Zan-Thint." I tried to sound casual. "I expected to find you here, but I'm not so sure how you expected me. By the way, it's 'Captain Alvarez' now."

"Congratulations on the promotion. I suppose you earned it after your exploits on Bathala. I would have been willing to wager my entire army that neither you nor your wife would have survived the Skrela outbreak. In fact, I was prepared to believe it would be the end of the entire planet, and perhaps your entire Commonwealth."

"Wishful thinking, General. Seems like it's the major failing of the Tahni as a species. It's why you lost two wars, and why you'll lose this one too."

Yeah, I was being cocky, taunting him even. But I wanted him to talk, because while he was talking, I was triangulating. That transmission was close.

"Alvarez!" Solano snapped on the command net. "What the hell's going on? Is that actually Zan-Thint?"

"It's not fucking President Jameson," I shot back, annoyed with the man for his failure to grasp the obvious. "Get me those charges. I'm trying to backtrace his transmission and I need to get through this fucking door."

I switched back to the general net, but Zan-Thint was already bloviating.

"You may have been right about the Imperium, *Captain* Alvarez. But I am not the Imperium, and I didn't survive the war by wishful thinking. I survived by being prepared."

The comm gear in my helmet was on the command net, which meant I had access to the feeds from everyone else in the company, and I was using their positions to triangulate the source of his transmission. It had to be microwave because there was sure as hell nowhere for a laser to come from in the bare walls, and if it was, it could be traced.

"You were prepared for this?" I asked, not trying to be too clever, concentrating on the shrinking circle on the comm display in the corner of my helmet screen. He was on the other side of the door, I could see that already, but I couldn't tell how close. "If you were prepared, why didn't you just move the whole damned thing somewhere else before we got here? And you still haven't told me how you knew I was coming."

"Who do you think organized the insurgents? Who do you think fed that venomous little turncoat Ven-Wan information to pass on to your intelligence agents? There's nothing that happens on Tahn-Skyyiah without me knowing about it. And there's nothing that happens on this world without me being prepared for it. As for why I didn't move my operations, well...I read of a human custom, back when you hunted predators on your world. To attract the predator, your people would tie a domestic farm animal to a stake and wait for the cat to attack. They called it a Judas goat."

There. He was two hundred meters away, past this door... and past another. And there was something solid in the middle. A *lot* of somethings.

"The charges are on their way," Solano interrupted. "Chartres is bringing them up. You sure you don't want me to bring up the rest of the company?"

"No. He's trying to bait us in, and I don't want us all falling into the same trap."

"I imagine by now," Zan-Thint went on, sounding far too amused for my comfort, "that you're getting ready to blow this door the same way you did the last. Let me save you the trouble."

The door began to move aside, the grinding of its motors

vibrating into the floor and up through the metal of my armor. A surge of fear bordering on panic rose out of my guts and up into my chest. This was bad. This was very bad.

"Solano! Get the fucking company out of here!" I switched to the company net. "Everyone! Get out of here!"

There was movement through the gap in the doors, skittering, like an insect but so much larger. I wanted to run, knew I should, but something about the motion teased at my memory, and I knew I had no choice but to hit the external lights. I didn't bother with infrared because they'd be just as easily seen by enemy suits as visible, and when the white light shone through the door, it threw sinuous, wavering shadows against the far wall.

The first thing it hit was a large, fibrous pod, two dozen meters long and split open right down the middle. I knew what it was...I'd seen another just like it, back on Hausos. And skittering around it, so thick I couldn't see the floor, were dozens of Skrela.

"Oh, boy," I murmured. "We are so fucked."

"Back! Get back!" I screamed the order, but I couldn't follow it, not until the others got clear. I had seconds until the doors were fully open and the Skrela rushed out, and I had to use it.

I had two missiles left and I launched them both, not at any one of the things, but directly into the open pod. The blasts were twin flashes of lightning, throwing everything into stark clarity for just a moment, a light shone on a nest of cockroaches. But these cockroaches were more like scorpions the size of a draft horse.

Scorpion wasn't an exact description. They had a tail reminiscent of one, and they had eight limbs, but these weren't life forms engineered from Earth originals like the flora and fauna on the colonies, not even anything as familiar as the animals on Tahni worlds. The most understandable analogy I could come up with would be insectoid, or maybe arachnoid, but they weren't strictly that either. Their legs were thick and digitigrade, the knees bent backwards, and the lower pair of arms were nearly as big around as the legs, one of them supporting some kind of energy cannon, the other armed with a large, serrated claw, while their upper set were much smaller, meant for manipulation. The heads were broad and flat, with mandibles that came together at the fore end, endlessly clicking as they moved...though I couldn't hear it in the vacuum.

And they could *live* in a vacuum, which I hadn't known before and which didn't make me feel any better about the situation. They spotted me a second after the explosions, probably following the thermal trail of the missiles—I didn't *know* that they had integral thermal sensors, but it wouldn't be wise to assume they didn't.

The creepiest thing about them was the energy cannon. Without it, I could have let myself believe they were nothing but mindless animals, biological robots created to kill whatever was in front of them, unable to think or reason. But they were carrying guns, and they obviously knew how to use them because they tried to shoot me. I don't know what the things fired, but I knew I didn't want to be in the way of one of the bolts. They *shouldn't* have been visible in a hard vacuum, but shouldn't didn't seem to matter to these things, and when I bounced out of the way of the shot, I could see the pale blue glow of its passage, and I don't think I was just imagining the feeling of static electricity dancing over my skin.

I risked a glance backwards, deathly afraid that the round had passed by me only to hit Vicky, but she was already moving. Not backwards, of course, because the idea that she'd actually listened to my order was too much to hope for. But she'd slid laterally, giving herself a boost with the small, onboard solid fuel supply left over for the jump jets. It wasn't enough for a drop, but it could give us a few seconds of boost when we really needed it.

She launched her remaining missiles through the yawning doorway, and then it was all the way open and the Skrela began streaming through.

"Volley fire! Now!" I hoped Wade and Fargo hadn't fallen

so far out of practice that they'd forgotten their Armor School training, but I squeezed off a shot from my plasma gun anyway, hoping they'd know to join me.

A plasma shot in an atmosphere was something to behold, a second sun rising, so hot the air itself leapt away from it in a panic, its passage a sonic boom that could burst eardrums if you were close enough, sear the skin right off an unprotected human from meters away. In a vacuum, it was less impressive, though not the ethereal phantom of a laser beam. The ionized gas provided its own atmosphere, short-lived as it was, but without surrounding air to react with, it was a pale, narrow corridor, a flashlight beam in a dusty room.

Until it connected. Then, it still put on a show. I didn't know what the chitinous exoskeleton that covered the Skrela was made from, but I knew it was tough. Heat-resistant, impact-resistant, probably so thick, it could shrug off a laser or turn a Gauss rifle round. Not quite thick enough to handle a relativistic stream of hydrogen plasma that could cut right through centimeters of BiPhase Carbide, though.

Four plasma beams struck out, because my team had been listening and, for once, had done what they were told. Where they hit, something, be it metal or polymer or biological chitin, vaporized with a flash of liberated energy and Skrela drones died. If you could honestly say they were ever alive. I still wasn't clear on that. Unfortunately, the barrage attracted even more attention, and a dozen pale-blue energy beams quested out into the darkness at us.

"Back, Goddammit!" I yelled, this time following my own orders.

The Vigilante's hip suspension was impressively robust, designed to take a lot of impact, and when I jumped backwards with all the might of those reactor-powered servos and a half-second burst from the jump jets, I nearly slammed into the overhead. But I had reflexes born of endless hours of training, a lot of it in simulator programs I'd written myself, and I hadn't neglected fighting in tight corners. I spun end-for-end in mid-air with an agility I couldn't have matched without the suit, and impacted the ceiling with my feet instead of my head, bouncing off the reinforced concrete before I spun again.

My gymnastics had rewarded me with time...the time my plasma gun's capacitors had needed to recharge. I fired in mid-air, the blast blowing the head off an alien warrior drone a split-second before I landed right on top of another. Tons of BiPhase Carbide, ceramic and metal slammed into the Skrela where its spine turned upward to support its torso and something broke. It wasn't me, though the hit was hard enough I thought I'd snapped my own spine and not just the Skrela's.

The blow didn't kill it, though its lower body went limp and it collapsed to the ground. Those load-bearing arms were still active, twisting around, trying to reach me, the serrated mandibles clacking together, trying to gain purchase on my armor. Revulsion twisted in my stomach and I acted out of an atavistic fear and loathing of the Other, slamming my left fist down over and over, smashing through that armored skull. It took three blows to crack it, another to split it wide open, and what came out defied description.

Black ichor sprayed across the metal of the Vigilante's arms and chest, and I fought an irrational fear that it was acid, that it would eat right through my suit. But I smashed it again and hit something that might have been metal or might have been bone, pulping the softer, biological material around it to mush. And finally, it went limp.

I'd taken too long. An energy beam sought me out, and the only reason it didn't burn me to cinders was the massive lower body of the Skrela blocking its path. Both rear sets of legs disintegrated in a flash of light that blacked out my camera view, and heat washed over the suit, turning it into a convection oven, taking my breath away.

I couldn't think, but I didn't have to. Moving came naturally, from a place deeper than thought, and if I managed any rational calculation at all, it was the decision to hit my jets again. I bounced away from the ruins of the alien monster, chasing the others, who had the good sense not to wait for me. Another recharge, another plasma blast, taking down the closest of the things, and I wondered idly if they had the same need to allow their capacitors time to top up between shots. It would have been good to know, but they didn't seem in the mood to share.

Something inside me rebelled at the notion of running, wanting to stand and fight with the things, but I had to yield to the rational, to the knowledge that there were already hundreds of the things, and even if we retreated to Solano's company and managed to take out three for every one of us, it wouldn't be enough. I had no confidence that a couple missiles were going to be enough to shut down the nanotech factory inside that pod that was cranking these things out...but I *did* have a firm conviction that Zan-Thint wouldn't have left it there unless he knew there were enough of them to take us all out.

"*Orion!*" I called, hoping to hell I had enough relay points between me and the surface to get through to the ship. "*Orion, this is Alvarez! Does anyone copy?*"

I was running backwards in powered armor, which sounds difficult but is actually *insanely* difficult, hopping like a man in low gravity except with the video streaming in reverse, firing off a plasma shot every time the capacitor reading went green, dodging and weaving and trying to keep up with Vicky and Wade and Fargo. It took somewhere north of one hundred percent of my concentration, so talking was a real effort and not receiving a reply was beyond annoying.

"Dammit, *Orion*, get off your ass and answer me! We're in deep shit down here!"

"Alvarez, this is Solano." Well, at least *someone* was listening. I checked my IFF transponder and was barely able to get a reading on Solano and the rest of the company. When I'd said to get the hell out of here, he'd taken me at my word. "We're back at the docking bay...the *Orion* is sending the drop-ships down for us. She's still tangled up with the Tahni destroyer, but Cam...there's another destroyer. It was tucked into the other side of the moon and there are landers taking off from the planet, heading for it."

"Zan-Thint," I grunted. A Skrela rushed forward, faster somehow than the rest of the group, and I boosted straight at it, coming underneath its firing arc and hitting it low across the front set of legs, a body block that struck with enough force to take it off its feet, send it tumbling forward so Vicky could jet up a few meters and come down on its head. "Zan-Thint is getting away."

"Maybe, but we can't let these Goddamned *things* off this planet. Colonel Hachette says they have enough raw material here to construct ships. We have to blow the place. Fusion missiles from orbit. And you have to get out of there while we still have ships to pick you up."

"There's a slight problem with that," Vicky interrupted. I checked the IFF display and saw that she'd bounced backwards from the Skrela she'd killed, to the rear of the formation. I knew her well enough to guess it had been a temporary retreat, that she'd intended to hop forward again to fight by my side. "The door is closed."

"What?" I blurted. "Didn't we just blow that damn thing with explosives? Fargo! Wade! Cover me!"

Which was more wishful thinking than anything, because there were hundreds of the Skrela and four of us, and the only thing keeping them from wiping us out in seconds was the constraints of the tunnel. But I had to see this for myself.

It didn't take long—I nearly slammed headfirst into the door. It wasn't, as it turned out, the one that we'd blown a hole through, though that was cold comfort. We'd missed the slot in the floor because of the darkness and the vacuum, or maybe because we'd been *meant* to miss it and it had been camouflaged. It was difficult to see, even with the illuminators still burning, mostly because of the annoying distraction of blinding energy beams trying to kill me.

It would be too easy to say I was afraid. But that would be a lie. Combat didn't scare me until afterward. Combat was easy. You had a lot of options, most of them shitty, and you had to choose the least shitty in about a half a second or you'd get yourself and everyone around you dead. This was even simpler than usual because there were only two options: either try to hold out until Solano blew this door for us or go out the other side. And since I was fairly sure we couldn't live long enough for Chartres to get back to the door with a breaching charge...

"Right through them!" I yelled, charging straight into the massed enemy. "We have to get through them and out the other side!"

"You must be fucking kidding me!" Wade exploded. But he did what he was told because what the hell else was he going to do?

I worked the radio while I fired and moved, hopping from one side of the passage to the other, falling into a pattern now, because the Skrela, as fearsome and relentless as they were, were also predictable.

"Solano," I said, grinding the words out, "we're cut off. Get to the lander. We'll try to find a way out."

He didn't say anything for the seconds it took my plasma

gun to recharge, and when he did, the words were bleak and hopeless.

"Copy that, Alvarez. Good luck."

Which was his way of saying we were all dead and it had been nice knowing us. I wanted to be mad, but he was probably right.

Vicky and the others were strung out behind me in a ragged line like a heartbeat on an EKG, the Skrela parting to either side of our column, waves crashing on rocks at the shore, going down to the volley fire of our guns. I don't know if we confused them by charging back into them or if they had a preprogrammed target, to get to the main body of the Marines, and we were just a distraction, but they didn't swarm over us the way they could have.

What were they used to facing? It was a horrible time to be speculating about extraneous shit like that, but thinking about our situation wasn't going to help. Thinking about it would only make it worse, make me hesitate when I should just go with my gut. So I shot and I thought. What kind of enemy were they used to facing? The Predecessors...those were the ones who they'd wiped out, if the Tahni were right. They'd overwhelmed them, forced them right out of this part of the galaxy, the Cluster, Dunstan had called it. How? The Predecessors had moved fucking planets. These things were tough and well-armed, but I would've put my money on a platoon of Drop-Troopers, even if the odds were three to one.

And that's just it, isn't it? By the time the Predecessors faced them, the odds weren't three to one. They were more like a thousand to one, or ten thousand to one.

The real threat wasn't these scorpion monsters with blasters; the real threat was the seed pods. They could nestle into some asteroid or moon and produce starships and warriors by the tens of thousands and no one would notice until they were swarming over a world. And how could anyone clean them all out once there were hundreds of thousands, or even millions of them on a living world?

By sterilizing it. The thought hit just as I fired my plasma gun into a wedge-shaped head, turning those click-clacking mandibles into a hot gas, wiping away whatever passed for a brain.

That was why the Predecessors had left, I realized. They'd made all these living worlds, put all that energy into a program of re-creation and re-engineering that must have taken millennia, and they couldn't bring themselves to reduce them all to cinders. They'd done what they could to beat the Skrela and then, once it became clear that the only way to do it was to destroy everything they'd created, they'd left it behind. Left *us* behind, us and the Tahni, hoping what they'd left us would be enough, that their departure would drag the Skrela threat along with them.

And it would have, if it hadn't been for Zan-Thint. *Sore fucking loser.*

I got caught between recharges, spun in mid-air to let the energy beam pass by only a meter away, close enough that a first-degree burn crackled across my left arm, like standing too long in the sun. When I touched down, the thing's tail snapped at me, a bullwhip that weighed a hundred kilos, the tip moving close to the speed of sound.

I caught it. I don't know how, because I didn't consciously decide to do it, could never have moved fast enough with my own muscles and reflexes. But my arms were raised to steady my descent and the suit must have read my intent before I did. The end of the tail wasn't a needle like a real scorpion's, and I doubted it was venomous, but it was a nasty spike as long as my arm, and going fast enough to penetrate the BiPhase Carbide over my chest.

The impact of the tail against the claw-like articulated fingers of my suit was a sledgehammer against my shoulders, enough force to slide the suit back against the stone floor, showering sparks from the spiked soles of the suit. I grabbed hold of it and jumped, with visions of carrying the damned thing into the air and dropping it on the others. It was a nice idea, but in practice, all I managed to do was twist it around and yank the spike out of my hands...and send me jetting into the ceiling.

No time to flip my legs around; I just clenched my teeth and slammed my shoulder into the polished stone. Bright lights and dull pain, and I was suspended in a haze that made it hard to move, impossible to think. I don't know how I managed to hit the jets to break my fall, but landing safely was only half my problem—the other half was the Skrela whose tail I'd grabbed. It hadn't forgotten the insult, and was skittering toward me at sixty klicks an hour...until a plasma shot blasted it in half. Vicky stood at my side, and even though I couldn't see her face, I knew she was glaring at me.

"Stop showing off and run," she snapped.

I did as I was told, trying to shake my head clear. The HUD informed me I was possibly suffering from a mild concussion and suggested that, when it was safe to do so, I should seek more comprehensive medical attention. It also told me that the right shoulder actuator on my suit was damaged and I needed to perform PMCS on it as soon as possible. I filed both of those under my to-do list and concentrated on what I could make out in the sensor display. The good news was, the Skrela were thinning out...we'd made it through the main body of the horde that had emerged from the pod. The bad news was...I had no idea where we were, or how to get out. And the clock was ticking.

[8]

Something glowed a dull red in my thermal sensors, growing hotter and closer with each long, loping step my Vigilante took. It was another five seconds before I realized it was the pod.

"Well," Wade said, an almost religious awe in his voice, "I guess this means we're going the right direction."

I'd expected that our missiles would have done significant damage to the pod, but that had been an underestimation of Skrela technology. The pod was charred, the edges ragged, but even as we approached, a double column of Skrela combat drones skittered out of the depths of it, so new, I could almost smell the cosmoline, to steal a phrase from Top. They seemed hesitant, as if they were waiting for guidance, and I didn't want to give them any reason to focus their efforts on us.

"Leave them," I snapped at the others, waving them forward. "Keep moving!"

Before the words were out of my mouth, Wade Cunningham blasted the first one out of the pod with his plasma gun. I wanted to curse, wanted to tell him off for being a moron, but I didn't have the luxury or breath or the presence of mind to come up with a good, scathing insult. I was ten meters past the pod and tried to skate to a stop, knowing what was coming. The converging barrage of actinic energy beat me to it.

We'd been living a charmed life up 'til now, one of those runs you have in combat when you make it through one impossible situation after another and don't get a scratch. And after a couple of those, it's easy to believe you're immortal, that nothing can ever happen to you, that you're a god of war. If you're lucky, you get that knocked out of your system by a smack to the ass, by a nasty burn, by something that doesn't kill you.

Wade Cunningham was many things, but lucky had never been one of them.

One heartbeat, he was there, boosting three meters off the ground, and the next he was gone, bits of glowing armor raining to the ground, the only evidence that he'd ever existed.

"Fuck!" Vicky screamed, and I knew she was about two seconds from charging in and shooting up the column of Skrela, because I was there myself.

"No!" The word wrenched itself out of my mouth, though I wanted to stifle it. "Move! Get out of here!"

Karen Fargo didn't protest. She hadn't known Wade that well. She sprinted past the two of us, ready to be out of the chamber as much as we were to go back and avenge our friend, but Vicky dragged her feet for a moment more, just past the edge of the pod, ready to turn back.

"He's dead," I said, the words harsher than they needed to be because I was saying them as much to myself. "And we will be too. Go."

"Goddammit, Cunningham." She was trying to make the words sound like a curse, but the sob burst through it. "You stupid son of a bitch."

I didn't move until I saw she was, and it was very nearly too late. The Skrela hatchlings were marching out of the pod, spreading out, and if they didn't detect us immediately, it was only because they still seemed disoriented. I sent my fervent hopes at their backs, wishing them forward, hoping they'd march all the way to the closed door and go have a long talk with the others.

Past the pod, the passageway opened up, as if it had been put in a chokepoint just to trap us...because that was exactly what Zan-Thint had done to us. This had all been about keeping us here. Why? The pods were to complete his revenge against the Commonwealth and the remains of the Imperium. Weren't they? Wasn't that the whole point of this?

Gears were turning inside my head and I didn't like the configuration they were coming in. Zan-Thint had done a lot of things and I had yet to find one of them to make sense to me. But the general wasn't stupid. He was smart enough to keep a huge web of connections going while in exile, while the whole of Fleet Intelligence was searching for him. He'd built up his own fleet, his own army, and he hadn't done it for nothing. He hadn't done it to try to fight his way back through the Skrela, and I didn't think he believed that one newly-hatched batch of them could take down the Commonwealth. If he'd wanted that, he would have planted the thing somewhere close to human space, somewhere far away from his base, and let it start brewing.

He'd left it here instead, left it where we would find it, used it to delay us. Why was he here at all?

"What's the purpose of this place?" I'd said it aloud, without meaning to.

"To get us all killed," Vicky answered.

The bare rock had given way to something else...something I didn't recognize at first. Buildings built under the dome as if they were on a habitable world under the light of a star, but the light came from above us, from a series of lamps built into the ceiling. They were constructed from local rock, black and unfinished, but there was something familiar about the shape of them, their configuration. I couldn't place it and I stopped trying, letting the details wash over me instead, hoping it would come together in my head on its own.

Nothing moved, nothing was left. It had been abandoned before the air had been drained, but there was still debris on the ground. Blocks of some kind, fashioned from plastic? Wood? Either way, they'd been brought along, not made here. They were small and oddly shaped, as if they'd been made to fit together through friction connectors. I stepped on one accidentally, not hearing or feeling the crunch beneath my foot but seeing the splinters left behind.

"I've seen this before," Fargo said, echoing my own thoughts. "On one of the Tahni colonies."

"That makes sense," Vicky snapped, "since this *is* a Tahni outpost. This is probably their living quarters."

"No." The firm note in Fargo's voice surprised me. She usually didn't sound this sure of anything. "No, this wasn't military quarters."

"She's right," I confirmed, kneeling down to take a closer look at the blocks. There were images on them, Tahni writing. "These blocks...these are toys they use to teach their young children." I waved an arm around us. "This is the sort of compound their females lived in, separate from the males."

"They brought their families here?" Vicky said, disbelief strong in the words. "Why the hell would they do that?"

"Cam?" Fargo said, fear vibrating in her voice so strongly that I didn't bother to remind her she should be calling me by my rank. "I'm picking up something coming this way."

And now that I was paying attention to the sensors instead of the buildings, I was picking it up too. And I knew what it was, recognized the thermal signature.

"Shit, they're coming after us."

They weren't marching like soldiers. That would have been less scary, less inhuman. Nor were they barreling headlong like wild animals. I could have lived with the idea of the Skrela as brainless, unguided beasts. No, this was worse. The Skrela drones weren't marauding anymore, weren't aimlessly firing their guns at anything that moved. They'd managed to organize themselves now and they were swarming, a horde of army ants advancing through this airless, lava-rock jungle, consuming everything in their path.

And we wouldn't be fighting our way through them this time.

"Solano said the Tahni escaped from another landing pad," Vicky reminded me. "We have to find it."

I didn't have to give an order. None of us was stupid enough to do anything but run.

"*Orion!*" I yelled into my audio pickup, not knowing if anything was going to penetrate the dome, get to any receiver on the other side of it. "Solano! Does anybody read me?"

More female commune-style buildings, a dozen of them. Hundreds of females had been kept here, hundreds more children. How had they gotten them here? Where the hell were they taking them?

"If anyone can read me," I went on, "there are three of us left and we're trying to make it to one of the other landing pads. We're being pursued by the Skrela and we need pickup!"

"They're not going to hear you," Vicky told me.

She sounded so composed, not even out of breath. I was panting already, from the adrenaline, the fear, and the exertion. My muscles weren't moving the suit, but they *were* moving. And even if they didn't have to support anything, just the motion was wearing me down and a thin sheen of sweat covered my head, my neck, the small of my back. We couldn't run forever in these things...eventually, muscles would cramp up, and if we counted on muscle relaxants to take care of that, we'd still be loopy from the drugs.

But, as my first trainer at Armor School was fond of saying, we could certainly run in them for the rest of our lives.

"Then we have to get outside," I told her between gasps of breath and hammer-blow vibrations up through my suit from long, leaping steps. Energy beams snapped out into the interior walls, vaporizing stone and plaster, leaving behind glowing craters but no smoke, coming closer with each second, each step. "They'll hear us from outside."

"They'll be getting ready to nuke the whole place by then." Her voice was flat, resigned. She'd given up and it was enough to nearly stop me in my tracks. Vicky *never* gave up. I didn't have the breath to debate it with her now, but I made a note to bring it up later, if there *was* a later.

We were running past one underground ghost town after another. It was utterly unlike what I would have expected from a human outpost under a dome. We would have maximized the space, building up the ceiling, connecting everything together, but that wasn't how the Tahni brain operated. To them, the dome was just a replacement for the sky, and they built beneath it the same as they would have on a habitable world, the blocks of structures discrete and closed off. Here, one of the combination mess hall/temples I'd seen on every Tahni base I'd ever raided; there, a barracks building.

I toyed with the idea of trying to take cover inside one of the buildings and let them pass us by, but if they did figure out where we were, that would only have made us easier targets. But those shots from behind were getting closer, and just running our asses off until they finally homed in on us wasn't particularly appealing.

"We're gonna need to find a place to make a stand," I said, reluctantly giving in to the inevitable. It meant we were probably going to die, since Hachette was going to nuke this place, and he wasn't about to hold up just because he had a handful of troops on the planet, not when the entire Commonwealth was at risk.

"What's that?" Fargo asked.

She was still in front, ahead of me by about twenty meters, coming around the edge of what looked like a storage building, stopped dead in the road. I came up quickly behind her, about to yell at her to keep moving, when I saw what she'd seen.

It was an airlock. Not one of the landing platforms we'd bombed to start the attack...those, I had mapped out, and I knew we were nearly a kilometer from the next one, if we could even reach it from a direct route inside the base. No, this was a utility lock, smaller, not visible from orbit...just big enough for one of our suits to get through it at a time.

I had about two seconds to consider the problem. If we tried to squeeze through it together, the Skrela would run right up our asses.

"Fargo," I said, keeping my words calm and steady, "get through this thing and call us a dust-off. Hurry. We'll hold them off."

Karen Fargo wasn't the quickest Marine on the uptake, but she at least had the brains not to waste time arguing with me.

"Yes, sir!"

She went to the controls and I hoped she could figure out how to use them, because neither Vicky nor I would be able to help her. I would have asked Vicky to go through the lock first, tried to keep her alive, but I knew her too well to believe she'd leave me here to die. Vicky didn't say a word, just took up a position behind the corner of the storage building. I wasn't sure how much cover it would provide against the Skrela energy weapons, but I didn't say anything. It wasn't as if we had anything else to hide behind.

I went the other way, boosting up on my jump-jets, coming in above the horde of Skrela as they rounded the curve. There was an art to picking which one to target, knowing where the lynchpin was, and it was little different for these things than it was for humans or Tahni...because when neither of the latter two had time to think, they acted on the same sort of hind-brain instinct that these things seemed to be operating on. They were in a modified wedge formation, crammed closer together than a company of Marines would have been, four abreast, just enough to keep from having to break up to go around buildings, but narrowing down to two and then to one in the front ranks.

I shot the right-hand Skrela in the second rank, aiming for his left front leg, counting on Newtonian physics to do the rest of the work for me. I'd caught Vicky watching footage of the *Tour de France* once back during the war, which I'd found odd, since neither of us had as much as ridden a bicycle in our whole lives, having grown up in the mega-cities. But she was watching it for the crashes. I thought it was a bit morbid, but we *were* Marines in the middle of a war, so lots of things we did were morbid, and I'd settled in to watch the footage with her.

The chain-reaction tumble that resulted from the fall of the Skrela I'd shot reminded me of one of those bike crashes, the jumble of skittering legs clashing and clawing for purchase and not finding it. The whole line of them piled into the ones in front and blue energy beams exploded outward in every direc-tion like sunbeams coming through the clouds at dawn. Most of them came nowhere near us, though one sizzled a glowing crater into the wall about a meter from me before I started my descent. What they mostly hit was each other, which I found perversely gratifying.

And their friendly fire also gave me the space I needed to recharge my capacitors, the indicator blinking green just as I touched down near the front of their broken lines. The Skrela at the point of the spear had been the only one unaffected by the crash, but I'd been counting on Vicky to take care of that one and she hadn't let me down. The thing was tottering, trying to move without a head and coming terrifyingly close to succeeding before it finally toppled. I watched it with a corner of my eye in the rear-view camera display of my HUD, putting the better part of my attention into picking my next target.

It was a matter of timing, just as before. The wave of collisions had traveled back through the columns of Skrela, but unlike a peloton of human cyclists, emotional shock wouldn't play a factor in how quickly they recovered. That was all a matter of leverage and untangling themselves from each other, and also unlike humans—well, okay, *most* humans—these things didn't care if they stomped on each other to get to their feet.

There was a tipping point, where the front rank was getting back to their feet, and another lynchpin, where a single shot could do the most damage. I took it and almost paid for it with my life. The plasmoid seared through the upper torso of a Skrela drone that had just managed to get back to its feet, collapsing it back on top of two others who had come near to righting themselves. But I'd stayed in one place a second too long and a pair of pale-blue beams converged at my position just as I hit the jets again.

Searing pain shot up my left side from my ankle to my hip and I didn't need to look at the damage display to know just how close the near-miss had been, but it wouldn't let me get away without the gory details. Third-degree burns on the outside of my left leg, not to mention that I'd lost a centimeter of armor and there wasn't a whole hell of a lot between me and the vacuum now. The suit was hitting me with painkillers, and the effects on the speed of my thinking be damned, but the numbness hadn't kicked in before I touched down again.

I screamed, and the only reason I didn't collapse was the

suit. This wasn't the worst injury I'd ever had, but it was beyond anything I'd experienced since the war, and if pain and I weren't strangers to each other, we certainly hadn't kept up lately. I might have passed out for a second. I couldn't be sure, but between one eyeblink and another, Vicky was at my side, pulling me back toward the storage building.

I wanted to tell her it was useless, that the Skrela would slice right through the lava-rock bricks the Tahni had used to make the building, but I couldn't speak. Everything was becoming hazy, clouded with gauze, and I wasn't sure if I was going into shock or if the pain medication was finally beginning to hit me.

Through it all, I knew we were dead, and I wished I could make my brain work long enough to tell Vicky I loved her.

The world exploded.

I was on my back and I was surprised. Not surprised to be flat on my back, but surprised I was alive to realize I was flat on my back. The haze was still there, but the pain was definitely gone. The drugs had kicked in. That was good. I'd be able to die without pain, which was more than I had any right to expect after the life I'd lived. But where was Vicky?

I tried to move and was even more surprised when I could. Vicky was right beside me, on hands and knees, which looked utterly ridiculous for a Vigilante suit, but she was in the middle of trying to roll to her feet, clawing her way out of piles of black brick. The building had collapsed. That meant the Skrela would be on top of us at any second. I jammed my eyes shut and tried to concentrate, gaining enough mental wherewithal to push myself over onto my good leg, hopping upright with a judicious burst of my jump-jets.

I was, at least, going to give these soulless bastards one last shot before they overran us.

But they *weren't* overrunning us. Most of them were

trapped behind a wall of rubble, and the first rank of the things didn't exist anymore, burned into a twisted, charred ruin by the same weapon that had blown a hole in the side of the dome. Through the glowing edges of the hole, blackness rushed in from the vacuum without...until the silver wedge of a starship floated across it, belly jets glowing.

A suit of Vigilante armor clambered through the hole, running over to us with awkward, bounding steps.

"Come on!" Fargo urged, grabbing at my arm. "We don't have much time!"

I still couldn't talk, could barely move, but the suit was doing most of the work. I had to use the jets to get through the hole because I didn't trust the suit's left leg, much less my own. It was surreal being outside the dome. It had only been minutes, yet it felt as if we'd spent weeks in there, like we'd never get out again. The planet glowered at me with harsh, black crags, as if it were pissed off that I'd made it out alive.

"Cam!" The voice was Dunstan's, and the realization gradually penetrated my drug-addled mind that this ship floating to a landing outside the dome was his, Intercept One. "Get up the fucking ramp! Missiles are inbound!"

Light flowed out of the gap where the belly ramp was lowering, already two meters and still opening before the missile cutter even touched the ground. I could have used the jets to fly through it, but my head was swimming, and as loopy as I was, I thought it was more likely I'd wind up slapping right into the side of the ship. I leaned on Fargo and Vicky and limped up the ramp, thinking how weird it was that I couldn't feel the left side of my body anymore.

The ramp rose beneath us, and Intercept One lurched forward, the belly jets vibrating up through the hull, though I still couldn't hear anything. The ship was in a vacuum, except for the sealed cockpit, and the crew chief was in a full vac-suit, motioning us toward the cargo anchors just inside the belly ramp. I wasn't sure what he wanted us to do, but Vicky guided me into one of the anchor points and magnetic locks snapped into place around my ankles.

Pain. Even through the drugs, there was pain, just from the slight pressure of the anchors against the weakened metal on my leg. But I forced it down and slugged my brain back into coherent thought long enough to tie my HUD into the ship's tactical feed.

My inner ear and stomach both told me we were ascending straight up, and the views from the hull cameras confirmed it. The dome was beneath us, two kilometers and growing farther with every second. And then it didn't exist.

Where it had been a moment before was an expanding hemisphere of pure white, swallowing up the whole valley in the fury of a multimegaton fusion explosion. Then another joined it, and a third, and I knew the only reason Hachette hadn't launched more of them was because that was all the *Orion* carried. She lacked any anti-ship missiles and the three Space-to-Ground weapons were for situations exactly such as this.

"We did it," Fargo sighed. "We got them all."

I frowned, but I couldn't remember why I'd been about to disagree with her. But Vicky reminded me.

"No, we got the Skrela. We didn't get Zan-Thint. The fucking bastard got away."

[9]

"It's a damn shame about Cunningham." Top sighed, leaning against the bulkhead in the medical bay. "He was a good Marine."

The medical bay was in the ship's rotational drum, for some health reason that had probably been explained to me at some point, but I didn't recall. At the moment, I wasn't that happy with the situation, since it meant I'd had to be carried into the ward by a pair of orderlies, because walking under my own power had been out of the question.

It all seemed like an old nightmare now, the pain a distant memory. My entire leg, from hip to ankle, was encased in a gel sheath, medical nano doing their work to regrow muscle and nerves and skin. They hadn't stuck me in an auto-doc, which had surprised me, but Dr. Halonen had insisted on doing things the old-fashioned way.

"Those damned auto-docs," she'd said, "turn medicine into engine maintenance. I'd like to think there's a little bit of human touch in my profession still."

Which I had been too loopy at the moment to appreciate, but currently didn't much agree with. I'd done auto-docs before and they had the advantage of keeping you asleep until the whole ordeal was over. You woke up and that was it, you were good to go, whether it had been two hours or two weeks. With this stupid gel pack, I'd have to sit around and deal with the constant phantom itch that I couldn't scratch.

Another advantage of the auto-doc would have been that I could have avoided this conversation. I was still trying to come up with a response when Vicky finally spoke. She'd been standing there since we'd arrived on the ship, silent, just watching the Doc treat me.

"Wade," she said, "was an idiot. He couldn't lead a platoon of corporals into a whorehouse and he couldn't recognize the smart choice if you drew him a fucking map." The words were harsh, but her tone wasn't. Her shoulders were shaking and if she wasn't sobbing, it was because she was forcing the tears back, reining them in because she didn't want to lose control of herself. "But he was a good friend."

"He was that," I agreed, trying to adjust my leg on the sickbay bunk. It itched and I scratched at my hip above the gel pack, hoping it would do something to stop the sensation. "I was talking to him just before all this, about what he'd do when the operation was over, when we got Zan-Thint."

"We haven't got him yet," Top reminded me, her frown turning into a scowl. "Fucking bastard got away, jumped to Transition Space while we were tangled up with his corvettes. But there's nowhere left for him to run to. Once we figure out where he's headed, we'll hunt him down."

"Where's left?" Vicky wondered. "Where's left he can hide out? His whole plan is shot, now that we got the last seed pod."

"I don't think that was ever his plan," I confessed, leaning back against the pillow. It was hard to stay awake. The drugs from the suit had worn off, but the gel pack had its own anesthetics, and between them and the crash from multiple adrenaline rushes, I was close to wiped out. "He had females down there with them. *Children.*"

"What?" Top asked, pushing away from the bulkhead, looming over the bunk despite the fact that she was a head shorter than me. "How the hell do you know?"

"We found buildings down there that looked like the female communes we've seen on Tahni worlds," Vicky supplied.

"And there were those plastic building blocks their kids play with. You've seen them."

We both had, after the Tahni had bombed their own civilians trying to get to us. Scattered in the wreckage alongside little, broken bodies.

"That doesn't make any fucking sense," Top rumbled, staring at the bulkhead as if the answer was written on it. "This was a bolt-hole for his troops, someplace he could launch the final attack from. Why bring families along?"

"Zan-Thint didn't come all this way to commit suicide," I said, scooting up in the bed. "It's not in his nature. He's out here because this is on the way to somewhere else. Somewhere he couldn't go unless we thought the war was over and we'd won." I shrugged. "Or we were dead."

Top's brow furled, like she was thinking hard or possibly trying to focus her psychic powers to make my head explode.

"You think you can walk on that thing?" she asked, nodding at my leg. "We need to go have a talk with the colonel."

I cocked an eyebrow and motioned at my lack of pants. They'd left me my underwear and a robe.

"I'm a little out of uniform, Sgt.-Major."

"Throw on your robe, boy," she said, snorting a laugh. "Nobody cares."

In fact, they *did* care, even if they didn't say anything. The sidelong looks and questioning glances spoke volumes, and my cheeks warmed with each crewmember we passed. It was worse once we left the rotational drum and started down the central hub to the bridge. I mean, it was easier on my leg since I didn't have to put any weight on it, but my robe kept hiking up in the microgravity.

Wade would have laughed his ass off.

Hachette was deep in a conversation with Solano and Captain Nance when the three of us arrived and arrested our momentum on the handrail surrounding the crew stations. Cold fire hit my gut at the sight of Solano. I hadn't realized until that very second just how badly he'd pissed me off.

"Glad to see you up and around, Alvarez," Hachette told me, nodding a curt greeting. "Though I *should* write your friend Dunstan up for ignoring an order to clear the area." He shrugged, which had the effect of pushing him down into his acceleration couch against his seat restraints. "Since he managed to save your lives, I'll give him a pass, though."

"Hey, Cam," Solano said, floating over to put a hand on my shoulder. "I'm really sorry we had to leave you in there when the doors came down. And I'm sorry about Sgt. Cunningham too. I was ordered to get my Marines out of there, or I would have tried to blow the door down...."

I regarded him with the same sort of cold, unyielding look that usually preceded an invitation for someone to go fuck themselves, but I refrained from the follow-through, given our ranks and the presence of Colonel Hachette.

"I thought we *were* your Marines, Solano."

"Yeah," Vicky growled from beside me, not even trying to sound neutral about it. "I mean, you put a couple of captains on point for you. I guess it was almost worth it to say we killed more of the Skrela than your whole company even *saw*, but I can't help thinking that if you'd taken the couple minutes to blow that door down for us, Wade Cunningham would still be alive."

Solano's hand moved off my shoulder and his eyes went

wide. I almost felt bad for him. If he'd acted angry and self-righteous, like I'd expected, I wouldn't have wasted a second of pity on the man, but instead, Solano's face was white as a sheet, filled with guilt and self-doubt. Not that he didn't deserve the slam, but he wasn't a total shitbag.

"Enough," Hachette cut the exchange off, glaring at us. "I ordered Captain Solano to withdraw and he followed my orders. If anyone's to blame, it's me. Understood?"

"Aye, aye, sir," Vicky said, though from the look in her eye, the end result of the transfer of responsibility wasn't likely the absolution Hachette was looking for. If I knew my wife, she was now royally pissed at *both* of them instead of just Solano.

"Colonel," Top broke in, exasperation rasping in her tone, "we have more important things to talk about. Captain Alvarez said the Tahni had females and children in the dome. They likely evacuated with Zan-Thint."

Hachette snapped around so quickly, I thought he might have pulled a muscle in his neck.

"What? Are you certain?"

"We both saw their quarters," Vicky said.

"That's...." Hachette stared at the Tactical display on the main screen, which was a spaghetti bowl of multicolored course projections through Transition space. "We've been assuming he's on the run, trying to find a place to hide since we took out his last Skrela seed pod." His eyes came back to Vicky and me. "Do you think he has another one, another pod stashed that we don't know about?"

"I don't think this has ever been about the pods," I said, trying to sound confident, which would have been much easier without the draft going up my robe. "I think there's something else here, something we missed." I kept one hand on the railing and used the other to pull my robe together, trying to organize my thoughts. The drug haze had faded, but my brain still wasn't firing on all cylinders. "Look, sir, he found out about the pods from his brother, the priest. They had secrets that were handed down in their religion, secrets not even the Emperor knew. The pods were one of them...but they might not have been the *only* one."

"What?" Solano blurted, earning a sidelong glare from Hachette. "You think he's got some other secret weapon? Something even worse?"

"It's not about a weapon. It's about those females. Their kids. Think about it, sir," I went on, addressing Hachette. "Zan-Thint isn't an idiot. You think he really believed that him and his half-assed fleet could clean up what was left of the Skrela after they multiplied enough to wipe out the Commonwealth?"

"Then what?" Top wondered.

"He's taking them somewhere," Vicky mused, eyes clouded in thought as she caught up with my argument. "Somewhere we can't get to."

I nodded.

"And this whole thing has been about distracting us, making us look for those Skrela weapons, while he built up a fleet and an army, and a *colony*." I pointed at the display, at the dozens of multicolored strands representing the Transition Lines available from this system. "You can leave off any of those lines that head back toward Commonwealth space. He's not going that way."

"You're that sure?" Captain Nance asked. I glanced over at him. He hadn't said a word until now and he generally didn't get too involved in strategic discussions, but I suppose charting a course for his ship was more in his wheelhouse. No pun intended.

"I am. Anywhere he goes from Tahn-Skyyiah right through to the Pirate Worlds, he's gotta know, someone is going to notice. Same with the new colonies past the Tahni home system. He's got to be going somewhere without a habitable, somewhere the opposite direction, inward toward the galactic center."

"That doesn't leave much," Nance warned us. He touched a control on the arm of his command chair and almost all the noodle strands disappeared, leaving only three, all of them stretching out on one side of the animated representation of the system. "We're at the ass-end of the Cluster as it is. No Transition Lines past these three stars."

"What do we have?" Hachette asked. He could have looked it up himself, but I guess that's one of the benefits of being a full-bird colonel, being able to get other people to do that sort of menial shit.

Captain Nance, having the same functional rank, albeit translated into Fleet terms, motioned to his ship's Helm officer to do the search for him.

"Lt. Yanayev?"

I'd never spoken to the woman, but she was tall and statuesque, with steel-blue eyes that would have been at home on the toughest Force Recon killer I'd ever met.

"No names, just numbers," Yanayev said immediately, as if she'd been anticipating the order. She didn't bother to recite the alphanumerical designators, but she touched a control and they sprang to life beside the display icons. "Only two of them have had Scout Service expeditions...the other is scheduled for the next circuit...." She looked down at her console. "Four weeks from now."

I frowned.

"Who would have access to that schedule?"

"Anyone with a low-level military or civilian government clearance," Hachette said, shrugging. "This sort of thing gets published a year in advance. Why?"

"He knew," Top murmured, something akin to admiration in the words. "That son of a bitch *knew*."

"He knew we'd find it eventually," I agreed.

"Find *what?*" Hachette demanded, his patience visibly draining away.

"I don't know what. I do know where." I jabbed a finger at the world Yanayev had told us about, VN-987. "That's where he's going. I'll bet you a year's pay."

"You're betting a lot more than that," Hachette snapped, but he was looking at the star map. "I thought you said," he reminded me, "that you were a Marine, not a spy."

"It doesn't take a spy to think like Zan-Thint. He's not a spy either. He was a groundpounder, like me."

"If I follow through with this and it turns out to be a bust, Alvarez, you won't be the one whose career is over. General Murdock will slice off my testicles and feed them to his fucking cat if I screw this up."

"And if you don't follow it through, and never find him," Vicky pointed out, "what do you think he'd do then?"

"If he's not there," Hachette responded, sighing in resignation, "then there's no way we're going to find him anyway." He motioned at Nance. "Recall the patrol cutters and secure for acceleration to minimum safe jump distance."

"Will do," Nance said with a curt nod, turning to bark out orders to his crew.

"I hope that leg of yours heals up fast," Hachette told me. "This is a short hop. Four days, give or take."

"They'll have a head start on us," I fretted. "We might be too late...for whatever it is."

"Maybe, maybe not. T-space is funny when it comes to time. They have a few hours on us, but we could arrive at the same time, relative to their arrival. If you believe in God, now might be the time to ask for a nudge in the right direction."

I didn't respond, just let Vicky tug me back toward the lift bank, muttering something about getting me back to the sickbay before the boost started.

I believed in God, all right. That much was left over from my mama's influence.

I just wasn't sure if He was very fond of me.

[10]

My leg did heal up pretty fast, as it turned out. I still grumbled about it to Dr. Halonen when she took off the gel pack, just because I didn't want her to think she could throw one of the damn things on me whenever I got hurt.

"If I get burned like that again," I insisted, slipping back into my utility fatigues, "you gotta throw me in the auto-doc next time. You have no idea how badly that damned thing itches."

"Oh, I think I have *some* idea," she said, chuckling as she tapped data into a tablet with a stylus, not looking at me. "I spent two weeks in a full body pack during the Pirate Wars."

I finished fastening my belt and looked up at her, blinking in disbelief.

"You were in the Pirate Wars?"

"I'm not as young as I look." Another soft laugh. She didn't actually look all that young, but I wasn't going to say that to the woman who'd be putting me back together if I got hurt again. "I enlisted in the Marines right out of high school." Now she did meet my gaze, grinning. "Scandalized my whole family, let me tell you."

"How'd you get hurt?"

"Oh, I was on a lander with the rest of my platoon, hot LZ." She shrugged. "The assault shuttles were supposed to have suppressed the enemy artillery, but you know how that goes. Mortar rounds started falling the second we cleared the ramp. I woke up on a medevac bird heading right back up the way I'd come."

"Wow." I wasn't as impressed by the extent of her injuries as I was just by the fact that she'd been a Marine. "Is that why you're a part of this operation? Your combat experience?"

"That, and four years as a Force Recon combat medic during the war, before they sent me off to medical school."

I shaped a low whistle.

"Okay, Doc, I won't complain anymore."

"Just don't be giving me any more business, Captain Alvarez," she said, pointing at me with her stylus. "That'll be thanks enough."

"I'll do my best," I promised.

Vicky was waiting for me outside the sickbay...and so were Dunstan and Fargo. I looked between the three of them, uncomprehending.

"Is there a mission brief or something?" I wondered. "Or did you guys just want to be the first to tell me how glad you are that I can wear pants again?"

Vicky had a shoulder bag hanging across her chest and she tilted it toward me, showing a glass bottle filled with a clear liquid.

"We'll be Transitioning in thirty-six hours," she said. "This is our last chance to give Cunningham a proper sendoff."

I nodded, checking up and down the passage to make sure no one else could see.

"Just the four of us?"

"No one else knew him during the war. Except Top and,

honest, I'm kind of afraid to ask her to go break regulations with me."

I got that. We might be captains now, but deep down, we were both still privates fresh out of Armor School, reporting to our platoons for the first time. I looked at Dunstan questioningly.

"I know," he said, raising a hand to forestall my protest. "I didn't serve with him in the war, but we did work together for a while here, which is more than any of Solano's company can say."

"Come on," Vicky urged, waving me toward the lift bank. "Let's get somewhere they don't have surveillance cameras."

"Somewhere" turned out to be a storage closet tucked into the docking bay.

"You find this place?" I asked Dunstan, cocking an eyebrow in his direction as I squeezed past a rack of cargo crates. The far side of the room had been cleared and someone had set up a folding table and light plastic chairs.

"Well yeah," he admitted. "I mean, you gotta have some-place to chill without officers looking over your shoulder."

I pulled out one of the chairs and sat down, taking the weight off my leg. It was pain-free, but it still felt a little numb and tingly, which the doctor had assured me was temporary.

"You *are* an officer, Kyler," I reminded him. "You're an O-3, and you've been one longer than either of us."

"And yet, here you are," he pointed out, the plastic chair creaking under his tall, lanky frame.

Vicky pulled the bottle out of the bag and set it on the table with a loud clunk, then retrieved four plastic cups and laid them out. Fargo was still standing off to the side, hands clasped in front of her like a schoolgirl outside the principal's office, and Vicky eyed her, probably noticing the same reticence that I was.

"What is it, Fargo?"

"I don't know if I should be here, ma'am," she admitted. "I mean, I didn't know Sgt. Cunningham that well, and you guys are officers and I'm just...."

"Wade wasn't an officer," I told her. "And he was our friend. You fought beside him and I know he'd be happy to have you take a drink for him."

She hesitated for another second, but finally pulled out a chair and sat down, her butt at the edge of the seat as if she thought she might have to jump up and stand at attention at any moment. Vicky rolled her eyes but poured the vodka into the cups, setting one in front of each of us.

"Where'd you get the vodka?" I asked.

"Oh, that's mine," Dunstan said, grinning.

"Why am I not surprised?"

"Yeah, I picked it up on the last colony world we stopped at. They blow the glass there themselves, which I still can't get over." He chuckled. "Can you imagine that shit? They blow their own glass, like it's the fucking Dark Ages or something."

I didn't bother telling him that people had blown glass long before and long after the Dark Ages, figuring that he wouldn't care and I'd sound like I was showing off. Hell, I only knew it because of Captain Covington and his insistence that I get a real education and not just OCS leadership training.

"The vodka was made from real potatoes too," Dunstan added helpfully. "Not synthesized bullshit like you get on Earth."

I picked up the plastic cup, staring at the vodka. I hadn't had a drink since...when had it been? Bathala? Hausos? There'd been a time when I couldn't get through a day without a couple shots of whiskey or tequila, when the memories wouldn't stop beating down on me and alcohol was the only thing that would force them to let up. And now, when I'd watched Wade Cunningham die in front of me like so many others had done back in the war, I was having another drink.

"It's okay," Vicky told me. I looked up sharply, wondering if I'd let some of that slip, said it aloud without meaning to, but I realized it was just her reading my expressions as usual. "I wouldn't let you do it if I thought you couldn't handle it."

I nodded, smiling gratefully.

"Absent friends," I offered, raising my cup in a toast.

"Absent friends," the others murmured.

The vodka had a homemade bite to it, feral and unrefined, and even if Dunstan hadn't told me it came from a colony, I would have been able to tell. I liked it. It wasn't entirely pleasant, but it reminded me that I was alive, which was a good thing for a memorial toast.

"The first time I met Wade," Vicky said, going first because she'd known the man the longest, "he tried to hit on me." Dunstan snorted amusement, but I just grinned. I'd heard the story before. "We were both right out of Armor School and had just reported to the company, and we were assigned to some bullshit cleaning detail that should have been handled by a 'bot, but they had to come up with something to keep new privates busy. We were both bored, and jazzed to be at our duty station, finally, but frustrated not to be doing anything useful." She shrugged. "And truthfully, he wasn't too bad-looking a guy and we were both young and stupid, and if he'd come across a little less obnoxious and demanding, who knows?"

I scowled at her, not at the thought there'd been guys before me—I wasn't *that* naïve—but at the thought she would have had the poor taste to sleep with Wade. At least with the Wade I'd known back when I first reported to the company.

"Oh, get over it," she said, pushing against my shoulder. "Anyway, Wade was Wade and he had to push things too far and get grabby and I popped him in the nose. After he'd stopped the bleeding, I told him if he needed a fuck that badly, he should go fuck himself."

Even Fargo burst out laughing at that one.

"Yeah, my first impression of Wade wasn't that great either," I said. "He'd got a look at my scores in Armor School and he thought he'd get all pissy and put the new guy in his place." I took another shot of vodka, draining the cup. "Then, after our first combat mission, he blamed me for the death of his friend, my team leader. Kurita. That was his name. He'd been my battle buddy and he'd taken a missile and I hadn't even realized it. My comm antenna got fried, but Wade thought I should have been looking out better for Kurita." I shrugged, the old scourge stinging my soul, not quite as painful as it had once been because of the callus built up over the intervening years. "He and a couple friends tried to beat me up in the shower, but it didn't work out so well for them, and then Scotty showed up and broke it all up."

"Jesus," Dunstan said. "He sounds like a gigantic asshole."

"He was," Vicky agreed. "But people change. And what changed Wade Cunningham was falling out of an exploding drop-ship and shattering his spine."

"Oh, my God," Fargo exclaimed, rocking back in her chair. "I can't believe he survived that!"

"He couldn't either," I assured her. I squeezed my eyes shut against a tear that had been about to leak out. "I think he didn't believe he deserved to. But almost dying mellowed him, humbled him maybe. He was easier to get along with after that, and I think we would have been closer friends if I hadn't gone off to OCS."

"I left not too long after you," Vicky reminded me. "When I came back, I was in a different company. I didn't see Wade again for months."

"By the time I got the platoon," I said, "he was a squad leader in another platoon. I barely ever talked to him."

"And then he dragged us into all this shit." Vicky snorted. "I know Top asked him to, but I think he did it more because he was feeling lonely and out of his depth."

"But it *was* good seeing him again." I pushed my cup forward and Vicky poured me another. "We'd been trying to get away from the Marines, the war...all those memories. But running from the memories didn't make them go away. It just made me more afraid of them. Maybe it was a good thing that he brought us back to the military." I took another sip and made a face, but still swallowed it. "I think facing what I was feeling about the war was better than pretending it hadn't happened."

"You think you can deal with it now?" Vicky eyed me sidelong. "Or do I need to toss you out an airlock and put you out of my misery?"

"I think I need to listen to the advice I gave Wade," I told her. "Maybe I don't need to be a farmer, but there are other things out there. I just need to find one we can do together."

"You know," Dunstan cut in, sounding a bit more serious than usual, "up until a few weeks ago, I thought Wade was dead. You guys told me he died at Bathala to cover the fact that you were all working for Fleet Intelligence. And when I *did* know him, it was as a Corporate Council Security Force mercenary." He chuckled. "I thought he was kind of a dick, but that might have been part of his cover."

"Or not," Vicky murmured.

"But when I found out he was alive again," the pilot went on, "I went and talked to him. You know, just to clue him in that I'd joined the good guys, put on the uniform again. He told me I was a great pilot and he was glad I was aboard." He grinned. "Then he said I needed to learn to keep my mouth shut or the sergeant-major was going to gut me and leave me for dead."

"That's almost the same as what he told me!" Fargo said, thumping Dunstan on the shoulder. "Why is everyone so afraid of her?"

I was going to answer that question when the hatch to the storage room thumped open under a heavy palm and Sgt.-Major Ellen Campbell stalked into the compartment, hands on her hips. Fargo jumped to her feet and so did the rest of us, despite our officer ranks. Some habits were too hard to break.

"What in the fuck is going on in here?" she demanded, her quarterdeck bellow echoing off the walls of the compartment.

"Um, Top," I stuttered, "we were just...."

"You were just having a memorial for Cunningham." She jabbed a finger at me in accusation. "And you didn't bother to come ask me to join you?"

I was, for once, speechless. That usually doesn't happen. Thankfully, it *never* happens to Vicky. She reached into the shoulder bag and pulled out another cup, then filled it with vodka and handed it to Top.

"We knew you'd come," Vicky told her. "But we also knew you'd like it better if it was your idea."

Top eyed her dubiously from under thick brows, but she took the cup and pushed the hatch shut behind her.

"Of the two of you," she said, glaring at me, "it's pretty obvious Sandoval was the better pick for OCS. She appreciates her NCOs."

"Yes, Sgt.-Major," I replied meekly.

Top downed half her cup in a single gulp, not showing the slightest effect of the bite from the cottage-industry vodka.

"I met Wade Cunningham," she began without preamble, "when he reported to our company. He was a cocky little shit, always sticking his nose into every argument, like he was trying to prove something. Finally, I got tired of dropping him for pushups and giving him shit details and I did a little digging, past the sterile pap they stick in the personnel files. Wade Martin Cunningham was born in the Greater Cleveland Metroplex, in the Underground. His father was already serving a fifty-year term in punitive hibernation when he was born and his mother was a chronic Kick addict who wound up letting her sister raise him."

Top grunted something that might have been a laugh, though there was no humor in it.

"She wasn't any better a mother than his biological one had been, though, and little Wade had already seen Juvenile Rehab three times before his eighteenth birthday, mostly for his involvement with the local gangs in his housing bloc. He was looking at a forced emigration at best for his latest foray into crime, which had involved aggravated battery against a rival gang member. He chose the Marines instead, figuring that it would be better to kick asses and take the chance of being killed rather than getting paid shit wages to work on someone else's farm."

A memory of our conversation about farming traced a stream through my thoughts, running like a video clip, and something tightened in my gut. Wade and I hadn't gotten along, probably for the same reason I hadn't gotten along with gangs like the one he ran with in Cleveland, but we also weren't that different. Neither of us had anyone around to raise us, no family to take care of us the way Vicky's had. The difference was, he tried to find a family in his Housing Bloc gang and I hadn't had that option.

"Not an uncommon story in the Corps," Top mused. "But it helped me figure out how to motivate him, and I shared that information with his platoon sergeant. He just needed to start seeing the Corps as his gang...the platoon leader as the shot caller, the rest of his platoon as his brothers and sisters, the same kind of replacement family his gang had offered him."

"Which probably explains why he blamed me for Kurita dying," I murmured.

Top did laugh this time, a sound so rare, I thought at first it was someone else.

"Yeah, I heard about that little dust-up."

"You did?" I squeaked. "Did Scotty...?"

"No, Sgt. Hayes didn't narc on you," she assured me. "Nothing happens in my company and I don't know about it. I thought you knew me better than that." I had no intelligent response for that, because I suppose I should have guessed that already. "You took care of things, though," she acknowledged, "which meant I didn't have to." Top tilted her head to the side in a shrug. "It's usually better that way. And by the end, he was a halfway decent human being. So," she said, raising her cup in salute, "here's to Wade Cunningham. He died doing his duty and we'll remember him that way. Semper fi."

We echoed the words and drained our cups.

"By the way, Dunstan," Top said, tossing her empty glass back to Vicky, "this backwater swill sucks. If you ever break regs again for anything less than Grey Goose, you'll be out on the street faster than you can spit. You get me, *Lieutenant*?"

"Aye, Sgt.-Major," he said, snapping the words out like he was on a parade ground.

"Damn right." She nodded, regarding each of us. "Colonel Hachette is going to want you all ready for a mission brief in twelve hours." Top rolled her eyes. "Well, not *you*, Fargo; the officers. Though I suppose you can tag along if one of them wants you there to take notes or something. Anyway, be there and be sober. If you're right about where Zan-Thint is running, this is our last chance to nail his ass."

And then she was through the hatch and gone. I shared a look with Vicky and Dunstan.

"Twelve hours," I said. "You wanna finish that bottle?"

"Might as well," Dunstan sighed. "I don't know where the hell I'm gonna get Grey Goose out here."

"I know what Wade would do," Vicky said, tilting the bottle up and taking a shot straight from it, then passing it to me. "And just this once, I'm going to do the same thing."

[11]

"I'd feel better," Vicky said quietly, close to my ear, "if we were in our suits, in a drop-ship."

Colonel Hachette looked out the corner of his eye at us, as if he'd overheard, and I waited until he turned back to Captain Nance before I replied, speaking even softer than she had.

"Solano and his company are stuck in their suits, jammed into their drop-ships like good little mushrooms." And Top was with them, though I didn't remind her of that. "I'd rather be up here. Anyway, if we need Drop-Troopers that quick after Transitioning, we're fucked anyway."

Besides, though I didn't want to admit it, I liked being on the bridge during Transitions, not just because we could see more of what was going on but also because it made me feel like we were part of the decision-making process. I'd come back to the military, but I hadn't done it to be just a trigger-puller.

"Thirty seconds to Transition," Yanayev announced.

"All hands secure for Transition," Nance droned into the audio pickup at his chair. Then he glanced up at Vicky and me. "If you two are going to be hanging out on the bridge, you need to find an acceleration couch."

My ears heated up as I shuffled to the rear of the compartment and folded down one of the emergency seats from the bulkhead and strapped into it. Vicky didn't look embarrassed at all, but then, she'd never thought much of Fleet types. Taxi drivers, she liked to call them, though I'd always thought she was being a little unfair. True, they didn't have to run and gun on the ground with enemy behind every corner, but they were stuck in a giant tin can and most of them would probably never see the shot that killed them.

"Transitioning now," Yanayev said, and at the sweep of her hand through a haptic hologram, our gravity field dissipated along with the nothingness of Transition Space, and my stomach tried to come up through my throat.

The main screen was huge, a hologram the size of the front bulkhead, and in the projection there, reality snapped into being as we emerged back into our own spacetime near the edge of the system. No alarms sounded, which I thought had to be a good sign, and I squinted at the sensor readouts on the screen, trying to make sense of them.

Apparently, Colonel Hachette was having the same problem.

"What have we got?" he asked Nance.

"White dwarf," the ship's captain reported. "No inner planets left, consumed by the red giant stage of its stellar evolution." He jabbed a finger toward the outer orbits. "All that's left are two ice giants with a few moons. No energy readings from either of the planets or any of the moons that I can see. Tactical?" Nance turned to the Tactical officer, a Lt.-Commander Wojtera, an eastern-European-looking man with a long face and pinched features.

"You called it, sir," Wojtera agreed, ignoring the main screen for his own individual console readout. "Not getting anything from here in the outer system. No signs of the Tahni fleet. Checking starward now."

"Is 'starward' a real word?" Vicky wondered.

"I'm sure it is. I mean, it *sounds* like something the Fleet would say."

"What's that reflection?" Nance asked, leaning forward in his seat as much as his restraint straps would allow. "Close in, near the dwarf."

"Is it the Tahni?" Hachette demanded, jerking against his chest straps like he wanted to bolt out of his seat and right through the screen.

"I don't...*think* so," Wojtera said, frowning, his already-pinched face squeezing into a few centimeters. "The readings I'm getting from there are weird. I can't use active lidar or radar, not from this distance, and the gravimetic readings aren't anything I've seen before."

"What are gravimetic readings?" Vicky asked me, and I stared back, surprised she didn't know. She rolled her eyes. "Oh, get off of it, I was a Marine officer. I never once had to read a starship's Tactical board."

"Well, so was I," I reminded her. "But I looked into this stuff when I was researching that operation we did on Ambergris."

"Jesus," she sighed, shaking her head. "I'd almost forgotten about Ambergris."

"It's big, I think," Wojtera said, their exchange going on much louder than ours, drowning out what I'd been about to say. "Going by the albedo and the gravimetic warping effect off the star, I'm thinking it's about asteroid size? Maybe? But its mass is all wrong for that."

"Thermal?" Nance asked, leaving Hachette's mouth hanging open like the Intelligence officer had been about to ask the same thing.

"That's messed up too, sir." The Tactical officer spread his hands in a helpless gesture. "Going by the gravimetic output, I think there's some kind of power source in there. But it should be glowing like a fuck...like a *freaking* Christmas tree ornament. But it's not. It's cold. Well, it's cold enough that the only thermal readings coming off of it are from the input from the star."

"What about the Tahni ships?" Hachette asked. "Are you picking up anything from them?"

"Nothing, sir. But we're four light-hours from that thing, whatever it is."

"Shit," Hachette murmured. He eyed Nance. "What do you think, Captain?"

"I think we're not going to find out a damned thing sitting out here, sir. Do you want me to have one of the Intercept birds jump in and bring us back a recon report?"

Hachette didn't answer immediately, staring at the screen.

"No. Right now, they don't know we followed them. If they're in there, we can still surprise them. We send in a scout, they'll catch his warp corona, and Zan-Thint could jump right back out of this system before we could fire on him. Take us in. But ready the Interceptors for immediate launch on my order."

"Right. Yanayev, are the capacitors recharged?"

"Aye, sir."

"Then plot us a Transition in as close to that...whatever it is." He nodded back to me. "I don't know if you were right about Zan-Thint being here, Alvarez, but there's something weird here and I don't believe in coincidences. Not this big."

"Take just a moment, sir," Yanayev told him.

"Gravimetic sensors," I whispered to Vicky, finishing my thought from earlier while Yanayev did her work, "use the gravimetic field generators in the Teller-Fox warp modules, the ones that we use to tear a hole into Transition Space, to try to pick up gravitational warping from any sufficiently large mass or from other warp modules that are active, like someone jumping."

Vicky blinked and frowned at me.

"You remember all *that* from one mission seven *years* ago?"

I shrugged.

"You know I don't forget something once I've learned it."

"I know it's annoying as shit."

"All right, we're set," Yanayev announced. "We'd normally have to Transition no closer than 150,000 klicks from the object, but it's fairly close to that white dwarf, and I've calculated the spot where the gravitational pull from the star evens out with the pull from the object. We should be good to go at just under 60,000 klicks."

"*Should* be?" Hachette repeated, an eyebrow shooting up. Yanayev smiled, seemingly unconcerned.

"Nothing is certain in hyperdimensional physics, Colonel, but I'd stake my reputation on it."

"And just how *is* your reputation, Lieutenant?"

"I'm the best Helm officer on this ship, sir."

"Right." Hachette smiled thinly. "Captain Nance, alert the Intercept cutters and take us in."

"Another fucking jump," Vicky said, making a face like she'd bitten into something sour. "I hate micro-Transitions."

"I don't think anybody loves them," I agreed.

"Tactical, arm the main gun and sound general quarters."

I had an idea that sounding general quarters would mean blaring klaxons and flashing lights, but it was just an automated announcement both over the PA speakers and the earbud from my 'link. It was kind of a letdown.

"Transitioning in thirty seconds," Yanayev announced.

She counted it down, but I tried to shut that out because people counting down wore on my nerves. Instead, I thought about the object.

"What do you think it is?" I asked Vicky, nodding at the glowing red icon the computer was using to simulate the thing on the screen.

"Something Zan-Thint wants," she said, "so it can't be good."

"What *does* he want?" I wondered, speaking half to myself.

"All of us dead."

"No, he doesn't." I shook my head, firm with sudden conviction. "If he'd wanted us all dead, he had the way to do that. He wants something else. My mama used to read to me from a book called *Paradise Lost*. The Devil said he'd rather rule in Hell than serve in Heaven. I think he's trying to find his Hell."

"What the fuck does that *mean*?" she asked.

I didn't get the chance to answer, because we Transitioned.

I was getting used to it again. The first time I'd Transitioned after spending over a year on Hausos, it had *hurt*. Not physically, but somehow spiritually. Now, I barely noticed, though I *did* notice when we jumped back out again a few seconds later. There was a wrenching feeling, like turbulence, and I winced. But the discomfort seemed as illusory as the time between jumps. One second, we were staring at distant glints of light, and the next, we were right on top of the thing.

"Holy shit." That was Yanayev, who didn't seem like an officer who would talk out of turn, but I didn't blame her. "What *is* that thing?"

The object filled the screen, even from 50,000 klicks away. More than anything, the thing reminded me of a beehive. Not that it was shaped exactly like a beehive, any more than the Skrela drones were exactly like scorpions, or the pods were really similar to seed pods. But it was the first thing that came to mind when I saw it. Narrower at both ends, broad in the middle, intermittently ridged in a pattern, though one I couldn't have guessed the reason for.

Its surface glowed in the light of the white dwarf, and yet I had the sense that it was putting out more light than it was taking in, though I couldn't have said how. And there was something else about it, something I felt at a gut level, though I couldn't put a finger on the why or how of it.

"That's not Skrela," I declared, the words cutting through the babble on the bridge. Hachette and Vicky both stared at me with equal doses of skepticism. I went on before anyone could ask me a question I couldn't answer. "I'm telling you, sir, whoever built that, it wasn't the ones who made the Skrela we fought. It's...different."

"It looks too natural," Vicky said. I was surprised to hear her agreeing with me so quickly, but she was staring at the screen, nodding. "It looks like something I'd *expect* to see. Everything I've seen of the Skrela feels wrong."

"That's not much to go on," Hachette said, snorting a derisive laugh. "What are we picking up?"

"I've got the Tahni, sir," Wojtera announced, and somehow, we all forgot about the artifact as red threat icons popped up on the board. "They were here already." He traced a line through his control board and the images grew on the screen. Two Tahni destroyers, one of them showing a lot more damage than the other, doled out, I assumed by the *Orion* during the battle over Firbolg. Nothing else, though their other ships could be inside their hangar bays. "They got here sometime in the last four hours, or we would have seen them when we were sitting in the outer system."

"Have they seen us?" Hachette asked him. "Are they adjusting course?"

Wojtera didn't answer immediately, his eyes narrowing as they flickered back and forth over the stream of data coming up on his station's readout.

"Sir, something...weird is happening."

"No shit," Vicky said quietly.

"The Tahni destroyers, sir," Wojtera went on. "Their drives are cold. They aren't boosting, but...they're *accelerating*. Toward that thing. And way too fast, hundreds of gravities. They're not using their Teller-Fox drives, not that they *could* that close to a gravitational mass the size of the object. It's fucking impossible, sir."

"Set course for intercept," Hachette directed, his jaw set in determination, ignoring the impossible and focusing like a laser on his mission. "Maximum boost."

"You heard the man, Yanayev," Nance snapped, though it seemed to me that he wasn't very happy about it. "Six gravities, set for intercept."

"At the acceleration they're going," Wojtera warned, "they're going to reach that thing before we intercept."

"Do it anyway," Hachette told him. "They're going to have to decelerate before they reach it. We'll catch them when they do."

"*Are* they going to have to decelerate?" Nance asked, a hard edge in his tone, something that might have been panic flaring behind his eyes. "Why would you think that when they're magically flying across space? Do we know what this thing is? Do we know that the artifact isn't doing this?"

"No, Captain," Hachette ground out. "I *don't* know. But what I *do* know is that Zan-Thint is out there and our mission is to kill that son of a bitch. And despite the fact that we share a rank, *I* am in charge of this task force and you *will* follow my orders."

"Shit." I said it low enough that only Vicky could hear it.

I thought for a second that we were going to have a mutiny, and I wasn't sure which side I would have taken. Hachette was bulling ahead and not thinking about this, but he was right that it was Nance's job to follow his orders. But apparently, Nance realized the same thing.

"Yanayev," he said, biting the words off, "intercept course."

"Aye, sir," she said, and there may or may not have been a tremor behind the words. "High-acceleration warning." There was a klaxon this time, if short-lived. This wasn't just about being ready for possible combat; it was to avoid serious injury. I tightened my restraints. "Accelerating now."

I braced myself, fingers clutching at the armrests, ready to get smashed back into the cushioning gel of the seat.

Nothing happened.

"What the hell is going on?" Nance asked, probably beating Hachette to the punch by half a second.

Yanayev didn't answer immediately, swiping her hand through the haptic hologram of her controls over and over, frustration building up in her expression with every second. When she looked up at Nance, the frustration turned to fear.

"Sir, the drive won't ignite."

"Engineering!" Nance barked at the red-headed woman sitting at the Engineering station. She wasn't the ship's Chief Engineer—that was Chief Patel down in the Engineering section. But Lt. Kelsey was the officer in charge of the Engineering section, which, in practice, meant she told Chief Patel what the captain wanted and told the captain what Chief Patel told her was happening. "What's wrong with the Goddamned fusion drive?"

Kelsey was a deer in the headlights, quivering in fright.

"The controls aren't responding, sir," she told him, her voice tremulous. "Chief Patel says that the reactor is functioning, but the signals to the drive aren't going through. He doesn't know why."

"Launch the interceptors." Hachette was trying to sound confident, trying not to come across as afraid, probably sensing the same panic spreading throughout the rest of the bridge crew and not wanting to feed the fire.

"Intercept cutters, launch immediately," Nance ordered over his station audio, not even bothering with the Flight Control Officer.

But it was that officer, Commander Ralston, who answered the order. Ralston was a stern-eyed man who reminded me of some of the cops who'd busted me when I was a kid.

"Colonel, the drives on the interceptors aren't igniting either. Not even the maneuvering jets." He pronounced the words like a sentence handed down from a judge. "The pilots report that they've tried bypassing the main control bus, but the signals aren't going through."

"How the fuck is that even possible?" Hachette exploded, finally losing his cool. I didn't blame him. I'd lost mine two minutes ago. "Is this Zan-Thint?"

"Not a fucking chance," I said, not caring that I was out of line. "If he could shut down our drives from a distance, he'd have already taken over the Commonwealth."

"It's that *thing*, sir," Nance declared. "It's gotta be."

"We're moving," Wojtera said. He sounded as if he was in awe more than afraid. Not me. I was afraid. "We're accelerating toward the object."

"Tactical," Hachette said, "target the object with the railgun and open fire. Continuous volley until I tell you to stop."

Wojtera shook his head.

"Weapons systems are down. Everything from the railgun to the Gatling lasers. Nothing is operational except comms and life support."

"That's fucking impossible," Kelsey blurted from the Engineering station. The color had drained from his face and I think if there'd been any gravity, he would have collapsed. "How the hell are they shutting down just weapons and drive systems? What the hell could even *do* that?"

Hachette's hands were shaking as he yanked at the quick-release for his seat restraints, floating free of his acceleration couch, his jaw working as if he were chewing at the problem. Apparently, it was indigestible, because when he turned to Vicky and me, he seemed totally lost.

"Alvarez, Sandoval," he rasped. "Recommendations? Should we try to launch the drop-ships?"

"It won't do any good," I told him. "If the interceptors won't launch, the drop-ships won't either."

"We should get the Marines off the ships," Vicky said. "Get them set up to defend the airlocks."

"Defend them from *what*?" Hachette asked her.

"From whatever's on that thing." She pointed at the beehive. "Because that's where we're going."

"Do you really think Drop-Troopers are going to do anything against whatever's pulling us into that?" I asked her. I wasn't panicking despite the roiling in my gut, despite images of alien monsters, mostly because Vicky wasn't and I didn't want to let her down.

"No," she admitted. "But I think Top and the others would rather go out that way than crammed into a drop-ship."

"Sir," Nance suggested, "maybe we should consider abandoning ship?"

Hachette finally seemed to get his shit together, disdain for Nance's suggestion doing what pure training and experience couldn't.

"And assuming whatever's pulling us in would even let us do that, Captain, where the hell would we go?" Nance had no answer for that, and Hachette shook his head. "No, I think whoever's inside that thing...." He nodded toward the growing shape on the screen. "...we're about to meet them."

[12]

No one spoke.

The ship moved in complete silence, missing even the distant vibration of the fusion drive, the image on the main screen sliding by with a velocity that seemed unreal, like we were watching a simulation at double-speed. Someone should have been asking what to do. *I* should have been asking what to do, but I trusted my own judgement as much as Hachette's, which meant the only person I would have asked was Vicky, and I could already tell what she was thinking.

"Are we picking up anything?" Nance finally broke the silence, looking to Wojtera and Yanayev. "Any effects from the... whatever's doing this?"

"The gravimetic sensors are down," Wojtera told him. He was holding it together better than his commander or mine. He would probably make a good ship's captain himself, if there were any chance in hell we were going to live through this. "Along with the Transition drive. We *are* getting some gravity waves, but I can't make sense of them. It's almost like there's a singularity out there."

"Medical?"

The medical officer wasn't the ship's doctor, just like the Engineering officer wasn't actually the chief engineer. I don't know why the Fleet does it that way...it's not the damned blue-water Navy. The captain could just as easily have called down to Engineering or the sickbay and talked to the HMFIC, but I guess maybe the idea was that it would be better not to have to bother someone who was busy doing more important things.

Lt. Tovar, the bridge medical officer, took a moment to answer, one hand to her ear, listening to a report over her earbud.

"There are no injuries or ill effects reported from anyone in the crew or the Marine contingent," Tovar said. She shrugged. "There are a few cases of people panicking, but no one has required medication yet."

I bet there were. I could see a couple people on the bridge crew who could have done with a sedative. Maybe me, in a second.

"Who's going to get there first?" Hachette asked, motioning at the front screens. "Us or the Tahni?"

"Looks like we're going to arrive at the object pretty much at the same time," Wojtera told him. "I think maybe the...thing...is arranging it so it happens that way."

"How thoughtful of them," I murmured aside to Vicky. I wanted to unfasten my seat restraints, but I didn't want to wind up thrown across the bridge if the alien assholes decided to play handball with us.

"Cam," Vicky said, grabbing my arm hard enough that I winced. Her jaw was clenched, nostrils flaring like she was about to throw down with someone. "What the hell are we going to do? I don't want to just sit here waiting. Let's go get suited up."

I wanted to argue with her, wanted to point out that our Vigilantes weren't going to do much good against beings who could shut down our weapons and drives, but I got the sense she didn't need me to reason with her. She was just as scared as I was, but she was expressing it with a need to act.

And why wasn't I? I hadn't considered it until that moment, but the whole thing seemed...revelatory. We'd been chasing the remnants of an ancient civilization since this had all begun on Hausos and now we were about to find the answers, and I would rather have stayed on the bridge to have ringside seats.

I didn't think that answer would convince Vicky.

"Okay," I told her, yanking the quick-release on my harness. "Let's go. Top's probably organizing boarding defense parties already."

"You may as well stay here, Alvarez," Hachette said before Vicky was halfway out of her seat. "We're going to be inside that damned thing in two minutes."

"It's unbelievable," Nance said, eyes glued to the screen. "We're travelling at nearly half of lightspeed. If they don't stop us, we'll be atoms in two minutes."

"They'll stop us," Hachette insisted, sounding more like a prayer than a prediction. "If they can do this, they could have just disintegrated us from 50,000 klicks away."

He was pulling himself together, finally. I guess I should have expected it. He was a Fleet Intelligence colonel, after all, and they wouldn't have sent him on an operation like this if he couldn't handle the unexpected. Maybe not something *this* unexpected....

Vicky had pushed out of her chair despite Hachette's advice and was heading for the bridge hatchway, but I stopped her and pointed to the screen. A few seconds before, the beehive had seemed a thousand klicks away, but it had expanded in those scant moments to fill the main viewscreen.

"Too late," I told her.

This close, the details of the structure should have been

clearer, more precise, but there was still a hazy quality to them, as if they weren't actually there. The glow I'd taken for a reflection wasn't. It was coming from somewhere inside, though how, I couldn't even guess. The surface of the thing wasn't pockmarked by micrometeorite impacts like I'd expected, given how long it had to have been out here. It was smooth, perfect, untouched.

And at the narrow end, where I expected an entrance... there was nothing. A blank hull. And we were heading straight for it at a good percentage of the speed of light.

"Shit!" I yelped. It wasn't my proudest moment, but I wasn't in a Vigilante suit and, if there'd been any gravity, I would have ducked behind something.

I wanted to say something to Vicky, something we could hold on to all the way through eternity, but I couldn't make my brain work fast enough. The wall of glowing green met us and we passed through it. And stopped.

"What the fuck just happened?" Vicky blurted, just one of a dozen voices chattering at once on the bridge, probably one of hundreds throughout the ship.

The screen had gone fuzzy when we'd passed through the wall, and when it cleared up, we were floating inside a giant hollow, surrounded by a latticework of glowing green webs and spiraling towers protruding from walls I couldn't make out past the verdant glow that seemed to come from everywhere.

And there was gravity. It slapped up against the soles of my boots as I dropped the half a meter to the deck, and I had to grab at the side of my acceleration couch to keep my balance. *How* there was gravity was a mystery, but not as big a mystery as how it was pulling us in the vertical orientation of the ship. There was no reason it should have. I was totally prepared to believe the aliens who could disable the ship's drives and pull us and the Tahni through space at relativistic speeds could generate gravity, but the gravity was perfectly aligned with the ship.

I wondered if it was aligned with the interior of the Tahni destroyers. They were so close to us, I felt like I could touch them through the viewscreen, wedge-shaped monoliths hundreds of meters long, yet even abreast with the *Orion*, they didn't come near the edge of the glowing webs or the twisted spirals protruding beyond them and through them.

"Status?" Hachette demanded, his voice cutting through the confused babble. "Do we have power to drives? Shields? Weapons? Anything?"

"Negative, sir," Kelsey replied. "Everything is still locked out except life support and comms."

"We could send the Vigilantes out with external fuel tanks," Vicky suggested, pointing toward the Tahni ships. "They could board the destroyers."

"You think whoever brought us in here would let us do that?" I asked her.

"Keep an eye on those ships," Hachette said to Wojtera. "If you see anything coming out of them, even a single Tahni in a space suit, you let me know."

"What now?" Nance asked. Hachette turned and frowned at him and the ship's captain expounded. "They brought us here. What are they going to do now?"

"Are we picking up anything at all inside besides the Tahni ships?" Hachette asked.

"There's all sorts of screwy gravitational wave readings," Wojtera replied. "Even stronger in here than outside. It's strong enough to be a singularity, but if there were a black hole inside the ship with us, I think we'd know about it."

"How big is this thing?" Vicky asked. Wojtera looked over at her like she was an elementary school student who'd spoken out of turn, but he answered the question.

"I couldn't get a clear reading before we went in, because we weren't getting any kind of radar or lidar return, but it has to be at least a hundred kilometers long and maybe seventy-five wide at the skinniest. And I have no idea what the hell it's made out of or what's producing the glow."

"We have comms," Hachette mused. He motioned toward Chase, the Communications officer on duty. "I want you to broadcast a message, omnidirectional microwaves. Make sure anything inside this object can receive it. Route the signal from my station."

Chase took a second to work the controls at his station, then nodded to Hachette.

"You're a go, sir."

The Intelligence officer took a deep breath and spoke with the sort of deep, self-important timbre I was used to from colonels.

"This is Colonel Hachette. I am an officer in the military of the Commonwealth. We come from a planet called Earth." Well, in the generic sense, anyway, though I was sure a good percentage of the crew had been born on the colonies. "We have come to this system in pursuit of war criminals who attempted to end all life in our section of space. We have no quarrel with you, nor do we wish anything but peaceful contact with you. We ask that you reply to our signal and let us know your intentions."

He looked as if he was about to say something else, but he shut his mouth and touched a control to kill his audio pickup.

"Do you think they'll be able to speak English?" I asked him, more curious than skeptical. It was hard to rule anything out.

"Something's happening," Chase announced, scowling at whatever he was reading in his display. "There's some kind of signal coming in."

"Is it a message?" Hachette asked, leaning forward in his seat.

"It's a computer networking link." Chase looked up at him, eyes going wide. "Something is trying to access our database."

"Shut down the computer networking!"

"Too late, sir. With the power of that signal, they've got what they were looking for."

"And what's that?" I asked, not expecting an answer. "Are they trying to look through our history and decide whether we deserve to live?"

"You've watched too many ViR-dramas, Alvarez," Hachette scoffed, but he didn't offer any alternative theories.

"Should we strap in again?" Vicky asked me, one hand still grasping the back of her chair as if she expected the gravity to shift any second.

"I don't think it matters at this point," I told her, stepping out into the center of the bridge tentatively, keeping a hand on my chair until I could grab the back of Hachette's, which earned me an annoyed glare.

"Sir," Chase said, "we're getting a comm signal."

"Another probe attempt?" Hachette asked him.

"No, sir...it's a message. In English."

"Well, I guess that's why they needed to access our database," I said, wondering why the hell I was acting so calm. I certainly wasn't *feeling* calm.

"Do you want me to send it to your earbud, Colonel?" Chase asked Hachette, and I couldn't help but shoot a dirty look at the man. This was the first contact with ancient alien gods and he wanted to make it a private call.

"No," Hachette said, acting as if he'd been seriously considering it. "Put it over the ship's intercom. Everyone deserves to hear this."

"Damn right we do," Vicky said, a bit too loud, but Hachette and Chase acted as if they hadn't heard and the Communications officer waved a hand through his control hologram.

The voice that came over the speakers was unmistakably female, and somehow very familiar.

"Greetings from the Corridor."

I expected the voice to go on, but it paused, as if waiting for us to respond, and Hachette eventually did.

"What is the Corridor?"

"The Corridor is where you are," the voice answered reasonably, if infuriatingly. "It is the path out of the Enclosure." Hachette opened his mouth, but the voice interrupted them. "You are about to ask me what the Enclosure is. I have reviewed your terminology while I learned your language, and you refer to it as the Cluster, the stars connected by the Transition lines. As some of your physicists have already hypothesized, this arrangement is not a natural one. It was put in place by the beings you know as the Predecessors."

Someone on the bridge gasped, though I don't know why. Anyone who'd been paying attention could have figured out that was the road we were on. We'd been tracking the weapons used to kill off the Predecessors, so coming across them now shouldn't have been a surprise.

"How did they engineer Transition Lines?" Nance asked, not sounding skeptical so much as scandalized. "How is that even possible?"

"Through the judicious placement of singularities. This was done to protect you and the species you know as the Tahni from the Skrela. It was the only way the Predecessors could defend their home and what they had created for their children."

"We're their children?" Hachette asked.

Now I recognized the voice. It was the same computer-generated voice I'd heard in every training video I'd watched in

Boot Camp or Armor School. Whatever this thing was, it had stolen the voice from our files along with our language.

"No, not you. You are the inheritors of their homeworld. The Tahni are their children."

Complete silence. Even Hachette couldn't think of anything to say to that, and if a full bird colonel was at a loss for words, everyone else surely was. I knew what the thing was saying, knew the implications of it immediately, and it wasn't anything I hadn't been thinking myself. But it was one thing to consider something that crazy a possibility, another to hear it declared as gospel.

"Are you a computer?" I blurted. Hachette and Nance both stared at me, but no one else had bothered to ask.

"I am a sentient system left in place by the Predecessors to guard the Corridor."

A sentient system. That was disturbing. I was a kid from Tijuana via the Trans-Angeles Underground, and then a grunt, so that sort of high-level political shit was well beyond me, but from everything I'd read and heard during OCS, there was a damned good reason why the Commonwealth heavily restricted research into sentient systems. Beyond the ethical concerns of actually creating and exploiting a sentient, thinking machine, there was the whole problem of taking the risk of trusting one of them. Humans were sentient, thinking entities and way too large a percentage of them were imbalanced, unstable, violent, unreasoning, and sometimes you couldn't tell which ones were problems until it was too late.

What happens if you build a sentient computer and then put it in charge of asteroid defense for Earth or one of the core colonies, put a bunch of high-powered weaponry under its control and then it goes nuts and decides it doesn't really like humans and they all deserve to die? It was bad enough we had to put humans in charge of shit like that, but at least with them, we knew what to look for to find out if they were headed around the bend.

"Corridor, you said your name was?" Hachette asked the thing.

"I do not have a name. Corridor is a description of what I am and the purpose I serve."

Hachette's face contorted as if he'd been about to snarl then remembered he was talking to a sentient computer capable of ripping the ship to shreds.

"What do you *mean* that we inherited *their* homeworld? What do you mean that the Tahni are their children?"

"He sounds like a fucking parrot," Vicky growled quietly beside my ear.

And she wasn't wrong, but I couldn't blame him. How many decades had we been asking these questions?

"You evolved independently on the same world as the Predecessors, after they had left your planet. The Tahni were engineered."

There was so much more I would have asked the thing. Like why? Like what the hell did it *mean* that the Predecessors evolved on Earth? But Hachette had other priorities.

"Why have you brought us here? Do you intend to hand us over to the Tahni?"

"I do not exist to serve the Tahni. Nor do I exist to serve you. I exist to guard the Corridor. The Corridor's existence is necessary to preserve the possibility of the return of the Predecessors to the Enclosure and their homeworld, once the Skrela have been eradicated, but if the existence is revealed to your Commonwealth, it puts you and the Tahni at risk. The possibility remains that the Skrela are out there, beyond the Enclosure, ready to finish what they started tens of thousands of years ago. It is my purpose not to allow this to happen."

What the thing was saying was damned important, both in

general and to me in particular, but all I could think of was its voice. I kept expecting it to lecture me on the military regulations for uniform wear or inform me that it was illegal to use my position as a member of the Commonwealth armed forces to try to gain favors from local businesses.

"Are you going to kill us?" Vicky asked.

"Damn it, Captain," Hachette snapped, rounding on her, but the Corridor answered her question with equanimity.

"I am discouraged from killing sentient beings except to guard this place. When I was constructed, there were no other spacefaring races in the Enclosure, but the Predecessors anticipated that you or the Tahni might find this place eventually. My creators were loath to take life, so they left me with but one option."

"And what's that?" Hachette didn't sound like a colonel anymore. He was as scared as the rest of us, facing a problem that wouldn't be solved by the eagles on his shoulders.

"You will be sent through. If I understand your culture correctly, I believe it would be appropriate to wish you good luck."

The hair was standing up on the back of my neck and I reached out to grab Vicky's hand. On the main screen, a blue halo flickered around the superstructures of the Tahni destroyers, just an almost-imperceptible glow at first, but cohering into streaks running vertically along the length of the things, then connecting with each other and forming spirals. They encompassed both ships, spinning ever faster, and static electricity crackled in the air on the bridge.

"Send us through what?" Hachette yelled at the screen, though I didn't think he was going to get an answer. "Send us through to where?"

The Tahni ships were swallowed by the blue glow, their details lost inside the haze of color and light, and the screen blinked. Everything was blank for nearly a full second, just the slate grey of the projector losing its link to the external cameras, and when the image returned, the Tahni ships were gone.

And the blue fireflies were flitting to life around us.

"All hands!" Nance yelled into the ship's intercom pickup. "Secure for Transition!"

The azure energy swallowed the view around the ship, and somehow, it penetrated the hull and the bridge and right into my brain. Everything went dark.

[13]

It wasn't a Transition.

I didn't know what it was, but I'd gone through enough Transitions in my life to know this wasn't one of them. I'd even transited a wormhole jumpgate once, but this was nothing like that either.

A Transition was experience but without duration. There was no sense of time to it, just a memory of experience that I was never quite sure I'd had. This sensation went on for several seconds at least, and the duration held the promise that it could stretch on into infinity. It was as if my soul was pulled from my body and stretched like taffy halfway across the universe, and when it stopped, it snapped back into me with enough violence that I spun backwards through the bridge compartment, back in free-fall.

Klaxons were sounding, automated warnings echoing on the bridge speakers and in my earbud, telling me what I already knew, that the ship was under stress, that it had gone through some sort of anomaly. No human voice greeted me on the other side of whatever had happened, not for several seconds.

I smacked shoulder-first into the far bulkhead of the bridge, less than a meter from the hatchway to the outer passage, and winced at the spray of light behind my eyes, the dull pain running through my back. Bouncing back the way I'd come, I pulled my knees to my chest and rolled in mid-air, trailing a hand downward to snag the railing around the command stations. A twinge of pain flared in my shoulder, but I managed to hold on, then reached up to catch Vicky as she was about to sail past.

By that time, the shouting had already started.

"...reading multiple bogies at ranges from ten thousand kilometers out to 300,000...."

"...no planetary formation in this system. Red giant star that may have swallowed them all up in its expansion...."

"...can confirm we are *not* anywhere in the Cluster."

That last was from Yanayev, and I paid special attention to it, since I had the conviction, through a veil of pain and shock, that this was the question that held the preeminent importance for us.

"I'm trying to run star pattern recognition to get us a more exact location."

I couldn't tell much from the images on the screen, the view from the external cameras, except that we weren't where we had been. The white dwarf and the object were both gone, replaced by the dull red glow of the giant star...and a wash of white where a nearby cluster of stars was close enough to nearly drown out the glow of the dying giant.

"All systems are back online!" Lt. Kelsey exclaimed, exulting as if the change was the result of something she'd done personally rather than just a report from the section. "Drives, sensors, weapons, everything!"

"Where are those damned Tahni?" Nance demanded. "Did we come out at the same place?"

"I've got them, sir," Wojtera whooped, pointing at the main

screen. "Both bogies are off the port bow at ten thousand klicks, drives still dark. Orders, sir?"

I don't know if he was talking to Nance or Hachette, but Hachette stepped back into the role of operational commander quickly enough, even if he hadn't commanded anything but jack and shit for the last few minutes.

"Half-G boost, Helm, and make me a course for the Tahni ships. Tactical, arm the railgun and prepare to take helm control for targeting."

"Half-G boost, intercept course, aye," Yanayev responded, not seeming to care which of them was giving the orders.

"Sir," I said, finally catching my breath, pushing Vicky back toward the spare acceleration couch ahead of me, "are the Tahni still the priority?"

"Zan-Thint is the mission, Captain Alvarez," Hachette snapped, not looking back at me, eyes fixed on the Tactical display as it began to repropagate on the main screen, fed by the newly-active gravimetic sensors. "You should know that better than anyone."

"Zan-Thint *was* the mission," I corrected him. "Shouldn't we be concentrating on how the hell we're going to get back to the Cluster from wherever we are?"

"I plan on giving it my undivided attention, Captain," he promised, "once we blow up those Goddamned Tahni."

I sighed but didn't bother arguing. Half a gravity of boost kicked in, pushing me down into the acceleration couch, and the view on the screen shifted, swinging the nose toward the enemy ships.

"The destroyers are adjusting course," Wojtera announced. "They've seen us."

"What the hell are we doing?" Vicky asked, not keeping quiet at all this time. "We just got thrown halfway across the galaxy by some alien avocado and we're worried about the Tahni still?"

Hachette might have ignored her carping before, but not this time. He rounded on her, fire licking at the sides of his ears, fingers curled around the ends of his armrests like he was prepared to vault right out of the seat at the wrong word.

"Captain Sandoval, if you suddenly have a problem with following orders and respecting your commanding officer, I suggest you take your opinions and get them the hell off this bridge! I'm sure Captain Solano has a spot for the both of you in a drop-ship and we may very well be executing a boarding action before this operation is over."

Vicky's nostrils flared, her eyes narrowing, and she was getting very, very close to saying something that would likely get her thrown into the brig. I didn't blame her. I thought Hachette was being an idiot. But I didn't want to watch what happened from the brig—if there *was* a brig—or confined to our quarters.

"Yes, sir," I said, jumping up, less worried about the Tahni than I was about Vicky's temper. "We'll go get suited up."

Vicky didn't look happy about it, but she got up to follow me since it was what she'd wanted to do from the beginning anyway. I was playing out the battle to come on a sand table inside my head as we headed for the hatchway, imagining the space engagement in vague terms since it wasn't my area of expertise, but putting more detail into the boarding action. We'd have to spread out our boarding teams to every airlock and hangar bay we could access, let the assault shuttles and the intercept cutters blow holes for us....

We didn't quite make it to the hatch.

The proximity alarms blared across the bridge, and by the time I turned back to the viewscreen, they were already there.

"Transitions!" Wojtera snapped, and I don't know how the

hell he kept his cool. "Multiple bogies transitioning within ten thousand klicks!"

We should have either gone down the passage, gone for the lift to get our suits on, or made our way back to the acceleration couches, but all I could do was stare at the screen, and if Vicky had any better ideas, she wasn't mentioning them. What stared back at me was something bulbous, twisted, deformed; shapes that had never come from the mind of a human, nor even a Tahni. The Tahni were technically aliens, but they shared a humanoid design with us, and form followed function. Whatever imagination had sculpted these ships hadn't come from a bilaterally-symmetrical biped, much less a human.

They should have been totally unfamiliar, but they weren't. There was some pattern to the twists and whorls and protuberances, not anything I'd seen before, not exactly, something that sparked a memory just out of my grasp, something that held me there, captivated and speechless long after I should have moved.

Lucky for all of us that Captain Nance knew his job.

"Helm, emergency boost! Ninety-degree maneuvering burn, south!"

Which meant that in about two seconds, Vicky and I would be dead, our necks broken as we slammed across the bridge.

"Go!" she yelled at me, as if I didn't already understand. She still made it to her seat before I did, and I'd barely gotten a hand on mine when the maneuvering burn slammed into the dorsal bow of the ship, pushing her downward relative to our forward motion.

The abrupt change of direction threw me toward the overhead and I only avoided the body slam by wrapping my arms in the harness straps. Pain tugged at my AC joints and my legs whipped upward, but I held on and pulled myself into the couch, buckling a fastener across my chest. I was breathing like I'd just run a hundred-meter sprint and every muscle in my body was sore, but I made time to check on Vicky as I belted myself in. She was strapped down to her acceleration couch and had the presence of mind to give me a nod before nine gravities of boost hit us with all the subtlety of a sledgehammer.

I blacked out. I'm not ashamed to say it. Maybe if I'd been a Fleet pilot, trained in how to keep my head clear during an emergency boost, I could have managed to clench my stomach or whatever it is they do, but I was a Marine, and no one was going to ask a Drop-Trooper to pilot anything bigger than a Vigilante, so I passed out.

The *bang-bang-bang* of maneuvering thrusters against the hull shook me awake, jolting me into the right side of my acceleration couch against a free-fall I hadn't realized we'd returned to. My vision cleared just ahead of the clouds over my thoughts, showing a side-on view of one of the ships. It was haloed in red on the screen, but it took me a moment to realize the color was a threat designator and not just more of the lights floating across my vision.

"Helm control to Tactical!" That was Yanayev, though I didn't look at her because my head was still lolling and I couldn't even put two words together. How the hell do those Fleet people do it?

"Tactical has Helm," Wojtera said. "Targeting...." Another series of hard bangs on the hull and just as I was finally getting my shit together.... "Firing!"

The hull vibrated like a gong and I thought we'd taken a hit before my boost-addled brain understood we'd fired the railgun. The shot was a blue star projected on the Tactical display and it didn't have far to travel. One of the weird, twisted ships was less than twenty kilometers ahead of us and the heavy tungsten slug traversed the distance in seconds.

I thought the bogie would somehow dodge the projectile, but it didn't even try. The slug was the size of a small groundcar and moving at over 3,000 meters per second, but it deflected away from the enemy ship, spiraling off into the darkness.

"Dammit," Wojtera hissed, the first time I'd heard him sound flustered. "Negative impact."

"Forty-five degrees port," Nance barked. "Emergency boost!"

The man was quick and decisive and better at his job than I would have been, but he was nearly too late. The energy beam was a pale blue and somehow visible in the vacuum, though I couldn't have explained how, and it passed close enough that I thought it had hit us. The *Orion* shuddered like an ancient sailing ship run aground.

"What the hell?" Wojtera said, looking around as if he could see cracks in the bulkhead. "What was that? It felt like something hit us!"

No one had the chance to answer because emergency boost cut in, squeezing the air from my lungs and, presumably, everyone else's. I didn't black out this time, but it was only because I was too miserable to nod off. We were a pubic hair shy of nine gravities and God was stomping me in the face, and I was pretty sure we were going to die anyway, so why did we have to be uncomfortable too?

"Kill the boost!" Colonel Hachette strained out the words, reading my mind. "Micro-Transition insystem, as close as possible to the star!"

It was a damned good idea, but I wasn't sure it would be any more pleasant than the emergency boost. Bile rose in my throat, trying to fight its way free without the acceleration to hold it down, and I clamped my jaws down against it.

"Transitioning now," Yanayev announced, and I wondered if there was some Fleet regulation that they all had to tell us what we all could tell we were doing anyway.

The first jump wasn't so bad...it never was. It was always the second phase of a micro-Transition that got me, and the closer they were together, the worse it was. Someone groaned in misery and I was pretty sure it was me.

But according to the Tactical screen, we were halfway across the star system from the attack, and the crew was delivering status reports, one almost stepping on the other, like they were afraid the enemy would drop back in on them if they didn't get the words out in time. But the one I was most interested in was the damage report from Kelsey.

"We have a burn through in the hull on Level Six," she said. She'd settled down from the shock of our trip through the Corridor, though there was still a tremble in her voice. "It's not big, and the automated repair systems have patched it, but from the sensors, that shot didn't even hit us directly and it still burned through Twenty centimeters of BiPhase Carbide. A direct hit would core us like an apple."

"It won't take them long to figure out where we went," Nance warned Hachette. "It wasn't a bad idea jumping inward, but we can't keep this up forever." He pointed at Yanayev. "Helm, get me gravimetic readings on the Transition Lines out of this system. We got here, so there has to be some way out of here."

"What do we have that can hit them?" Hachette wondered. "The railgun is useless."

"We could try the main lasers, sir," Wojtera suggested.

"I want to know who the hell they are," Vicky added, apparently having learned nothing from her last go-round with Hachette.

"They are," the computer-generated female answered from the bridge speakers, "the Skrela."

"What the fuck is that?" Chase exploded, looking around the bridge as if he thought someone had walked in while he wasn't looking and answered Vicky's question.

But I recognized that voice. Again.

"That's the Corridor," I said. "The AI that was talking to us."

"You're correct, Cameron Alvarez," the voice told me, and I didn't know if I was more freaked out that I was right or that the thing knew my name.

"How are you communicating with us?" Hachette demanded, not bothering to try to deny the obvious. "Is there some sort of FTL comm system connecting you to us?"

"No, Colonel Hachette. When I accessed your computer systems in the Corridor, I downloaded as complete of a copy of myself as your technology is capable of containing into your quantum core."

Hachette scowled at the bulkhead then snapped his fingers in the direction of Lt. Chase.

"Run a systems purge, get rid of this thing."

"You won't be able to purge my data without wiping clean your own...if you can even find me. You don't have that sort of time to waste. Those ships are the Skrela. I told you they were out here. They hover at the border systems, cut off from communications, cut off from the resources to build more of themselves, frozen in preservative stasis until they sense new life in the system...and then they pounce. You have seconds. Perhaps a minute."

"Why are you here?" I asked the thing, since Hachette hadn't bothered to. "Why did you download a copy of yourself into our ship?"

"Guilt," the AI admitted. "Though the term isn't an exact translation, since I do not experience the emotions you do, it is, as you say, close enough for government work. I did my duty, but you are the first of your kind I have encountered, and I knew you wouldn't survive long without guidance."

"The thing's right, sir," Chase told Hachette. "I can tell it's using our processing power, but its engrams are tied into the main computer system. We'd have to take it offline and purge all data and subroutines, then reboot from a clean backup. That would take hours and we'd have to be in a safe harbor."

"Are we still picking up the Tahni ships?" Hachette asked, still stuck on his mission like a tick on a dog.

"They're way out of visual range now," Wojtera told him. "I was too busy trying to keep us from getting blown up by the aliens to pay attention at the time, but the recordings of the sensor readings before we jumped showed they were taking some damage."

"Maybe the Skrela will take care of the problem for us." Hachette growled, still looking as if he wanted to punch the AI and was searching for the best way to do it. "Corridor, do we have any weapons that can kill those things?"

"Corridor was the designation of the sentient system guarding that area. I have chosen the name Dwight."

"Why?" I asked, but this time, everyone ignored me, even the computer.

"I have analyzed your weapons systems," Dwight went on, not waiting to see anyone's reaction to his choice of names, "and your best chance at defeating a Skrela warship is your lasers. However, by the time you were able to focus the beam for long enough on one ship, the others would destroy you. You would require a dozen ships to overcome their numbers, and even if you were to join forces with the Tahni, the result would be the same. You need to Transition out of this system while you are still able."

"That thing is trying to get us out so we can't find a way back to the Cluster," Hachette snapped. "We need to stay here. We *know* there's a connection from here to the system where we jumped from."

"You lack the technology to get there from here. The

Corridor uses captive singularities to establish a wormhole through the Enclosure. Your species is, as of yet, incapable of containing a singularity."

"Helm," Nance broke in, "do we have a read on the Transition Lines?"

"There's a grand total of one coming out of this system, sir. I haven't been able to zero in on our exact location, but I can tell it's toward the galactic center, and I'm sure that this line doesn't head back the way we came."

"We can't do it," Hachette declared. "This is a trick."

"I'm picking up multiple Transitions from out-system," Wojtera said. "I think it might be the Tahni destroyers making a run for it."

A thought struck me, something disturbing enough that I had to share it.

"If they were the only thing distracting the Skrela, and they took off...."

I hate it when I'm right. My eyes had been locked on the main screen so I didn't even need the alarm or the blurted exclamation from Wojtera. They'd found us. More than I could count, red halos popping up across the screen all around us.

There was no time to think, no time to target them all, and I think Vicky and I and Nance all yelled at the same time.

"Jump!"

Reality twisted around itself, warping two dozen azure energy beams away from us, and the universe disappeared into nothingness.

[14]

"We are so screwed," Kyler Dunstan moaned, burying his head in his hands, elbows resting on the galley table.

"That about sums up the situation," I agreed around a bite of processed soy masquerading as chicken and not doing a very good job of it.

I must have made a face because Vicky nodded my way, gesturing with her fork.

"You'd better enjoy that," she warned me. "God knows how long our stores are going to last. Or if there'll be any place to find more."

"Jeez, aren't you little Miss Mary Sunshine," Dunstan whined. "There's gotta be some way to get out of here. We have to be able to find a way back."

"Not without help from Dwight," I told him, shaking my head.

"Dwight?" he repeated. "Who in the hell is Dwight?"

"The Predecessor AI," Vicky supplied. "The alien computer that took over our damned ship. Didn't you get the memo?"

"The fucking *what?*"

"Anyway," I went on after Vicky had explained the situation to him, "Dwight claims that we don't have the technological capability to get back from here, that we'd need to be able to create a black hole to do it."

"So where *are* we going, then?" Dunstan glanced down, seeming to just remember that he was supposed to be eating dinner, and shoveled a few bites of noodles with peanut sauce into his mouth. The man ate like a steam shovel.

"The only system we can reach from the red giant where we came out." I rolled my eyes. "It's another three days in T-Space and we have no clue what's in it."

"Doesn't this Dwight know? Did he just stow away to laugh at us?"

"It's been stuck in that Corridor system for over ten thousand years," Vicky reminded him. "It doesn't know anything it wasn't told before its installation." She squinted at me. "Why did it call itself 'Dwight' when it picked a woman's voice?"

"It's an alien computer." I shrugged. "Maybe it doesn't know the current trends in girls' names. Look, the bottom line is, we're flying blind and..."

I paused and looked around the galley. It was...*shit*, I didn't even know what the ship time was. My 'link was still set to Tahn-Skyyiah time. But even in a situation like this, we were only on half shifts, which meant half the crew was off duty and it seemed like most of them were here grabbing a meal. There was always chatter and small talk at dinner, but the buzz in the compartment was almost incessant, and more than one of them were halfway to shrieking.

No one around us seemed to be listening to us, so I lowered my voice and continued.

"Colonel Hachette is freaking out. I'm not sure how well he's going to handle this. Nance is keeping it together, but in the end, he's not the one who's going to be making the decisions."

"If we're stranded here," Dunstan said, twirling noodles around his fork, "who's to say that Nance shouldn't be in charge? I mean, Hachette was in charge for the operation against Zan-Thint, but that's history now. We're in another freaking part of the galaxy with these alien goons hunting us down. It's not like Hachette is an experienced combat leader either. He's just Intelligence."

Vicky and I shared a look: half "oh shit" and half "he may be right."

"I think it's a little early to be planning a change of command," I said, choosing my words carefully. "Especially since Solano and the Marines are probably loyal to Hachette."

Vicky tilted an eyebrow at me, mouth opening slightly like she couldn't believe I'd actually said that.

"Is this table only for officers," Top asked, "or can a lowly NCO join you?"

I was about halfway out of my seat before I stopped myself. How the hell did she manage to sneak up on us?

"Sure, Top," Vicky said, waving at the chair across from her. "Have a seat."

Top looked haggard, exhausted, and I wondered how much convincing the Marines had taken to not panic. Vicky and I had been prepared to jump into a planning meeting after the Transition, but Hachette had snapped shut any suggestion of it by Nance or me and told everyone not on shift to go back to their compartment and get some sleep while he did some thinking. We hadn't done much sleeping, just lay next to each other in the dark for a few hours, too stunned to even talk, until hunger had driven us out. It had probably been just as well, because I was sure there'd been a lot of drama among the ship's crew and I could barely keep my own shit together.

Top had brought a tray with her and she didn't say a word

for a couple minutes, eating quickly and methodically, as if she were attriting the food's ability to make war with her.

"Colonel Hachette would like to see you two in his quarters after dinner," she said, once the rice and beans had been reduced to a third of its original size.

"Just us?" Vicky wondered.

"No. I'll be there, along with Captain Nance, Captain Solano, and Gunny Pineda. This is supposed to be a planning session, or so I've been told."

"Why has he taken so long to have a planning session?" I asked her. "We should have done this the minute we jumped."

The muscles beside Top's eyes tensed, and if I hadn't known her, I would have thought it was a sign she was getting angry. But I did know her and I was sure it was the result of her trying not to roll her eyes.

"We should have," she agreed. "However, the colonel took the time to bring in computer technicians and an Engineering tech to...*harden* his private quarters against intrusion by our new guest." She shrugged. "He wants to be able to plan without Dwight listening in."

"I guess that makes sense," I allowed. "He doesn't trust the thing to tell the truth and God knows, I don't either."

"Why would this thing bother to hitch a ride with us," Dunstan wondered, "just to lie to us? It could have just let us just die when those Skrela things attacked."

"I'll be sure to bring that up when I talk to the colonel," Top said, scowling at the man.

"What happens," Vicky asked, her voice soft and subdued, eyes on the table, "if we're really stuck out here? If we can't get back?"

I covered her hand with mine, squeezing.

"We're going to find a way back." I didn't make it a promise because I had no idea if it was even possible.

"And what if we don't?"

She speared me with a glare, daring me to answer, and I couldn't.

"Top," I said, slow and hesitant, not liking how this was going to sound and liking even less what her response might be, "this is a really...unusual situation. Not something any of us trained for. Do you think Colonel Hachette is up for it?"

She didn't explode, which was a good start. I don't know if it was because of our rank or her experience with us in the war, but a deep frown was the only clue that the question upset her.

"I don't know that *any* of us are up for this, Alvarez. But Colonel Hachette is a superb officer, and I have to believe he's going to react as well as any of us could under the circumstances." Her smile was wan, but not hopeless. "Would I rather have Captain Covington here, in charge? Of course. But he's what we got. I'll tell you what, though." She raised a single finger. "I'll promise you this. One thing. If, at any point, I see the colonel fucking up, and he won't take my advice to change his mind, I will let you know."

Top leaned forward, fingers interlaced in front of her on the table.

"I hope to God it doesn't come to that, children. Because as bad as things seem now, having to try to deal with a bad CO right in the middle of it all would make it a million times worse."

———

"Shut the door, Alvarez," Hachette snapped.

"Yes, sir." I squeezed in behind Vicky and pushed the hatch closed behind me.

Hachette's private berthing on the *Orion* was large compared to everyone else's quarters, but this was still a starship, and not a cruiser. It was small enough that the seven of us were about all that could comfortably fit into the compartment, and even that was stretching the definition of "comfortably" past its limits.

Vicky and I were last to arrive, despite getting there fifteen minutes before the announced time. I suppose that was a testament to how little else there was to do, or maybe how little everyone cared about anything else right now. It sucked, because that meant there was nowhere left to sit. Hachette was already taking the edge of his bunk, Nance had the chair by the work desk, and Solano had grabbed the emergency fold-down acceleration couch on the bulkhead, which left Sgt.-Major Campbell, Solano's Top Kick Gunny Pineda, and the two of us to stand.

I fought an urge to stand at ease and deliberately leaned against the hatch, letting Vicky lean into my shoulder. I thought I caught a hint of irritation in Hachette's eyes, but it might have just been general displeasure with the situation. I didn't care either way. If he didn't want me leaning against the wall, he should have made sure there were enough chairs.

"Now that we're all here," Hachette went on, "I'm going to give everyone a run-down of our situation as best as we can tell." He closed his eyes as if he was trying to remember the details, then gave up and grabbed a folding tablet off his bunk and read from its display. "The senior Helm officer had another go at determining where we were before we Transitioned, the system with the red giant. The navigational programs weren't able to zero in on a particular star system due to how dim the giant would be from Earth, or anywhere in Commonwealth space, but we've managed to narrow it down to the Perseus Arm of the galaxy, somewhere on the order of 7,000 light-years from Earth."

"Shit." It wasn't me who said it, that was all I knew. I think it might have been Pineda. The man was a good Marine, but he was also a career NCO, and swearing came like breathing to him, no matter what the company.

Hachette didn't bawl him out, just nodded agreement.

"Quite. Even if we knew the correct route to take, the Transition Lines that would get us back, it would take us decades to get back using our drive. Dwight...." He spat the name out. "...at least isn't lying about that. We need Predecessor technology to get back. Assuming he's telling the truth about being a creation of the Predecessors."

"I don't know if he's telling the truth," I put in, "but I've fought the Skrela more than once now and I can tell you, sir, whatever manufactured those things did *not* create anything that could understand humans well enough to talk to them."

"That doesn't mean that it was the Predecessors," Solano argued, though it seemed as if he was just doing it pro forma.

"No," I admitted, "but if it's not the Skrela, and it's not the Predecessors, then we have to postulate a *third* non-human species that had the technology to build that gate thing that took us here."

"Occam's razor," Captain Nance agreed. He spread his hands in an encompassing gesture. "Everything we've seen so far agrees with what this AI has told us. Until we receive data that contradicts that, the simplest and safest assumption is that he's told us the truth. Maybe not the *whole* truth, but at least some of it."

Hachette grunted noncommittally.

"Perhaps. Moving on, the Transition Line we're traversing currently is going to take us to a system with a single G-class star. We don't know much more than that at this distance, just what the gravimetic sensors can tell us."

"G-class might mean habitables," Nance pointed out. "Not a sure thing, but it's been that way in the Cluster."

"Of course," Vicky cut in, "it was probably that way in the Cluster because the Predecessors engineered those habitables."

"Oh, come on, Sandoval," Solano sneered. "Don't tell me you believe that conspiracy-theory bullshit."

The hackles rose on my neck and I was about to tell Solano exactly where he could stick his opinion, but Vicky beat me to it.

"Really?" she snapped, pushing away from me and standing up straight. "Really, Solano? We're in another fucking galactic cluster seven *thousand* light-years from home, because a sentient computer sent us here using its tame black hole, and the only reason we wound up in this shit is that we were trying to stop a rogue Tahni general from setting loose ancient alien clone monsters and destroying our civilization. What fucking part of this do you think *isn't* conspiracy-theory bullshit?"

"Enough," Hachette barked. "Whether or not the Predecessors terraformed the habitable worlds in the Cluster, we can't say for sure that there will be habitables where we're going. If the Predecessors *did* get chased out of the Cluster by the Skrela, then they might have done the same thing out here. But if they built the Cluster to keep us inside and keep the Skrela out, then there may be things out here we've never dealt with."

I nodded, almost reluctantly. It was a good point.

"We also have the AI. Dwight." Hachette rubbed at his temples, eyes pressed shut. "Which was also the name of the kid who bullied me in elementary school for three years, coincidentally enough. He says he tagged along because he feels responsible for us, because we're the first sentients he's tossed out of the Garden of Eden, and he didn't want the snakes getting us. I'm not sure I buy that. I mean, his motives for downloading a copy of himself may not be malevolent, but I'm not convinced they're altruistic either."

"It," Top corrected him. At Hachette's confused expression,

she clarified. "You're calling the thing 'he' and 'him.' Dwight is an 'it.' Let's not anthropomorphize a computer that wasn't even programmed by humans."

"Nice catch, Sergeant-Major," he acknowledged. He leaned forward, resting his elbows on his legs. "That's the external forces working on us. Let's talk about what *we* bring to the table. We have one reinforced company of Drop-Troopers, a platoon of Force Recon, two Intercept cutters, four assault shuttles, three drop-ships, and six landers. The *Orion* has a full load of metallic hydrogen reactor slugs except for what we burned on this last operation, which should last us a while as long as we don't get into any more running battles with the Skrela. We're Winchester on missiles, but we have enough Gatling laser ammo to start a war." He sighed, as if running into a fact that derailed his thoughts. "We have enough food stores for approximately four hundred days without resupply. That's soy paste and spirulina powder. There are emergency rations as well, which could stretch that out for another two hundred days, though God knows, it wouldn't be pleasant. Water won't be a problem for a long time, with the recyclers." He scanned the compartment, meeting each of our eyes. "Am I forgetting anything?"

"We have spare parts and patching materials for the repair 'bots," Nance put in. "Enough to keep us spaceworthy for a long time, if it comes to that."

"That's our situation," I said, putting it into terms I understood, an op order. "But what's our mission?"

"Stay alive," Solano said, chuckling humorlessly.

"No." I cut him off harshly, earning a dirty look. "Any idiot can survive. We're not just stranded colonists. We're Marines." I shrugged, motioning at Nance and Hachette. "And Fleet, of course. We're not here to just survive."

"As of now," Hachette declared, "our mission is to try to get back. There are people on this ship who have wives, children. And we all have a duty to the Commonwealth and the military to try to return and report. We have to find a way to get back."

"And as far as we know," I cut in, "there's only one way to get back."

Six pairs of curious eyes stared at me and I shrugged as if it was obvious.

"We have to find the Predecessors."

[15]

"*That* is a Predecessor?" Colonel Hachette blurted, goggling at the projection in the conference room holotank.

The thing was tall, depicted next to a stylized human for scale, two meters tall or maybe a hair more. Its knees were bent backwards like a kangaroo's, digitigrade I think the term is, its feet long and split-toed. A narrow waist expanded into a deep chest, twice as large as a human's, with shoulders set far back from the ribs. The arms were long and bony, the fingers strangely agile, reminding me of a pianist. But the head...that was the real difference. The face extruded from a long and bulbous skull, the nostrils flat above a too-wide mouth lined with pointed teeth. I couldn't see the ears because they were hidden behind a swept-back mane of what could have been hair but what I sensed were more akin to feathers.

The clothes were tight sleeves, encasing forearms, upper chest, groin, and thighs, colored a slightly darker grey than the skin. From appearances alone, it was impossible to tell how they went on and off. Something that looked like a cross between a bandolier and a vest went from left shoulder to right hip, lined with pouches.

"This is what was in my memory banks," Dwight told us. Its tone and cadence were becoming more casual the more it talked to us, as if it needed the practice. "I have no reason to doubt it, though I understand you might, Colonel Hachette."

"You said they evolved on Earth," Vicky mused, walking around the table, looking at the image from every angle. "I was thinking you meant like Neanderthals, or some other hominid that somehow developed a civilization we hadn't detected."

"That wouldn't be too likely," Captain Nance said with more confidence than I would have felt. "Neanderthals disappeared recently, on the geological scale. If any of them had developed a technological civilization, we would have found traces of it."

"Are you an amateur anthropologist, Captain?" I asked him, hiding a grin. I was constantly amused by the unexpected hobbies senior officers had the time to pursue. Top had told me that Hachette was an accomplished sculptor, and when I'd stared at her dubiously, she'd shown me pictures of some of his work.

"Not quite that," Nance replied, waving it off. "I just dabble."

"You're quite right, Captain," Dwight assured him. "No other hominid species would have been able to develop a space-faring civilization without your species discovering it."

I frowned, my brows knitting.

"What's wrong?" Vicky asked, apparently noticing my expression.

"It's starting to bug me having a conversation with the damned bulkhead," I admitted.

"Is this better, Captain Alvarez?" Dwight asked. Only this time, it wasn't a disembodied voice speaking; it was a hologram standing beside the notional Predecessor in the projection tank. It was a man, a human male, dressed in a Commonwealth Space

Fleet uniform, his brown hair cut to regulation, his face bland and unremarkable.

"No!" I exclaimed, half startled by the sudden appearance of the image, half annoyed. "If you're calling yourself Dwight and appearing as a human male, why do you insist on using that voice?"

"It was a voice I knew all of you would be accustomed to hearing, since it is the default setting for your computer learning programs." The bland-looking Fleet tech cocked his head to the side. "Would you rather I chose a female form?"

"I'd rather you chose another voice."

"Is this pertinent?" Hachette ground out.

"As I was saying," Dwight continued, now with a male voice.

I recognized this one too. It was the one the Fleet used to warn recruits at the in-processing station that they weren't allowed to use the staff lounge, the same one that I heard at the Fleet Headquarters station at L5 when I got off the shuttle from Trans Angeles, telling me and all the others that our transport to Inferno would be leaving in thirty minutes and we could either be on it or face charges. I think I preferred the female voice.

"The Predecessors were not Neanderthals, nor were they descended from any hominid species."

The shape of the Predecessor morphed into something else, something I'd only seen in my high school classes and barely remembered even then. The feathers were still there. It was bipedal, but it didn't stand upright, using a long tail for balance. Its legs were digitigrade like the Predecessor, but they were more muscular, the arms shorter and less useful. The head still protruded out from the back of the snout, but those sharpened teeth had once been daggers.

It was a dinosaur.

"I don't recognize this species." Nance alone was unfazed by the revelation, peering intently at the image.

"You wouldn't," Dwight confirmed. "It lived very close to the asteroid impact which you call the Chicxulub Event. Very few land species survived, and almost none of the dinosaurs. But this one did. And its ancestors, forged in the scrabble for survival following the extinction, developed intelligence. And technology."

The dinosaur was replaced by an image of Earth, except the continents weren't quite right. And where green should have been was, in too many places, brown and white. The picture soared through the dust-choked atmosphere and showed clusters of the bipedal dinosaurs digging tunnels beneath the earth, living in the burrows. Showed them using rocks as tools, chipping them together to sharpen them. Showed them making fire.

Their shape changed gradually along with the images around them. The sky cleared, the rain fell, grass grew again. And cities began to grow as aeons passed. Time sped up and cities of stone changed to cities of concrete and then of metal. Rockets launched and stations were built in orbit, spaceships heading out from Earth.

"What did they call themselves?" Vicky asked, transfixed by the footage in the holographic projection.

"You couldn't pronounce it. Nor any of their language. But the closest you could come would be *Resscharr*. It means *life-giver*. And the difference between your species and the Resscharr is that, once they left your world for the first time, they knew they never wanted to return. For them, Earth was a death-trap that had tried to kill them much too recently. They knew from the very steps they took off their world that the stars would be their home. They devoted themselves to spreading life throughout the galaxy, all of it engineered from the DNA of their homeworld...and yours."

"Did they...." I swallowed hard, not sure if I wanted to know. "Did they interfere in our evolution?"

"No." I wanted to sigh with relief, but I held it in and let Dwight speak. "Once they saw the evolution of hominids beginning, they decided to step away and let the random hand of nature make its own way. It was, I believe you would say, a control group. And the experimental group was the Tahni."

More images, of Tahn-Skyyiah this time. Of something large and anthropoid being walked down the ramp of a spaceship.

"They used species from your world as the base, and re-engineered their genes, creating the modern Tahni."

"They did more than that." I wasn't trying to make the words sound like an accusation, but they came out that way, just the same. "They gave them a religion. They gave them a society based on separation of the sexes, on sublimating aggression into something constructive."

"And they gave them the stars. The Resscharr created the wormhole jumpgates for the Tahni. They left a map for them concealed in their religious texts, left them the stars as their birthright."

"But what about the map on Hermes?" Hachette finally asked, sounding as if he was reluctant to engage the AI but couldn't tamp down his curiosity anymore. "That was only four light-years from Earth."

"The map on Hermes was, indeed, left for you," Dwight confirmed. "But you were meant to find it once you'd managed to travel to your nearest star via a slower-than-light spaceship. It would have been expensive, wastefully so, would have required a dedication to the future, to exploration that the Resscharr had worked to instill in the Tahni and wished to make sure you possessed as well before unleashing you on the rest of the worlds in the Cluster."

Dwight smiled sadly, a very human expression for an alien sentient computer.

"As I have learned from your historical records, fate intervened. You stumbled on the jumpgate in your asteroid belt by accident, traveled through to Hermes and found the map. It was not meant to be so, but even my creators could not claim to be omniscient. And they were long gone by then."

"Because of the Skrela," Hachette presumed.

"The Skrela spread like a virus. We never knew where the first of their pods originated. They were simply there, and once they hatched, they were unstoppable."

"We stopped them pretty well," Solano said, puffing out his chest a little. "At Bathala, we kicked their asses."

"They need resources," I pointed out. "Raw material. We caught them on a planet without readily-accessible mineral resources. If they landed on an asteroid, they'd have starships in a week."

"And that's exactly what happened," Dwight took up his explanation once again. "They rained down pod after pod, overwhelming our defenses, and it only took one to land somewhere ripe for reproduction. They would swarm across living worlds like locusts, killing everything in their path, using whatever they found to make more of themselves, to build ships, armadas of ships, then to move on to the next world."

"They had the Transition Drive?" I wondered. "The Skrela?"

"That was something that the Resscharr debated for many years." If it was possible for a holographic projection to look pensive, Dwight pulled it off. "Our final conclusion was that they did not. They had no technology of their own until they copied ours. The consensus was that they were some sort of failsafe weapon sent to cleanse the entire galaxy of technology-using intelligence."

"Sent by who, though?" Captain Nance asked. "Did the Resscharr…." He stumbled over the word, trying to add a Spanish roll to the "r," then abandoning the attempt. "…have any ideas where they came from?"

"There were two competing hypotheses," Dwight said, smiling thinly. "Neither had a scrap of data to support them, because acquiring such data would have taken time and resources, and once the Skrela became a threat, both were in short supply. The first was that they came from another galaxy, that they'd been sent out across the universe to eradicate all advanced civilizations for some reason. The second was that they were a doomsday weapon left from a war between two combatants lost to the ravages of time."

"This is all so…impossible," Vicky said softly, leaning on the conference table, looking closely at the Predecessor. "You said it yourself, Dwight. If it had been Neanderthals, we would have found their remains. But dinosaurs even, wouldn't we still see something left? If not on Earth, then the Moon? Mars?"

"You would have," Dwight agreed. "If they'd left it there for you to find. It was important to the Resscharr to allow you to develop on your own without even the knowledge of their existence interfering. They cleaned out the system of every trace. And when they began doling out bits of technology to the Tahni —in secret, through their priests, in traditions that would never be lost—they made sure that the Tahni never used high-power microwave communications by making it taboo."

"They were pretty serious about this whole control group thing," I said, running the whole scenario over and over in my head, trying to figure out if the AI was lying. "So tell me, Dwight. How long ago did the last of the Predecessors leave the Cluster and seal us all in with you as the gatekeeper?"

"Ten thousand years ago." He shrugged, a very convincing imitation of a human. "Give or take a hundred years. At least, that's approximately when the Corridor was built, assuming I was activated at the same time as its completion. If there were any more Resscharr left in the Cluster after that point, they didn't exit it through the Corridor."

"Ten thousand years." I whispered the words like a prayer. "The Tahni have had the same religion for ten thousand years."

"They always *said* so," Hachette told me. "We thought they were exaggerating."

"Dwight," I said, finally getting to the point, the reason I'd suggested this *tete-a-tete* to begin with, "you said you came along because you wanted to help us. We all want to go home." He opened his holographic mouth to protest, but I held up a hand to stop him. "And I *know* you can't do it, that we don't have the technology, that you wouldn't be allowed even if we did. But you serve the Predecessors, right? The Resscharr?"

"I do. Just as you serve your own Creator."

Well, maybe. Sort of.

"And the Resscharr would be the only ones we know of that have the technology to send us back," I went on. "And we know which way the Resscharr went when they left the Cluster. Can you help us find them?"

Dwight was silent. I wondered if it was for effect, so we'd know he'd taken the time to think about it. Or maybe even a sentient AI needed a few seconds to process an ethical decision.

"I can try," he finally said.

Shit. Now I'm calling Dwight a "he" too. I needed to watch that. He *wasn't* human. He wasn't even *programmed* by humans.

"However," he went on, "it has been ten thousand years since they left the Cluster. Though the Predecessors did not advance as quickly nor change as often as your own society, it is possible that they may not be the same beings I once knew. I may not even be able to communicate with them."

"You'll be able to communicate with them a hell of a lot better than *we* would," Hachette said.

"You never did tell us," Vicky cut in, "just why the Predecessors left the Corridor in place after they left. I mean, you—and, presumably, they—were so concerned about anyone on our side of the passage finding out about it and maybe letting in the Skrela, that you chunked us right through it without even asking us to keep it a secret. So why didn't they just blow the damned thing up? Or let that black hole inside it swallow the whole structure?"

"For their children," Dwight said as if it was the most obvious thing in the world. "The Tahni. They had to leave the Tahni a way to come through. Otherwise, they would never have known how the experiment turned out."

The rising sun struck me in the face, blinding me with what should have been obvious, and it was all I could do not to smack myself in the forehead. My only excuse was, things had been kind of stressful and panicked, but I was still pissed at myself.

"Zan-Thint didn't just stumble across that passage," I realized. "It wasn't an accident, wasn't his last resort in case everything else failed. It was always where he wanted to go."

"Of course. Zan-Thint had contacted me years ago. He knew that the Tahni would never be able to take back what your people had seized from them. At best, they would be subordinates, poor relations. He would have saved all his people from that fate if he could, but instead, he chose to bring with him a small group of the faithful, to seek out the only gods left he could believe in."

Dwight paced across the projection, hands clasped behind him, his bland face thoughtful, an odd look for a holographic icon.

"I feel you may want to rethink your plan to find the Predecessors and ask them for help in getting you home, though."

"And why's that?" Hachette demanded. The man didn't have a great poker face, particularly for a Fleet Intelligence spook. He resented having to talk to the AI, and he wasn't worried about showing it.

"If they still remember you," Dwight explained, "and still remember the Tahni...."

The AI's hologram shook his head, giving Hachette a look filled with a very good imitation of pity.

"They may not like what you've done to their children."

[16]

"This is not," Colonel Hachette admitted, "what I expected to find."

And whatever differences I might have with the man, I think that was a statement all of us agreed with. Nothing about this system was what we'd expected to find.

The G-class star we'd come upon at the first available Transition Line had proven to be a bust, not just lacking habitables but devoid of planets altogether. The letdown had hit us like a gut punch, doubly so because we'd been all set for something mind-blowing. Instead, we'd been faced with the choice of three lines from that system, one heading for a white dwarf, one for a K-type star, and the third for yet another G. Hachette and Nance had talked it over for nearly three interminable hours before they'd decided on the obvious choice, and then it was back into T-space for another sixty hours.

That had sucked. It had given us all two and a half days to ruminate and be scared and talk about what might be out there, and whether Zan-Thint and his ships had gone some other way. Vicky and I had spent most of our time either in bed or performing PMCS on our Vigilantes...except when Top requested oh-so-nicely for us to supervise an ammunition inventory. We had a depressingly-low number of suit-launched missiles, but everything else was good to go.

There were three separate fights between Drop-Troopers and Force Recon, but those were barely worth mentioning. That sort of shit happened every cruise.

And now, we were finally out of Transition Space, ducked out as far as we could manage and still get a good look at the inner planets. The system had an asteroid belt between the three inner, rocky worlds and the three gas giants of the outer reaches, and we'd taken the risk of Transitioning at the inner edge of the belt, just half an Astronomical Unit from the farthest out of the rocky planets.

I'd been simultaneously worried it was too damned close and that it would be too far to see anything. And I'd been half right.

The world was lush and green in the south, islands dotting the pristine blue oceans around something that might have been a small continent or a really big island, a little smaller than Australia. The northern continent was vaster, rugged and rocky, white with glaciers near the pole and brown with deserts farther south. We'd sat and watched it for a full rotation, about twenty hours, before we'd received the final report from Tactical.

"I'm not picking up any spacecraft," Wojtera had told us once everyone was back on the bridge. Wojtera hadn't been there for the entire day, of course, but he'd had the report from the junior Tac-O on his computer station. "No orbital stations, no satellites, no defense platforms. I'm picking up thermal readings consistent with small cities, maybe a couple reactors. Nothing indicative of anti-spacecraft weapons." He'd turned back to Hachette and Nance, looking between the two as if he still wasn't sure who should be giving the orders. "Do you want to try moving in and dropping a drone?"

And if it hadn't been clear which one he was asking, it had been Hachette who'd answered.

"Take us into a high orbit and launch a surveillance drone."

Which meant another Transition, as close as the drive would deposit us, and then a three-hour routine of burn-braking burn-orbital insertion before we'd even been able to send out the drone. It was disposable, dropped in a sensor-absorbent sheath that burned away on atmospheric entry, leaving a simple isotope reactor powering an air-breathing jet and a laser line-of-sight transmitter. It would have been shot down by even the most basic anti-aircraft weaponry, but we weren't detecting any from orbit, so it was worth a go.

"You know," Vicky had whispered beside my ear while we'd waited for the data to come back, "I'm happy as all hell to be officers now and here in grown-up land for all the big decisions, but I'm going to be honest with you, Cam, I'm getting damned bored of sitting on this bridge waiting for something to happen to somebody else."

I'd been about to commiserate when the first images had come back from the drone.

"This is the largest settlement," Wojtera had supplied. "The one on the west coast of the southern continent."

It was night over this part of the world, but the drone's optics lit the area up as if it were noon. I didn't know who lived there, but I knew they must be diurnal, like humans, because the only movement the drone caught was a few small animals flittering around corners and over rooftops. They were too far away to make any sense of them, though my brain wanted to shove them into a cat-shaped hole.

The city had a cyclopean look to it, carved from large, almost unfinished blocks of grey stone, laid carelessly at odd angles, as if some ancient god had discarded them and people had crawled into the gaps between. There were what I guess could be called streets, though they were too narrow for any sort of public transportation and I didn't see any personal vehicles parked outside. I knew I was anthropomorphizing an alien society, but just on a practical level, people and things had to get from one place to another somehow.

"I don't see any lights," Hachette observed. I watched him watch the screen for a moment. He was intent, focused. I liked that. I didn't know if I agreed with Hachette on military matters, but it was at least good to see that he took his spook job seriously.

"There are a few buildings with lights," Wojtera told him, tracing a line through a control hologram.

The view from the drone shifted as it spun in mid-air, and a taller building rose above the rest, no rhyme or reason to its placement. It reminded me of a ziggurat, though the comparison was inexact. Ziggurats didn't have windows, and they generally weren't lit up from the inside. The glow was gentle, a soft yellow, flickering a little as if it were torchlight rather than electricity, and glimpses of patterns carved into the interior walls were visible through windows that had to be two meters wide, either open to the night or the clearest glass I'd ever seen, lacking even a hint of reflection.

"Wait," Vicky said, pointing down at the bottom of the projection. "Can you pan downward?"

Wojtera did and the rest of us saw what she'd noticed first.

"There's some kind of patrol down there," I guessed. "A night watch, maybe."

They were bipedal, humanoid. I could tell that much immediately, even from a couple hundred meters up. They were shrouded in the shadows, the glare from the interior lights drowning out the drone's initial attempts to clarify their appearance.

"That's not a coincidence," Vicky said and I tilted my head toward her in a question. "Humanoid."

"Get closer, Wojtera," Hachette ordered.

"They might see it," the Tactical officer warned, but did it anyway.

Dark faces grew lighter as the drone descended, shadow stick-figures filling out with sharp, bony joints and dense muscles, made even bulkier by their dark-hued body armor. They carried rifles of some kind, though I couldn't tell much about them except that they were long and seemed heavy and unwieldy. Open-faced helmets hid their features in shadow even with the enhanced optics of the drone, until one of them looked up like he'd heard the whine of the drone's engines, and instantly, I knew.

He was a Tahni. They all were, the four of them standing at the main entrance to the building.

"Oh, shit," Wojtera murmured, maybe because of the revelation or maybe because they'd seen the drone. "Should I pull it out, sir?"

"No," Hachette said quickly, nearly cutting off the end of the question. "Wait. See what they do."

What they did was shout, and point, first with their hands and then with their rifles. The barrel of one flashed, the report deep and thunderous, and the drone zagged to the side as Wojtera's hands jerked it away despite Hachette's orders. More rifles fired, but the Tahni apparently weren't used to shooting at moving aerial targets and none of the rounds came close.

"Now, sir?" Wojtera asked, sounding as anxious as if he personally paid for every lost drone.

"No. Wait. Circle around." Hachette's eyes didn't move from the screen.

More Tahni rushed out the doorway, and I finally noticed there wasn't actually a door, just some sort of curtain, maybe beads or string, maybe fabric, but nothing solid. The guards kept firing and I was frankly shocked they didn't hit the thing just out of dumb luck.

"Those bullets are gonna come down somewhere," Vicky commented, shifting in her seat as if she would have liked to be anywhere with gravity. "Someone's going to have a bad night."

"These guys need remedial time at the range," I replied.

Wojtera took the whole circling thing to heart and the view bobbed and tilted, though the software in the camera kept the Tahni in the center of the picture. Finally, the lot of them realized they weren't going to hit the drone and the firing tailed off. One of the Tahni stepped through the others, and just by his gait and the deference the others showed, I sensed he was an officer or a senior NCO.

He watched the drone, just waiting, and I wondered what he was waiting for...until someone else came through the doorway. It wasn't a Tahni, that much was clear immediately. It was taller, broader in the chest, narrower in the waist. I don't know if the mane of feathery hair would have given away what the newcomer was, but the backward-bent knees did. There'd been nothing else I'd seen that struck me as so unnatural, so jarring to my senses.

It was a Predecessor.

"Oh, my God," Nance gasped, almost with reverence.

The Predecessor raised his long, oddly-jointed arm, and I noticed, for the first time, that he held something in his three-fingered hand. I didn't recognize it, couldn't have guessed what it did, but there was only one thing that any humanoid being would hold that way, and it was a weapon.

"Get the drone out of there," I warned Hachette.

"Wojtera..." Hachette didn't get the words out before the Predecessor fired.

The air between the weapon and the drone wavered, and then the image went dark.

"And that's that," Wojtera sighed. "What was that thing?"

I'd nearly forgotten that the Tactical officer hadn't been part of our private chat with Dwight.

"Dwight, are you hanging around in there, watching this shit?" I asked the air.

"Of course, I am, Captain Alvarez."

This time, Dwight used the communications display for his holographic avatar, which made Lt. Chase jerk in his restraint harness and curse reflexively.

"Why does he look like a human?" Chase demanded. "And why has his voice changed?"

"Was that a Resscharr?" I asked Dwight, ignoring Chase and hoping Dwight would ignore him too.

"It was." Dwight was getting damned good at the whole trying-to-be-human shtick. He had the look of concern down pat. "I find this disturbing. This was not how I anticipated finding my creators."

"Why the hell are there Tahni down there?" Hachette demanded, though whether it was of me, or Dwight, or perhaps God in Heaven was up for debate. "That's not Zan-Thint's people, is it?"

"It can't be," Vicky answered the second of the two questions. "Those Tahni had been there a while. They were like armed guards. Even if Zan-Thint had come straight here instead of jumping out into the red giant system, he couldn't have arrived more than a few hours before us."

"Well, what the hell, then?" Hachette followed up quite reasonably.

"Captain Nance, Colonel Hachette," Wojtera said, "I'm picking up aircraft launching from outside the city."

"Aircraft?" Nance asked, almost a yelp. "Why didn't we pick up their airfields if there are aircraft?"

"They didn't come out of an airfield, sir," Wojtera said, shrugging. "They just...appeared out of a wooded area right outside the city." He pointed to the Tactical display, to three red icons rising into the air above the tall building we'd been watching. "They're coming fast...way too fast for conventional jets. Gotta be running at enough acceleration to kill a human."

"Shit, if they can do that...." Nance looked back at Hachette, a plea in his eyes.

"They are utilizing Predecessor technology," Dwight supplied helpfully. "Though I do not recognize their energy signatures, and they seem primitive compared to what I recall. As does everything else. Still," he allowed, "if they're using gravitic drives, there's the possibility they might have gravitic weapons...which would destroy this ship."

I had one of those feelings in my gut, the kind where things are out of control and everyone can see it, but no one's trying to change course.

"Get us out of here," Hachette told him. "Break orbit and get us to a safe jump distance, just in case."

"One gravity boost, Helm." Nance almost stepped on Hachette's order with his own. "Take us out of orbit."

"One gravity, aye," Yanayev said, but the fusion drive was already pressing us back into our seats, and the acceleration was welcome for more than just how much better it felt for my inner ear.

The planet pulled away from us on the screen, the shadowed circle of darkness twisting into the nearly solid blue hemisphere of the other side, lit by the distant sun. Only a few island chains dotted this side of the planet, the ones near the poles swallowed up in white. What swam in those oceans? What roamed the forests and the pack ice? Everything we'd seen so far had, I realized abruptly, in a flash of insight, been based on life taken from Earth. The colonies, the Tahni worlds, everywhere, every scrap of life. Everything except the Skrela. They were the first true aliens we'd ever encountered. Was the life down there more like them? Or had the Predecessors engineered this world as well?

It was an odd thing to be, considering when we were trying to outrun the Resscharr ships, but there was nothing else to do, and I wanted to be distracted, to just look up and find out we were safe.

"They're catching up with us," Wojtera said, ending any hope of that. "At this rate, they're going to catch us before we've reached minimum safe jump distance."

Shit.

"Six gravities," Nance said, not waiting for Hachette to steal his thunder. "Colonel, we're going to micro-Transition out of here. Where do you want us?"

I don't know if the tremor of emotion I saw pass across Hachette's face was resentment at Nance for assuming he was going to okay the micro-jump, but if it was, he didn't waste time arguing.

"The second planet. Take us to just inside its orbit. Put it between us and this place."

"Calculating," Yanayev said. Then she added, "six gravities, aye."

I'd been hit in the face a lot as a kid. I could tell when it was going to happen and kind of prepare myself, tuck my chin into my chest, tilt my forehead toward the blow, but it wasn't something I'd ever gotten used to. High-grav boosts were like that. I knew what was coming and I clenched my stomach muscles, but when my weight suddenly increased sixfold, not all the preparation or all the cushion in my acceleration couch could alleviate the sheer misery.

I was able to keep my eyes focused on the main screen and I at least had the consolation of watching the threat icons fade behind us. Not that they wouldn't have caught us eventually—we couldn't keep up this sort of boost long, not without burning through our fuel stores, and apparently, they could keep going indefinitely. But we didn't need to do it for long.

Just long enough.

"There's some kind of energy buildup on the lead ship," Wojtera said, straining the words out as if he was deadlifting his body weight. "I think they're firing on us."

Something shot out of the enemy ship, something I could see even in the vacuum, a shimmer of reality, and the hull shuddered as if we'd run into something solid. It was just a gentle shake, but it carried with it the promise of something much worse if we let them get closer.

"Now," Nance said, belting out the word like he was the tenor in an Italian opera. "Jump."

"Not yet, sir." Yanayev barely sounded winded. "Ten seconds."

"We may not *have* ten more seconds," Dwight warned, not even having the courtesy to pretend that the boost affected him.

"We'll die either way," Yanayev shot back. "Five seconds. Four...three...two...one. Transitioning."

And the bottom dropped out.

[17]

"Thank God," Vicky sighed, barely audible above the whine of the landing jets tailing off as we touched down.

"Let's not be thanking anyone just yet," I cautioned, unstrapping and slinging my borrowed pulse carbine over my shoulder. "I don't like not being in my suit. Every time we go anywhere without our suits, someone winds up shooting at us."

"Oh, stop whining, Alvarez," Top admonished, pushing past a squad of Force Recon Marines as they scrambled to be the first down the slowly-opening ramp. "You're the one who wanted so badly to be off the ship and doing something useful." The Force Recon platoon sergeant nodded to her in apology then barked something obscene at his troops, warning them of the dangers of jostling a sergeant-major. "Besides, this is a diplomatic mission, sort of. We don't want to go scaring the shit out of the people we're supposed to talk to."

"Like the shuttle won't do that all on its own," Vicky shot back, laughing sharply.

A warm breeze wafted in through the lowering ramp, carrying with it the smell of the ocean. It reminded me of Bathala, though I hoped that would be the only thing about this world that reminded me of Bathala. The platoon of Force Recon tromped down the ramp, forming a security perimeter, and Top waved at the two of us to follow her.

"Don't forget," she said, putting a guiding hand on my shoulder as we emerged into the diffuse haze of mid-afternoon, "you're the ones doing the talking. I'm just here to make sure you don't fuck up."

"You're a comfort, Top," I assured her. I leaned over to Vicky, our shoulders touching. "I blame this on you."

She snorted a laugh and elbowed me in the side.

"Get your head in the game, Alvarez."

The field where we'd landed the shuttle was open and empty, smoke rising from charred grass where the belly-jets had set a few small fires. It was a good kilometer between us and the first sign of habitation. The buildings were mostly wood, which made sense, since there didn't seem to be any nearby rock quarries. The nearest forests were at least twenty kilometers inland, but from the drone footage, we'd seen the remnants of the ones that had been closer before they'd been logged out, replaced by farmland.

We'd seen the town from orbit, one of a dozen different settlements on the northernmost continent of the second planet. Individual structures, discrete and shaped to their purpose, easily identifiable even from the air. Most were single-story, though some climbed taller, reachable from ladders built into the wall.

This time, there'd been no shots taken at the drones, although a few tiny figures had run away, screaming. There'd been no aircraft launched, because there'd been no aircraft at all, Tahni or otherwise, unless we wanted to count a few tethered balloons. We figured those were used to spot schools of fish for the fleets of fishing boats chugging in and out of the harbor daily.

Steam-powered boats. The dark smudges from their smoke-stacks were visible over the horizon, as faint as the far-off roar of the surf. And their bounty was shipped back to the town and then out to the other towns on steam-powered trains. Farther inland, we'd spotted coal mines—not the open sores I'd seen in historical records, the pit mining that removed the tops of mountains and left huge scars. No, these were the older, more dangerous kind, tunnels dug into the hillside, the black anthracite coming out on metal handcarts.

This was the cutting edge of technology here, as far as we'd been able to tell from orbit. No refined oil, no wind beyond mill-powered water pumps for cattle, no geothermal. If it kept up, the haze over the primary star would eventually be a blacker color, but that was in a far future where the population had quadrupled over the current five or six million we'd estimated from the *Orion*.

I was more interested in their weapons technology than their fossil-fuel dependency. Whatever it was, we were about to find out. I'd expected some sort of steam-powered, coal-fueled armored personnel carrier, but perhaps that was a bit too fanciful. What we got instead, rolling down the packed-earth path from the town, were pedal-powered tricycles, each complete with baskets on the sides and back for carrying cargo. And riding those trikes, dressed in wool jackets that seemed to me like they'd be miserably hot in this climate even with the sea breeze, were...humans.

"You know what this means," Vicky said, speaking softly beside me, still staring at the thirty or forty people riding toward us.

"Of course, I do. We all do." We'd talked about it ad nauseam back on the ship before Hachette had decided to send down a delegation. "They took Tahni and humans with them when they left."

"Dwight didn't think so," she reminded me. "He said he never heard of any plans to do that. I think they cloned them from genetic material when they got here."

"What's the difference?" Top sounded as irritated with us now as she had at the endless debate on the subject on the *Orion*.

"The difference is," I told her, "if they cloned the humans and Tahni once they got here, it might mean they did it because there was nothing else out here. No other intelligent life, no competition. Everything out here might be just as engineered and tailored as it is inside the Cluster."

"Nothing else out here means fewer wildcards," Top said, grunting a dismissal. "Tahni and humans, we know how to deal with. We already have the Skrela and now the Predecessors, and that's about as much as I want to wrap my head around."

The pedal trikes stopped in a long, ragged line about fifty meters away. At this distance, I could make out the faces even without the enhanced optics of the glasses I swore I would wear next time I was on a planet without my armor. Top had vetoed them—sorry, she'd *suggested* that they'd make our hosts nervous, and we, as good little captains, had taken her suggestion. I still had them with me, though, stuck in a pouch of my tactical vest.

I didn't need them to see that the men and women getting off the trikes were nervous. Or that they were armed. The rifles looked to be single-shot gunpowder weapons, the pistols something similar to the old pepperbox revolvers I'd seen in museums, though their mechanisms were different. I reckoned the tactical vests could stop the bullets from something like that, as long as they weren't lucky enough for a headshot. They wouldn't even raise a bruise against the Force Recon armor, not even if they hit them right in the faceplate. None of them were actually pointed our way...yet.

The one I took to be either the leader or the appointed

spokesperson was a woman. That was pretty enlightened for people at this technological level, which gave me some hope. She was tall and slender, with a stern face and hair pulled into tight, blond braids running down her back, and I might have called her long, black dress Victorian if it hadn't been fairly similar to what the men were wearing.

She said something, raising her hand in what must have been a universal gesture, showing she wasn't armed. Her language was flowing and smooth, maddeningly similar to the little Russian I'd heard but also bringing to mind the Spanish I'd been raised speaking.

I carefully and slowly unslung my carbine and handed it back to Vicky, then did the same with my sidearm. I raised my hands in an imitation of her gesture and stepped forward, trying to keep my eyes locked on hers, but inadvertently straying to the guns in the hands of her people. One wrong move and the Force Recon troops would likely do something very rash.

"I am Cameron Alvarez," I told her, touching a palm to my chest. I repeated it again, then waited, making an expectant face that probably looked pretty damned goofy. She made the same hand-to-breast gesture and said something I didn't catch until she repeated it.

"Aldona."

"Hello, Aldona," I said, smiling, motioning toward her. "We...." I swept my arm back at the others, the shuttle, its metal still pinging as it cooled. "...are from Earth. We come as friends."

Another long line of the maddeningly familiar language and I tried to keep smiling despite the fact that I couldn't understand a word she was saying.

"Are you guys getting anything?" I asked softly, between my teeth, hoping my throat mic would pick it up and relay it via the shuttle to the *Orion*.

"Yeah, we are," Lt. Chase replied after a moment's light-speed delay. "But this can't be right."

"What can't be right?" I blurted aloud, accidentally interrupting the monologue by Aldona. But Chase didn't answer me…Dwight did.

"Captain Alvarez, your records should have no frame of reference for their language. The Predecessors left the Cluster *ten thousand* years ago. That is enough time for any language to have gone through dozens of mutations. Even if they'd spoken modern English, ten thousand years would be enough to make it gibberish to you."

"But they're *not* speaking gibberish," Chase interrupted, sounding annoyed at the AI. "And they're not speaking anything from ten thousand years ago. They're speaking something fairly close to Lithuanian."

"I don't even know what that is," I admitted. Aldona was staring at me now, frowning as if she sensed I wasn't talking to her.

"No reason you would." That was Top, who'd apparently been snooping on the conversation. "Eastern European country near Russia. *Too* damn near, once the Chinese MIRVs started falling. There's not much left of it. But I *have* heard the language, and this is close to it."

"Lithuanian," Colonel Hachette broke in, "was one of the most stable languages in history. Its origins go back to the Indo-European languages dating back to around 2,000 BCE. But not much before that. Nowhere near ten thousand years ago."

"Which means the Predecessors were on Earth as late as four thousand years ago," Vicky deduced. "What do you have to say to that, *Dwight?*"

"I have nothing to offer," the AI confessed. "I can only say that, if this is the case, they did not exit through the Corridor."

"Which means there are *other* exits—and entrances!"

Hachette exclaimed, more excited than I'd heard him since we'd met.

"That's all well and good," I snapped. "But this lady is looking at me like I just grew a third head, so how about doing some fucking translating?"

"All right, we can't do this through the speaker," Chase reasoned, "or they'll really freak out. So, I'm going to feed you the lines and you repeat them very carefully."

"Wonderful," I murmured. If I got the intonation wrong, I could start a war. I sighed. "All right, go ahead."

"*Sveiki, mano vardas* Cameron Alvarez..."

———

"You come from the sky," Aldona said, blowing steam off the top of her mug before taking a sip. "We have seen this before."

I took a drink myself to give the translator time to feed me the lines Hachette was giving it as a response. I was apparently not trusted to talk for myself.

No, that's not being fair. There was no way to make the conversation sound natural if I spoke every line in English and then repeated it in Lithuanian a moment later.

Not actually Lithuanian. We'd found that out fairly quickly, when some of the words and phrases hadn't translated. It was an ancient Indo-European language with many differences from the Lithuanian we had stored in the databanks of the *Orion*, but the translation program had been designed with just this sort of thing in mind.

I made a face at the drink before I spat the words out, wishing I could do the same to the broth.

"Who else have you seen come down from the sky?"

"The demons," she confided, making a sign of horns with her hand and spitting to the side. "They come in ships like yours..." She shrugged, an expressive motion of shoulders and hands. "...and *not* like yours. Theirs do not roar and spit fire as yours did."

"She's talking about the Resscharr," Top said, not looking up. She sat cross-legged on the matted floor of the...*office? Study? Conference room?* There was no exact word to describe the place where Aldona had led the three of us.

The building was one of the larger in the city, though it was near the edge of town, which I guessed had been intentional, to keep from parading us through the center of the place and scaring the children. We hadn't seen any kids, hadn't seen anyone other than our armed escort, except for a few furtive glances out of quickly-closed shutters on upper floors. I didn't have much to compare the layout of the place to, since the only cultures I was familiar with were my own and the Tahni, but it seemed strange to me, like someone had set up a business or a government office in their house. But I guess that was how they did things here in Laisvas Miestas. It meant "Free Town," which was one of the things I'd discovered in our "me-Tarzan, you-Jane" conversation.

"Why do the demons come?" I asked her for Hachette. "What do they want here?"

"They take our people. Not often, but the tales have come down through the mothers of our mothers. Every few years, they come and take the strong as slaves."

"Slaves?" I blurted in English. "Why the hell would the Predecessors need slaves?" Thankfully, Chase had the courtesy to translate it for me and I repeated it in Aldona's language.

"We don't know." She wrapped her hands around the mug, like she was drawing warmth from it. Not that anyone needed extra heat here. It was already warm enough, and without the sea breezes, it would have been damned uncomfortable. "None are ever seen again. But the Island People tell us this is why they come."

"The Island People?" At least this time, Hachette anticipated my question and fed it to me in their language before I could ask it in English.

"They are not as we are. Domantas." She turned and spoke to one of the three men present in the room, none of whom had said a word up until now. "Can you find the drawing Jurgis made of the Islander trader last summer?"

"Yes, ma'am." I was only going by the translator, but the man's tone seemed deferential. He was a good deal older than the woman, his long beard shot with grey, yet he treated her with the respect I thought might be due an elder. Was this place a matriarchy? Or was Aldona just a VIP here?

Either way, Domantas scrambled to obey, shuffling through a sheaf of papers in a cubby hole tucked into the far wall of the room. He returned with a charcoal-pencil sketch and held it up for us. There was no mistaking the face, the steam-shovel jaws, the flattened nose. It was a Tahni.

"You trade with the Islanders?" I asked, echoing Hachette's words.

"Once or twice a year. Their lands are far from ours and the journey is long...and they have no seams of coal in their islands, no steam ships. They use sail and the storms take many of their ships."

"How do they know anything about the demons?"

"They say it has been passed down to them by their priests. There is much they won't tell us, but they used to worship the demons, I think. The Islanders tell us that the demons used to snatch up their people as well until they scattered from their cities and took to the seas."

"Do they say where the demons come from?" I wondered.

"The sky." She motioned above us. "The stars."

"And where do you think your people came from?"

"We were brought here by the gods themselves. They plucked us off the steppes, the grasslands, where the horizon had no end, where we followed the horse herds, and taken to this place where the land and sea meet. The gods gave us the secrets of the black stone." By which I assumed she meant coal. "They shared with us the art of steam and of steel. Without them, we would be as the Islanders, adrift and at the mercy of the waves."

Interesting. I slipped into English, speaking directly to Chase.

"Hey, ask her if they have any record of what the gods looked like."

He grumbled at me going off-script, but he did it anyway.

"No," she admitted. "Only that they were beings of light, beautiful as the sunrise." She tilted an eyebrow toward me. "But we have talked much of us and nothing of you. You come from the skies, from the stars. Are you as the gods, or as the demons?"

Now that would be a long story. But not one Hachette was ready to tell her, so I just repeated the words I was fed.

"We are nothing like the demons. We don't want to take anything of yours or harm you in any way. We're only here because we're lost, very far from home, and we need to understand this place."

Eyes bluer than the ocean pierced through me, and I understood why she was the leader of this town.

"And when you understand, what then? Will you stay here? Share with us your arts as the gods once did?"

"That," I said in English, not caring if Chase tried to translate it, "is a damned good question."

[18]

"We need to think about it," Vicky said.

"No," Captain Nance insisted, pausing in his caged-lion pacing to slash the air with a hand. "Our priority should be doing everything we can to get back home."

I don't know what it is about senior officers and pacing. They just love to pace while they think. It was probably the main reason Hachette had asked for a rotational drum on the *Orion*.

"And if we can't *get* home?" Vicky shot back. "Sir," she added after a moment, blinking as if she'd just remembered she was back in the military and speaking to a Fleet captain.

For some reason, the five of us—six if you counted Dwight—had become the go-to brain trust for the mission. That worried the hell out of me. Any brain trust that wanted me in it was sorely short of brains.

"This is a whole *galaxy* we're talking about," Vicky went on. "We could wander around the rest of our lives and never find anything like the Corridor again. We don't have unlimited reserves. Our reactor fuel won't last forever, and neither will our food. We *know* this system has food. What if the next one doesn't? What if the next *ten* systems don't?"

Vicky was on a tear, and I didn't want to step into that field of fire, so I trod carefully when I replied.

"That's true. But we *do* know where the Predecessors are. Sort of."

"What you saw on the third planet," Dwight said, his holographic avatar pointing at an image of the third world out from the primary star, "were indeed the Resscharr species, but I question whether this is the same as what you would call the Predecessors."

"I would be giddy as all hell," Colonel Hachette said, cradling his head in his hands, elbows on the conference table, "if you didn't just help yourself to our communications displays every time you felt like it."

"It is the only way I have of communicating," Dwight replied, reasonably if not at all apologetic.

"What do you mean they're not Predecessors?" I asked him.

"The level of technology on that world was puzzling. I noted only two reactors in the city, and though their thermal signatures were similar to the self-contained slow-decay quark flux power plants that were standard for small-scale power production on Predecessor worlds, they're not being *used* for anything. There are no fabrication plants, no food production facilities other than the farms we spotted from orbit, and those were small parcels without any visible powered machinery to maintain them. The shuttles that chased us away were the only thing I could truly say was representative of their level of sophistication."

"Maybe it's on purpose," I suggested. "Maybe they're trying not to attract the attention of the Skrela."

"That is not an unreasonable speculation," Dwight acknowledged. "There was some speculation that the Skrela were drawn to the use of the Transition Drive or other residual effects of high technology."

"So, they might still have the means to construct another Corridor," Hachette said, seizing on the slender thread of hope like a drowning man. "Or maybe know where one is. We need to talk to them."

"They didn't seem too eager to talk before," Top pointed out. She had been unusually silent since our visit to the human settlement on the second planet. Not that she could have talked to the people there, but she'd said little since then as well. "They blew our drone out of the air and then sent interceptors after us."

"We didn't exactly *try* to talk," Hachette said. "We were spying on them with a drone. If the situations had been reversed, would we have done anything differently than they did?"

"The question is, will they want to talk to us now?" I asked. "Even if we can. Dwight, could you make us a translation program for the Resscharr language?"

"Of course. Though my files are ten thousand years out of date, I'm sure I can write a progression algorithm to track the changes."

"It's settled, then," Hachette said, not bothering to ask for any more input on the subject. "Alvarez, any objections to running point on this?"

"None at all, sir," I said. "But I do have a suggestion. We don't need to be worried about freaking out primitives with an excessive show of technology, I think we should go down in full Vigilante armor, maybe with a platoon of Captain Solano's Drop-Troopers for backup."

"Fine with me," Solano declared. "I'll command the platoon myself."

"Get ready, then," Hachette told us, pushing himself to his

feet. "We'll break orbit in two hours. I want a drop-ship prepped and ready to go before we Transition back to the third planet." He did that colonel thing where he made sure to look each of us in the eye to let us know he was watching us. "Even if they don't have a gate to send us back home, they may know where we can get one. And even if they don't, they might be able to help us get our hands on fuel and food. We're all counting on you, Alvarez. Don't fuck this up."

———

"I'm not sure why we're suddenly the ship's fucking diplomatic corps," I said to Vicky once we were out of range of Hachette's preternatural hearing.

"It's the same old story," she replied, eyeing me sidelong. "The reward for a job well done is a harder job. You and I have been the official factotums for this operation." I stopped walking and stared at her.

"The official *what*?"

Vicky rolled her eyes.

"Don't tell me you've never heard the word before. You're the one who's always been a walking garbage pail of trivia. Factotum is like a jack-of-all-trades."

"I said I read a lot." I shrugged, feeling guilty but not knowing why. "I never said I read a thesaurus."

"It's also because the only one Hachette would really trust for this job is himself, but he can't put himself in harm's way unnecessarily because he's the commander."

I checked carefully around us before I answered that point. Some things weren't for anyone's ears but Vicky's.

"As fucked up as the situation is, I think maybe he shouldn't worry so much about risking the commander's life. This is some lifeboat ethics here."

She cocked her head to the side, uncomprehending, and I sighed.

"Don't give me shit about factotum if you don't know what lifeboat ethics means, woman!" But I grinned and she did too, elbowing me in the side. "It means, this is an emergency situation and he should be more worried about survival and less about regulations. Going by the book isn't going to do us any good if we're stuck here."

She was silent for a moment as we hit the lift and headed back down toward the armory. The car was empty except for us. Most of the Fleet types used the central hub to get around in free fall, but I was out of practice and didn't want one of the hotshots to run headlong into me at forty klicks an hour.

"What if we can't get back?" she asked, abruptly, catching me by surprise. "What if we're here for good?"

"I know you'd miss hearing from your family," I said, cautious, like I was tiptoeing through a mine field.

"I would. But what about you?"

"You're my only family," I reminded her. "Wherever we are is home."

"You'd be okay with being a dirt farmer here but not on Hausos?"

"Oh, I don't think we'll be dirt farmers," I assured her. "Something tells me this place is going to need our other special-ties a lot more."

"I guess that will fit right in with your need to get yourself killed."

I winced at the bitterness in her voice.

"I haven't felt that way since..." I didn't finish. I felt guilty for what I was thinking and I didn't know if I wanted to say it aloud. But she wasn't going to give me the choice, not by the glare she was fixing on me. "I haven't felt that way since Wade died."

That rocked her back, and since we were in free-fall, the motion sent her back against the bulkhead and she grabbed at a handhold.

"Why?"

"I don't know. I think maybe I was trying to talk him out of being guilty for surviving and I...talked myself out of it. But I know I would have been feeling it after he died. And I didn't."

"That doesn't mean it's forever." She put a hand on my arm, squeezed. "But I'll take it for now."

"Hey!" I wasn't sure which came first, the door opening or Dunstan assailing us. Either way, it took nearly psychic levels of anticipation. "So, what's the op?" He was connected to the deck by ship boots, his arms spread in a question. "Are we settling down with the weird fish people and living in hovels or what?"

"Negative," I told him, brushing past in the passageway toward the armory. "We're going back to the Tahni goons and the dinosaur aliens and trying to make friends. Keep your ears open. You're probably going to be on high cover duty."

"Tahni goons and dinosaur aliens." Dunstan sighed. "Joy." He waved and hopped into the lift. "I'm heading down to the hangar bay."

"Solano will be down in a minute," Vicky said, pulling me toward the armory. "Once he spreads the word, the whole bunch will be getting geared up. Let's get into our suits and get to the drop-ship."

There were other Marines in the armory because there *always* are, anytime the ship wasn't under way. An NCO's favorite pastime is making the enlisted do PMCS, and since there wasn't enough room for the whole company to do it at once, one squad or another was always breaking down and cleaning Vigilantes. This one was Third squad, First Platoon, or at least I thought so from this one particularly trollish private from some heavy-grav world called Canaan. He was unmistakable.

And Karen Fargo. She was there, cleaning grit out of her suit's knee joint with a wire brush, and she didn't look up until we were almost past her and to our suit cradles.

"Oh, hi, sir, ma'am," she said, waving with the brush. "I was getting bored waiting around for the word to come down, so I thought I'd clean my suit. What are you guys doing down here?"

"We're going down to the planet with the Resscharr, to try to see if they're going to send us home," I told her. "You're going with us."

"Really?" Vicky asked, cocking an eyebrow.

"Why not?" I shrugged. "It's better than sitting around here waiting to see if the ship gets ripped apart by alien shuttles."

"You know," Vicky said, shrugging as she pulled down the restraint bar from the chest plastron of her suit, "if the Predecessors actually *are* native to Earth like Dwight says, they're not really aliens."

"Technicalities," I scoffed, moving to my own suit.

It was waiting for me, good as new, the damage from the battle with the Skrela repaired by the armorer. I needed to buy her a drink because she'd fixed it up quickly and well. I ran a hand down its leg, the metal as smooth as if it were new. The feel of the suit beneath my hands woke an old fire in my belly.

I'd lied to Vicky. Maybe the first lie I'd ever told her, though it hadn't been intentional. I'd said that wherever we were together was home. But the truth was, that suit was home. It was who I was. I'd tried to deny it and that hadn't worked so well for me.

"Hey, Cam." I looked over at Vicky, realizing she'd been talking and I hadn't been listening. "You there?"

"Sorry," I said, chuckling. "Just lost in a memory."

I threw open the plastron and stripped off my ship boots,

stuffing them in the locker next to the cradle, then twisted my way into the suit. It was easier in free-fall. I'd done it both ways, done it in high-gravity boost when we didn't have any choice, and I liked it in free-fall. Going inside the suit in free-fall was like climbing back into the womb, away from the chaos being wrought in my inner ear, the feeling of drifting lost. The suit held me like my mother's arms...like Vicky.

I closed myself into it and plugged the 'face jacks into my implant sockets. Maybe they were the reason I felt about the suit the way I did. Maybe it wasn't just the womblike dark, the cushioning gel cradling me. Maybe they'd done something to my brain when they'd implanted those jacks. But if they'd done that, they never would have let any of us go. I shouldn't try to blame anyone else. I was good at killing people and blowing shit up, the one thing I'd ever really been good at. There was no use denying it.

"You copy, Cam?" Vicky asked me.

"Five by five," I confirmed.

"You think these freaky-looking toads are going to talk to us?"

She was talking to me, but the suit was too. Flashing green indicators to assure me that my missile launch racks were loaded, that the plasma gun was functional, that it was ready to do its job.

"Honestly?" I said, shaking my head just slightly, as far as it would go in the padded rest. "No. I'm not counting on it."

"Well, then, why the hell did you volunteer us for it?"

"Because if it goes wrong," I told her, "we're the best ones to handle it."

She laughed softly, the sound like a crackle of static over the suit radio.

"Now that," she admitted, "I can't argue with."

I engaged the magnets in the soles of my boots and stepped

out of the cradle, the stomp of metal on metal a thump I could feel in my chest.

"Come on, Fargo," I said to the Marine, seeing her IFF indicator light up on my display, the sign she was sealed into her armor. "Let's get to that drop-ship before some assholes grab all the good seats."

[19]

"You think they've seen us yet?" Fargo asked.

I closed my eyes and counted to ten, but it didn't work as well this time as it had the first two times she'd asked.

"If they have," Vicky answered for the both of us, "then they must have decided we come in peace, since they haven't launched their ships. But I'm gonna go with no, they haven't."

"How could they have not seen us?" Fargo's tone was plaintive, as if she was complaining about the incompetence of the people who might try to kill us. "It's broad daylight and we're coming right down on top of them."

She was right about that. We'd arrived at near noon local time and the view from the drop-ship's cameras showed a sky painfully blue, shining off the stone city like it was a jewel set in the green and brown backing. The farms were cut into squares a few kilometers on a side, starting just outside the city walls and reaching out until the land turned into hills and the river went from a broad, watery highway into a narrow and winding serpent heading up into the mountains.

There was something different about the farms. I hadn't noticed it before, when the closest we'd come was orbit. They were laid out differently than the city, fewer curves and more straight lines. The buildings were dissimilar as well, less haphazard and more squared off. But there were farmers tending those crops at high noon, their plows pulled by something that might have been oxen, or the local evolutionary equivalent.

I had access to the camera controls, since I was linked into the command network for the drop-ship, and I zoomed in to the view showing me the farmers, as close as the optical lenses and the computer enhancement would take me. Most of the figures were dressed in loose grey clothing to shield them from the harsh light of the star, floppy hats hiding their faces from view. But one wasn't. Smaller than the others, running beside the plow like it was fun, arms and legs moving awkwardly, coltish.

It was a child. Maybe a young teenager. And he was human.

"You seeing this, Vicky? Solano?"

"We're seeing it up here too," Top assured me. She was up on the *Orion* with Hachette, analyzing from afar, and I wondered if that chafed at her the way it would have me. "Am I the only one thinking this might be where the humans end up who get snatched from the fishing towns?"

"Makes sense," Hachette put in. "It's probably just as well you're in the armor, Alvarez. They might not take you seriously if it was obvious you're human, not if they consider us conscripted labor."

"I'll stay buttoned up until we have a good conversation going," I promised. I didn't mention how unlikely I thought that was.

"I'm gonna set you guys down in that open field just outside the front gates," Lt. Pearl told us. He was a good pilot, for a Fleet jock. I was used to Marine drop-ship crews, but for some reason, Hachette had brought along all Fleet flight personnel. "Doesn't seem to be any traffic there, so you should be able to set up a security perimeter before anyone reaches you."

I switched camera feeds, trying to find the field he was talking about. I hadn't realized the city even *had* walls until about two minutes ago. It seemed anachronistic. Of course, the Tahni had put up wire fences on occupied colony cities during the war, but that had been to keep the captive humans inside. Stone walls were to keep things out. Maybe the humans here, as well? They might be second-class citizens, if not slaves, and maybe the Predecessors wanted to make sure they didn't bring down the property values.

"Looks good," I told the pilot. "At least we won't be landing on top of anyone. See if..."

"We have a bogie incoming!" That wasn't from Pearl; it was Wojtera, watching over us from orbit like a guardian angel. "Taking off from that same wooded area on the other side of the city! You need to get out of there!"

"If we just run at the first sight of them," I cut in, frowning at the feeling of the drop-ship banking away from the city, "we'll never get to talk to them."

"I'm not going to set you down in an open field with one of those ships ready to blast you to vapors, Alvarez," Hachette told me. At least the Predecessors weren't bothering to jam our microwave signals.

"The farms," Vicky suggested. "There are other humans there."

"Yeah," I agreed. "We'll drop from three hundred meters and Pearl can take the drop-ship back up to orbit."

The hesitation from Hachette was barely a second. "Do it."

"Get ready to drop!" Solano barked at his platoon. "Drop on my mark."

"Ten seconds," the transport's crew chief warned. "Ten seconds 'til drop."

The bogie was visible on the tactical display, a red dot rising above the city. My insides twisted at the thought of the weapons the alien ship carried tearing the drop-ship to shreds with us inside of it, ripping us all limb from limb like some deranged child destroying his toys. But not for long.

"Drop! Drop! Drop!" Solano's command merged with the crew chief's announcement and I hit the control.

We were low. Low was good, or at least better than too high, but urgency quickened my breath and put just a little more of a stomp into my heels as I hit the jump-jets. My spine shortened a centimeter, felt like it was being pushed upward through my skull, and the roaring filling my ears could have been from the air-breathing jets or could have been my blood rushing away from my head. Colors flashed outside, blurred together in a kaleidoscope of green and blue and brown, and the ground rushed against my feet, the battlesuit's hips creaking as they absorbed the impact.

I was down, left hand sunken four or five centimeters into the loamy soil, and Vicky and Fargo were to either side of me. I didn't look back at Solano's platoon, just noted them filtering down in a V-formation in the IFF display, but most of my attention was on the drop-ship. It had goosed its engines the second we dropped, and the jets were rolling thunder across the fields of grain as the drop-ship ascended on shimmering waves of superheated air. It was going as fast as one of the massive armor carriers could accelerate, yet it seemed to be crawling across the sky.

And behind it was something featureless and cylindrical, glowing a fluorescent green with a light that seemed to come from within and engulf the air around it in a verdant halo. It was far behind but making up the gap every second, close enough now that I knew in my gut it was already in range for that gravity weapon.

"The lasers," I shouted, knowing it was triply useless. "Use the lasers!"

Shouting on the radio was idiotic, and even if it hadn't been, the only way to relay a transmission to orbit from here would be with the drop-ship, and it was already too far away. The third reason it was useless was that we'd already gone over this with Hachette and Nance, and they knew damn well to use the lasers.

Dwight had told us those were the only weapons that stood a chance against the Predecessor ships, but we hadn't wanted to use them, hoping they'd give us a chance to land and talk. But Pearl and his crew were dead if the *Orion* didn't intervene, and Colonel Hachette's instincts were no more diplomatic than my own. Lightning flashed in a clear sky, a sheath of plasma forming around the superheated path of the *Orion*'s primary laser battery, the air crackling with the static electricity as peals of artificial thunder shattered the sky.

When the beam hit the alien ship, the thing shuddered, listing in mid-air as if it were an ocean-going sailing vessel from centuries ago, running aground on shoal waters. I knew what was happening, sort of. Dwight had told us the ship propelled itself via a gravitic drive, and that same drive field acted as a defense shield. When the laser hit, the drive field had tried to shunt it aside, but the energy beam dumped too much heat and radiation into the field and even the half-magic technology that could keep a micro-singularity in check couldn't shrug off the blow. The field attenuated, and without it, the ship faltered and lost ground to the only other gravity field around, the one holding my feet to the deck at approximately one Earth gravity. It didn't crash, but only because the *Orion* cut off the beam. We didn't *want* to kill them...it might complicate asking them for help. But we also didn't want our drop-ship blown up. It had been a diversion, and it had worked...the drop-ship was gone, disappeared into the blue.

Though maybe it had worked a little too well.

"Oh, shit," Vicky murmured, and I didn't have to ask her why.

The alien ship had recovered its bright green glow and was rising again, and it wasn't alone. Two more had joined, rising straight up, less like an aircraft than a rocket, or an arrow loosed from the bow of a giant.

"Cam," Hachette told me, his transmission reaching me easily, though I couldn't answer it, "we're going to have to micro-Transition once we take the drop-ship aboard. Try to stay clear of the Resscharr for a couple hours until we're back in position to support you."

"Stay clear of the fucking Resscharr?" Vicky repeated in a tone that might have gotten her an official reprimand if she'd had to worry about Hachette hearing it. "Then what's the fucking point of this little jaunt in the first place?"

"Improvise, adapt, and overcome," I reminded her. "Let's just hope the big green weenie ships are too busy to notice us."

"Alvarez!" Solano called from behind us. "We got company."

Oh, great. My first thought was that I'd jinxed us and the damned Resscharr or their Tahni soldiers had already seen us, that we were going to be forced into letting them take potshots at us while we tried to talk to them.

But it wasn't a Tahni and it wasn't a Resscharr. It was a man, one of the farmers I was sure, given his rough, homespun clothes. He peeked out from behind the unfinished wood of a hand-built shed, his face so pale, I thought he might pass out, eyes wide. He was fairly young, not more than thirty, I imagined, given the fact that he probably wouldn't have access to advanced health care. I mean, these guys were plowing with oxen. There was no grey in his short beard or his bowl-cut brown hair, but he had the weathered, leathery look of someone who's spent their whole life working outdoors.

"Time to find out whether these guys speak the same language as the Victorian fishing village," I muttered, tapping a control with my left hand, the menu scrolling across my HUD until I came to the translation program. I raised my suit's left hand, which was less intimidating than the right only because it wasn't filled with a plasma cannon. "Hello. My name is Cameron. We mean you no harm." The suit spouted the words out in the proto-Lithuanian we'd picked up on the second planet and the farmer's eyes got even wider, if that was possible.

"Who are you? *What* are you?"

The questions reached my ears a second after his lips had stopped moving, an annoying incongruity that I had to work to ignore.

"Vicky, keep on eye on this guy and make sure he doesn't do anything stupid."

"Why?" she asked. "What stupid thing are *you* going to do?"

"The only stupid thing I can think of."

I yanked on the release and my chest plastron swung downward, the humid midday air slapping me in the face. The farmer seemed even more shocked to see a human sitting inside the giant metal ogre.

"My name is Cameron Alvarez. We've come to this place from far away...from the place where your ancestors lived before you were brought here."

"Did the gods bring you?" If the man had been pale and fearful before, now his face shone like a religious fanatic. "They promised they wouldn't leave us alone...yet it's been generation upon generation and all we have seen is slavery and toil."

"Alvarez," Solano said, his voice buzzing in my ear, unheard and untranslated. "I'm deploying the platoon in a security perimeter along the road coming in from the city. Try to stay out of sight."

I didn't answer, not wanting to confuse our new friend, just motioned toward Fargo. She was smart enough to understand what I meant and hustled off toward Solano and his platoon to take up a position in the defense. I frowned. I *wanted* to get out of the armor to put the man at ease, but that would take away the speakers, and I couldn't be understood without them.

"What's your name, friend?" I asked him, trying to sound calming, though I didn't know if it would come through the translation. "Were you born on this world?"

"Matis. No, I was taken from Laisvas Miestas by the Resscharr when I was barely a teenager." He scowled. "They came down in their ships over one of our schools and took everyone old enough to work, boy and girls both. My wife was one of them."

Interesting. He clearly differentiated from what he'd called *the gods* and the Resscharr. Matis shrugged.

"Now, we are no longer of the Laisvas Miestas. We are *Vergai*, and our children and their children will be Vergai, just as the rest of us here, growing crops and raising cattle to feed the Resscharr and the Karai."

I blinked, wondering if the software wasn't working right.

"The Resscharr aren't the gods who brought you here?"

"Those?" Matis scoffed, then glanced around as if worried someone might have heard. "No, they want us to *think* they are, but the gods would not war amongst themselves. The gods would not scrabble for bits of the old magic like dogs fighting over scraps."

They have dogs here? I'd no sooner had the thought than I saw a redbone hound in the near distance, trotting from a barn or outbuilding toward the house. A woman waited there in the doorway, wringing her hands anxiously, staring at Matis.

His wife, maybe.

"You mean like the ships?" I asked, then rephrased it, thinking someone from the fishing village might equate ships with ocean-going vessels. "The ships of the air? The ones that glow green and make no sound?"

Matis made a sign of the horns, just like Aldona had done back in Laisvas Miestas.

"The flying ships are the work of the gods." He whispered of them reverently...or maybe fearfully. It was hard to tell. "None of the Resscharr are worthy of them, but especially not the pig Zemekar."

"Who's Zemekar?"

"The lord of that grand pile of shit," Matis snarled, motioning back toward the city. "They call it Yfingam, though I don't know if that's a Resscharr name or Karai."

"Who are the Karai?" I felt like I was interviewing the dude for the Commonwealth News Net, but the more I talked, the more relaxed he seemed to get. He'd come out from behind the corner of the shed and was at least standing up straight, though he seemed to be unsure what to do with his hands.

"The Karai were brought here as the Vergai were, by the gods, for their purpose." He made a gesture that might have been a shrug filtered through a couple thousand years and a culture that didn't even exist anymore. "Though the gods alone may know what that was. Now they are the soldiers of the Resscharr, fighting each other because the Resscharr would never risk their own lives." He motioned at the fields, golden with grain. "Nor would they dirty their hands growing their own food. We are their servants, as are the Karai, though they think otherwise, think they are noble and honorable, serving their masters." He spat aside. Now he wasn't even fidgeting, winding up for a good rant. I wasn't about to discourage him. People reveal more than they want to when they get pissed off.

"They're fools, dying for the glory of false gods. And if any of the Vergai disobey, or fail to show them proper respect..."

"The Tahni," Vicky said privately in my earbud. "He's talking about the Tahni. Those are what he's calling the Karai."

"What about the magic?" I asked him. "How much of it do the Resscharr have? Just the ships? Do you know how many Resscharr lords there are? Do they all have magic?" I shut my mouth. I was blathering, asking too many questions at once, and I needed to give him time to answer. Matis shrugged.

"No one knows all the magic. Not even the seven Resscharr lords who rule the seven lands." I hadn't seen any seven lands from orbit, but God knew how they ran things here. Maybe there were only three lands but the Resscharr liked the number seven better.

"They fight over the magic," Matis told me. "It's all they do. But Zemekar has the flying ships and none of the others can invade this place as long as he does. He's the most powerful."

"Great," Vicky murmured. "Lucky us."

This was, I decided, the worst-case scenario. The Resscharr were the Predecessors, or at least that was what Dwight had told us, but according to Matis, they weren't the same sort of "god" that had brought his people here. They fought over high-tech items like the ships, which meant they couldn't make new ones. They didn't have decent security or surveillance sensors, no drones, no signal jamming, no heavy industry. Which meant that the likelihood that they could get us back was almost nil. But they did have the "magic," the high-tech items, probably left over from when they'd come here. It wasn't likely, but there was a chance that, if we could get our hands on them, we might be able to figure out...something. I had no idea what. I just didn't want to give up hope.

"Have you ever been inside the city?" I asked Matis.

"Cam," Vicky said softly. "People are getting curious."

I looked up, handicapped by not having my Heads-Up Display or access to my sensor suite. The woman was coming out of the farmhouse, and with her were two other men. Brothers? Workers? No way to tell and it wasn't important enough to ask.

"Never," Matis answered my question. "None of us Vergai are allowed, except the few who deliver the food to the city, and even those are closely watched. We are not trusted by either the Resscharr or the Karai."

The woman was running now and I cursed softly, hoping the translator wouldn't catch it so I wouldn't have to explain to Matis why I'd said "fuck" when his sister or wife or whatever was coming toward us.

"Janus," he called, waving to her, and I thought it must be her name. "It's all right, they are men, like us. They're not our enemy."

"Matis!" she said, breathless, digging in her heels to stop herself as she reached him, sparing me a fearful and unsure glance even with her obvious urgency. "Lukas and his cousins were playing at the drainage ditch...they just came running back. It's the Karai! Many of them, with guns! They've left the city! They're heading this way!" The Tahni guards. Oh well, it wasn't the end of the world.

"It's a not a problem," I told them, gesturing with the plasma gun. "We can take care of them."

She stared at me like I'd grown a second head.

"A Resscharr is coming with them."

Oh, shit.

"We can't stay here," I said, tromping up to Solano, glad to be buttoned back up in my suit. "We don't want these people to get caught up in the middle of our fight."

"We'll move the platoon up onto the road," he suggested. "Maybe a klick north of here? We don't need cover against those rifles we saw in the drone video."

I didn't contradict him, but I remembered the weapon the Resscharr had used against the drone and hoped he was right.

"Right," I said. "Fargo, you stay with Solano. Vicky, let's go scout ahead before we let the platoon walk into anything."

"Isn't that what corporals are for?" Vicky grumbled, but only half-heartedly.

The path out of the farm settlement couldn't honestly be called a road, though it was rutted by what I assumed were wagon wheels. It hadn't been paved by anything except repeat usage, feet and hooves stomping the dirt flat and packing it down for a few thousand years. There was an almost permanent wind whipping across the open fields between the farms and the city, concealing its distant walls with a haze of yellow dust, but the thermal signatures of the approaching Tahni were already visible.

The reds and yellows blended together and I couldn't have counted them myself, but the computer told me there were an even two dozen. And that one other thing, the thermal signature different enough that I could have identified it without the computer's help. It was a devil from an old fairy tale, some dark, pagan god that had clawed its way up from Hell or been thrown out of Heaven.

These were the mysterious Ancients we'd been speculating about for a hundred years, since we'd first found the wormhole map on Hermes…except they weren't. It was like finally getting to meet your childhood sports hero and finding out they'd gotten hooked on drugs and gained fifty kilos of blubber. Worse than that, because now we really needed them to be that hero again.

And the worst part was, I didn't even know who to be angry with. With the Predecessors for leaving the Corridor AI to send any nosy idiots through to this hellhole, with Dwight for being a constant reminder of that, or with Wade for roping us into this mess to begin with. Or with myself, because this was mostly my own fault.

Maybe that was why I kept volunteering to walk point.

"We need to keep them as far away from the farms as possible," I told Vicky. "I'd rather not kill anyone if we don't have to."

"Always making things more complicated than they have to be." She sighed. "All right, I'll be gentle with them."

I didn't jump because the dust and haze worked both ways and they didn't have thermal sensors. Best to have as much surprise on our side as we could. The Vigilante looked awkward when it ran, like a toddler, but its legs ate up the meters, the spikes on its soles churning up even more dust, adding to our camouflage. The lead Tahni, or Karai, or whatever they were called here, didn't see me until I was fifty meters away. I found out he saw me when his big-ass bullet spanged noisily off my chest plate like someone had rung a gong inside my armor.

Noise was all it accomplished. It didn't register on the suit's damage monitors, not even when two more of the heavy, soft-metal slugs ricocheted off my left arm. The plasma gun called to me, wanting to be fired, wanting to do what it had done so many times before and kill Tahni, but I resisted the siren song. I swung my left hand slowly, not wanting to crack any skulls, aiming low.

Something *did* crack—I could hear it clearly above the gunshots and the shouting—but it was a thigh bone and I hoped for the Tahni warrior's sake that the Resscharr had a good health plan. He went flying, tumbling to a stop ten meters away, and I swept my arm back across the trail and took the legs out from another of the Karai. No broken legs this time, but his head was going to hurt where it smacked into the ground, helmet or no.

"Stop trying to hog all the fun for yourself," Vicky said, moving past me, arms and legs flashing, the speed of the suit belying its mass.

She didn't even have to swing a fist at them, just brush the Karai with her shoulder. Hundreds of kilos of BiPhase Carbide grazed the soldier's chest hard enough to knock the Karai off the road into the runoff ditch beside it, and I wondered if I wouldn't rather get a broken leg. Vicky stuck the turn, her pivot foot digging into the dirt, sending red clay and packed brown earth spraying in a semicircle, then spun and grabbed for another of the Karai.

They weren't stupid, and they were pretty quick on the uptake for a bunch of half-savage barbarians whose highest technological accomplishment was chemical-propellant firearms. They scattered, moving out of our grasp, not bothering to shoot at us, and it took me nearly a full second to realize that the Resscharr was yelling at them in a language the translator didn't understand. It wasn't anything like the Predecessor dialects that Dwight had shared with us, and I had a glimmer of a notion that it might be some proto-Tahni, but I didn't waste a second thinking about it.

My focus was on the device in the Resscharr's left hand, something built for his three-fingered grip. It resembled neither metal nor plastic nor anything I'd ever seen, looking more like it was a holographic projection, but I'd seen it before...in the drone video.

"Jump!" I told Vicky, taking my own advice, hitting the jets and hopping backwards, intent on getting back to cover.

Vicky listened, or else she'd had the thought just after I had, but she was a half a second too late. Whatever the weapon fired sent a shimmering tunnel through the air between the Resscharr and Vicky's armor, making the hair on the back of my arms stand on end through my Vigilante's skin from nearly a hundred meters away. She'd been in mid-jump, jets spinning up, only a couple meters off the ground when it hit her.

My gut clenched at the expectation that the beam of whatever it was would burn a hole right through her chest or simply disintegrate her and the Vigilante together, but instead, a halo of green light surrounded her armor, crackling with static electricity. And she fell.

Not far, just two meters, but the crash was a solid thump I could hear over the roar of my jets, and when she hit, she lay motionless...not stiff, like the armor was unguided, but slumping and slack, as if there were no power to the joints, nothing to move the heavy limbs. Her IFF signal flickered black and rage and pain and fear screamed in my head.

And I had to shout it down.

"Solano!" I said, touching down, falling into a crouch. "Get your platoon out of here! Fall back to the river and take shelter in the tree line. Don't fucking come out until the drop-ship comes back for you!"

"What about you two?" he asked, like I'd known he would.

"Do it! Go now while you can!"

I had one chance, time for one shot, though taking it would make our mission an utter failure. I didn't hesitate for a heartbeat on that account. Vicky was more important to me than this mission, than Solano's Marines, than this whole fucking galaxy. My only hesitation was a shuffle to my right to keep from catching Vicky's motionless armor in the fringes of the plasma blast, but it was enough that by the time I fired, the Resscharr had moved as well.

The incandescent spear of ionized hydrogen hit dirt instead of dinosaur-alien, heating the moisture in the packed earth past the boiling point in a fraction of a second, blowing a crater a meter deep where the Resscharr had been a moment before. The Karai were scattered between fifty to a hundred meters away from the blast, but its heat and concussion still knocked them flat...and the Resscharr too.

I *should* have finished him off, should have jetted straight up and squashed his elongated skull like a fucking melon, but the cold, calculating section of my brain wasn't quite able to override what the Bible my mama read me would have called the heart. I hopped over to where Vicky had fallen instead, needing to make sure she was still alive. She'd fallen on her side, her suit's arm draped across its chest, and I pulled her flat, freeing up the chest plastron if she was conscious to work the manual release.

The plastron separated from the rest of the suit by a few centimeters and fingers pushed past the edge of it, trying to work the thing open. My shoulders sagged as I let go of the breath I'd been holding.

"Are you all right?" I asked over the external speakers, realizing a moment too late that I'd had it at maximum volume *and* I'd still had it set for the proto-Lithuanian language.

Her head squeezed through as she forced the chest plastron open, her face screwed up in a wince.

"Stop yelling at me," she snapped, "and help me get out of this thing. Every system is totally dead."

Mistake number two. Like most of the worst mistakes I'd made, I didn't realize it until later. What I *should* have done, after first making sure the Resscharr was dead, was to call Fargo and get her to come help me carry Vicky in her armor, get her away from the battle. The Vigilante, unpowered or no, would have protected her from the Karai weapons and we could have tried to get it working at our leisure.

But I was still thinking the way I'd been trained, thinking I was still fighting in the war , where the priority was getting a Marine clear of their armor and back behind the lines. There weren't any lines here. And the Resscharr wasn't dead.

I caught just a flicker of movement in the suit's motion detection sensors and tried to raise my plasma gun. Its capacitors had recharged and all it would have taken was another degree of rotation to get close enough to char the Resscharr to cinders even without a direct hit, but I didn't have the rotation.

Energy blasted from the muzzle of the Resscharr's weapon and everything went black.

———

I'd figured we'd both be dead by now.

I hadn't had any choice but to come out of my armor. Not just because my oxygen would have run out eventually, without the fan motors to bring in fresh air, but because Vicky's top was already popped, and I knew for certain that they wouldn't hesitate to use her against me. And I would rather have been dead than listen to her die while I sat inside my armor, hiding.

That left the other question, though, one I thought about for a good ten seconds before yanking the quick-release. I had a pulse carbine in a niche built into the side of the Vigilante's torso compartment, and if I took it out and popped out of the suit shooting, there was a chance—a small chance, but a chance, nonetheless—that I could have gotten enough of them to make a run for it. It would most likely be suicide, which also might be an acceptable outcome, at least when compared to leaving both of us to the tender mercies of a Resscharr warlord and his Tahni mercenary army.

But I couldn't be sure Vicky would do the same thing, and if she didn't do it, then I couldn't, because I couldn't leave her alone. I'd left the carbine in its slot and opened the chest plastron, putting my hands out first, hoping that the gesture was universal. My hands had been grabbed roughly and I'd been yanked out of the suit by my arms, and I'd thought the Tahni would throw us both on the ground and blow our heads off.

And they might have, left to their own ends, because not a one of them looked happy. I'd had nightmares during the war of being surrounded by angry Tahni faces, though I hadn't imagined them looking like 19th century grenadiers. But the Resscharr had barked something at them in what I couldn't even recognize as being related to the Tahni language I'd learned during the war or after, and the Karai had hauled us both to our feet and started us marching.

They hadn't said a word to us, or maybe they had and I just didn't know who they were talking to, and we certainly hadn't said anything to each other. We knew better than that. I could see the accusation in Vicky's eyes, though, and the glare was as plain as any yell.

You shouldn't have surrendered, dumbass! You should have stayed in your suit and let me die!

And, of course, she knew I couldn't have done it any more than she could have let that happen to me.

So, we walked in silence, a dozen gun barrels pointed at us, and the Resscharr in the lead. They all towered over us, the Tahni and even more so the Resscharr. His gait was unnatural, bobbing up and down like a trotting horse. Just looking at him sent a chill up my spine, and I could understand how the Karai thought of him as a god...how I might have myself.

I was properly intimidated, but not scared. It was strange how much I wasn't scared. I'd expected to be. I was outside the suit, as vulnerable as I ever had been. Even the air felt wrong, laced with strange smells, cloying and humid, like it was designed to start us hyperventilating. But it was just *too* damned strange to be real, a waking nightmare that had overloaded my senses, left me drifting in the yellow haze of dust and dirt obscuring the landscape around us.

I didn't even see the city walls until we were less than a klick away, coming over a rise, their bulk too much for the wind-blown veil to hide. They seemed taller now than they had from the air, more imposing, their stone slab walls so huge, they must have been put in place by more of the Predecessor "magic" Matis had told us about. I'd seen a few humans on the way in, in the distance, leading oxcarts stacked high with wooden barrels. Probably food, given what he'd told us.

We'd outdistanced them, walking at the long-legged pace of the Karai, each of their steps two of ours, leaving Vicky and me nearly jogging to keep up. Sweat was streaming down my face faster than I could wipe it away, the small of my back soaked with it, dark stains on my fatigue top at my armpits. I wasn't out of shape, but we'd fast-walked or jogged five kilometers, maybe more, and adrenaline had ceased to be my friend nearly an hour ago.

I saw no more humans once we reached the main gate. Karai guards stood watch, their weapons held across their chests, and I finally took the opportunity to have a good look at them. I'd been under the impression they were semiautomatic, maybe gas-operated, but they weren't even that sophisticated. They were operated, as near as I could tell just from a cursory examination, by some kind of pump action, a curved handle on the foregrip, and they looked to be made by hand.

No fabricators at all, then, not even for weapons.

The Karai weren't as numerous as I'd thought. Once we were past the defenses, the only ones I saw were the males guarding Resscharr VIPs or escorting the ox carts the humans had most likely brought to the gate. Those went to storehouses, dome-shaped and sunken into the earth, and they were also guarded.

No females, though. They lived apart, but where? Where did they keep their females and children?

The Resscharr, though...there was plenty of those. I saw my first females, or I *thought* they were females, at least if sexual dimorphism was a thing for the Resscharr. They were shorter, thinner, their feathery hair hanging down rather than spiked backwards like a mane. Their clothing was different, covering more of their bodies. Maybe their breasts?

Hell, I didn't even know if they had mammaries. Did something that had evolved from a dinosaur have mammary glands? They weren't *mammals*, after all. They weren't *anything*. Closer to birds than any other modern animal, I judged, but even that resemblance was only surface-deep. Maybe I had it wrong. Maybe the smaller ones were the males and this one escorting us was a female. Maybe they were matriarchal and Matis had just made the same assumption I had.

The children were easy enough to spot. And the sight of them disturbed me even more than the adults. It was easy to think of the adults as monsters, mutations, lost alien creatures. But the children told the truth about them, miniature devils, somehow putting the lie to the idea that babies are always cute.

And it doesn't mean a damned thing, Alvarez. You're not throwing the damned things a baby shower. Get your head in the game.

Most of the Resscharr weren't visibly armed, particularly not the smaller ones, the ones I was calling the females. A few of the males were, but their weapons varied wildly from one to another. Some wore blades, long enough to be swords but oddly curved. Others had sidearms strapped to harnesses across their chest, and one or two had rifles so large, a human couldn't have even lifted them, much less fired them. None carried the same sort of EMP weapon as our guide.

Did that make him the second-in-command? The warlord's right hand? The Karai treated him with deference, but I didn't know enough about the Resscharr culture to say whether the others we passed were regarding him with reverence, respect, or derision. I couldn't even tell what they were doing. They were clustered in open areas, paved over, with trees growing up through patches where the gravel pavement gave way to dirt and grass. Gardens? But there were in groups, some of them females, some children, being addressed by a male. Classes? Churches?

I'd assumed the place we'd be taken to, Zemekar's palace, lair, or whatever, would be at the center of the city. That was a human conceit, and apparently, not one the Resscharr shared, because the largest structure inside the walls was less than a third of the way into the city. I kept wanting to call it a tower, but that was more an attempt by my anthropomorphic brain to try to fit this place into some conventional human design. It was more like a steppe pyramid that had gone on an unhealthy crash diet and I couldn't tell from the outside how anyone could build a staircase that would fit inside it. That was another human conceit, though. Maybe they used ladders for people and dumbwaiters or something for food and supplies.

More Karai stood guard at the long, narrow entranceway of the palace, the interior hallway shaped like the inside of an hourglass. The way it narrowed at the center, only a meter and a half wide, bothered me, not for the enclosed space but for the incongruity of it, the feeling that others might be fooled into thinking they could pass because the top was wider and then we'd wind up stuck.

No Resscharr or Karai ventured into the hallway until our party had passed through it, though a female and child waited at the end, staring at the two of us like we were a display in a museum of natural history. Vicky made a face at the kid and if the child responded in kind, I couldn't tell.

Through the entrance hall was a twisting, nonsensical chamber, walls at the center that didn't reach all the way to the ceiling, not seeming to have any possible use except maybe to some alien aesthetic. Nothing I recognized as art decorated them, not so much as a paint pattern, though perhaps the very shape of the wall was considered an art form. A Resscharr female lounged across a piece of furniture that was molded out of the same stone as the floor, her posture more akin to a patient being examined by a proctologist than someone relaxing on the couch.

Must be the backward knees.

"You could make a fortune designing more comfortable couches for these assholes," Vicky said, quietly but not quietly enough.

One of the Karai guards barked something at her and smacked her across the shoulder with the back of his hand. It was an odd gesture, something purely Tahni, but it sent Vicky sprawling forward, barely catching herself on her hands before she could smack face-first into the floor.

"Take it easy, fuckwad!" I snapped at the Karai, spinning on him, squaring off.

He was shorter than the others, a little skinnier, and maybe it made him more aggressive. He swung his rifle around, pointing the muzzle at me, and I was sure he was about to put one of those heavy slugs through my chest, but the Resscharr stepped between us, grabbing the barrel and forcing it upwards. He said nothing to the Karai, but motioned at Vicky to get up. She was smart enough not to say anything else, but there was murder in her eye as she pushed herself to her feet.

I made a note of the Karai, tried to memorize his appearance, difficult as that was with a nonhuman species. Not that I wanted revenge, though I wouldn't have turned it down if the opportunity had presented itself without jeopardizing our lives or the mission, but more that I wanted to remember which of them was most likely to take a shot at us if the shit went down.

I also had a thought. Our suits had been taken down by the EMP device, but we were still wearing our earbuds and throat mics connected to the 'links on our belt, and the mic would pick up subvocalizations. They wouldn't have worked inside the suits, not without a relay from the Vigilante's comm systems, but now that we were out...

"You copy?" I said under my breath, counting on the 'link's software to turn the vibrations from my vocal cords into something like my voice.

"Yeah," she said immediately. "Shit, I should have thought of these. Would have saved me a sore shoulder." Her gaze flickered back and forth. "You think they can pick up our transmission?"

"No." I fought an instinct to shake my head. It would be best if they didn't even have an inkling we could communicate.

"From what Matis told me, I'm guessing these guys don't even understand the technology they're using."

"That's a hell of a thing to guess at, sweetie."

I choked back a snorted laugh. She only called me pet names when she was being snarky.

"If I'm wrong," I promised, "I'll let you hold it over my head for the rest of my life."

She didn't have a chance to remind me how short that might be. We cleared another set of too-short, needlessly-curvy walls and reached what a chamber that was part throne room, part great hall and a little bit cage-fighting pit. I couldn't describe the shape of the room exactly, but it was approximately ovoid at the base, though as it rose, the walls twisted and curved until they met in a hole at the center. Not a smoke hole, though that had been my first thought. This building didn't have any fireplaces that I could see, nor did it have the torches I'd assumed the existence of from the flickering lights in the drone video.

There was a green crystal at the center of the room, in the middle of what reminded me of a fighting pit from the illegal bare-knuckle matches I'd seen in the Underground. It was two meters across, blistering out from the stone like it had burst through from below. And maybe it had. It glowed brightly from within, though I couldn't have sworn as to what caused it, and the light it produced somehow did *not* throw a green cast onto everything else. Instead, it was as if we were standing outside at high noon, despite the room's lack of windows.

And as we approached it, the room grew cooler. I was sure it wasn't my imagination, wasn't a delayed reaction to drying sweat or the shade inside the building. It was like going from mid-afternoon in the dog days of summer on Inferno into the air-conditioned offices of battalion staff.

"How the fuck is that happening?" Vicky blurted, and from

the lack of reaction by the Karai, I was sure she'd had the presence of mind to do it subvocally.

"We detected a couple reactors running," I reminded her. "Just looking at it, I'm going to bet they built this whole place over the top of one of them."

We were so enthralled by the green crystal and the cool air, neither of us noticed the Resscharr male until he stood from what passed for a chair among his people. Stood is an inadequate word. It would be more accurate to say he *unfolded*, like a praying mantis. He was taller than any of the others I'd seen, more skeletal. They all had striations in their cheeks, leading from flattened nose to fan-like ears, but his were deeper, and there was more white in his feathery mane than the others.

"He's old," I told Vicky. "The oldest of them we've seen."

The old Resscharr towered over us, looking down his long, horsey face at us, then over at the one of his race who'd brought down our suits. The old one spoke and the younger handed over the EMP device, long fingers lingering on its grip as if he was reluctant to let go. The old one set the device on a platform beside his chair and focused his golden gaze on us.

It was frustrating. Our 'links didn't have the computing power to translate his language because it was too different from the base Predecessor tongue Dwight had given us. The suits' comm systems would have been able to do it, but there was nothing we could do to make ourselves understood to him.

I didn't know if it was possible for the Resscharr to smile, but he did. Don't ask me how I knew, I just did. He reached behind the platform and pulled a crystal out, a smaller version of the one set in the floor. He spoke into it in the same rough, growling tones that the other Resscharr had used before when speaking to the Karai...and the crystal spoke to *us*.

In *English*.

"Greetings, people of Earth," it said. "I am Zemekar, supreme lord of the seven."

He held the crystal high in the air, and if the room had been bright as day before, now it was filled with the glare of nuclear fury seen from the inside of an atomic core.

"Welcome to my world. Welcome to Yfingam."

[21]

I don't know if they had flies on this planet, but I remembered to close my mouth before one flew into it.

"How do you speak our language?"

"The Vergai call it magic," Zemekar said, the translation from the crystal giving the words a dismissive tone. "The Karai say it is a gift of the gods. But the truth, as we both know, is that it is a remnant of a time when we were once the gods ourselves."

I nearly let my mouth drop open again. I hadn't expected the Resscharr here to be so cognizant of their origins.

"This is one of their artificial minds." The tone changed, the timbre of the voice, and I knew immediately something else was speaking, not a translation of the Resscharr's words, but the crystal itself speaking to us. "I am a sentient AI. I accessed your language via your personal datalinks the moment you entered this place."

Vicky and I exchanged a glance, and I wondered if she was having the same thought I was. If the thing was a sentient AI like Dwight, did it consider these Resscharr to be the same as its Predecessor creators? Because I knew Dwight didn't. And I was also thinking how grateful I was for military security, as nonsensical as that thought would have been to my younger self who always despised the paranoia of Fleet Intelligence. Our datalinks were restricted from any strategic or tactical details about our mission, our crew, or the ship.

Zemekar rumbled on, and when the crystal spoke again, it was a direct translation as before.

"The Karai think you are nothing but Vergai. They think you are farmers who've stumbled across a cache of lost Predecessor technology, but we both know that isn't true. I know the art of our ancestors better than any alive on this world, in this whole system, and I have seen nothing like the suits you wore. You are from Earth, the world my ancestors abandoned, but you are far beyond what they recorded of that place when they brought us the Vergai. How is this possible?"

I debated for a second whether I should lie to him. Whether there was some fiction that would get us out of this. Once upon a time, I could lie with the best of them. It was how I'd stayed alive. But I was out of practice, and the one time I'd attempted it recently, back on Portent, it hadn't turned out too well. Not to mention that I had no freaking clue exactly what lie would work. I waited a second longer, hoping Vicky could come up with something, but she was silent, eyes on me.

"Humans are adaptable." I shrugged, wondering if the machine would translate that too. "We work best under pressure, and our world has been under a lot of pressure. Plagues, volcanoes, earthquakes, tsunamis, famines...every single one of them made people come up with better ways to do things. For us, knowledge built up like an avalanche, each rock with the weight of all the ones behind it."

I was leaving out some details, like how that had only worked after we'd figured out a way to write things down and a system for keeping it so the next generation could draw on the knowledge of the one before, but this wasn't an essay for a grade.

Zemekar went on for several seconds, but when the crystal took over, it was the AI again, speaking for itself.

"He's going on and on about how grand his ancestors were and how you owe your existence to them. But I have questions. The Resscharr, my creators, were as your people, building new learning on old, but it took them tens of thousands of years to go from the level of advancement the Vergai showed when they were brought here to their first steps off their world. How is it that you were different? I know we offered you no aid, not as we did the Karai."

I shook my head.

"It's just who we are."

Zemekar made a face, something that looked to me like a giraffe biting into a cactus, and I thought he was frowning at the fact I'd spoken but the crystal hadn't translated.

"Why have you come to this place? What do we have that you would want?"

"We were looking for your people," I said. "We were hoping they might help us return home."

"You came here in a ship," he said. "You travel between the stars as we once did. You will tell me how."

Now I was really confused and I waited for the AI to explain to me why Zemekar didn't know this already, but it was silent. Maybe it thought it had been pushing its luck already.

"It's the Transition Drive," Vicky supplied. "It works by creating a wormhole into a reality where the laws of physics work differently. Didn't the Predecessors—your ancestors—use the same thing?"

"None of us know how they were able to achieve such things." That face again. It wasn't a *good* expression, I gleaned that much from context. "I have asked Presteri, but he will say nothing."

"Who?" Vicky frowned.

"Presteri is what I have named myself for the convenience of these primitive savages," the AI supplied, and if I'd wondered before, I had no doubt anymore. He thought of these Resscharr just as Dwight did.

"But you have the ships," I said, though I wasn't sure anymore if I was primarily addressing Zemekar or this Presteri AI. "The ones you used to chase off our shuttle. Can't you use those to travel to the stars?"

"If I could, would I be sitting here on this pile of shit?"

The words were explosive, both in their original Resscharr and again when Presteri translated them. Zemekar kicked backwards and knocked the platform sideways, spilling the EMP device to the floor. It didn't clatter, as plastic might have, nor did it clank like metal. When it hit the stone, it was a solid thump like a sandbag.

"We are the children of *gods*," Zemekar went on. "Yet we are imprisoned on this one world...and the only other we can reach is even poorer, mostly water, with not even the hidden gems of our ancestors' technology to dig up from their graves." He gesticulated with the crystal, as carelessly as if he were about to throw it against the wall in disgust. "Presteri claims that the ships I have found, the ones he has taught my nobles to fly, even to the Ocean Planet, are no longer capable of doing as you say." He jagged a long, multi-jointed finger at Vicky. "They will no longer go to this other reality, and that he lacks the raw materials to repair them."

Zemekar collapsed backwards into his seat, the strength gone out of him.

"I know not if he is lying to me, nor is there any threat I could make against him if he did. And he is quite aware of this."

He made a zigzagging motion with his left hand at the other Resscharr in the room as well as the Karai. "Understand, I would never admit to this sort of weakness to my subjects. Weakness is not something tolerated, not on such a harsh world. And while I may lack any way to threaten Presteri, the two of you are another matter."

"What do you want from us?" I asked him, though I had a pretty good idea.

"You will do for me what he can't. You will give me the stars. I want your ship."

"We're ground troops," Vicky scoffed. "We don't have the ship to give you."

"And yet, you could contact it. Order them to land, to surrender it to me."

"Our ship can't land," I informed him. "It's too large. You chased our landers away...that's why we have them."

"Then you will order me a lander and have me taken aboard, with my personal guard." He threw his head back, puffed up his chest, and squawked, a feral sound. "My birthright is out there, the land of our ancestors. I will partake in the riches of their gifts and be made young once more, as immortal as they were."

"We don't have the authority to bring you aboard or to give you our ship," Vicky insisted. "And even if we did, we have no way of talking to them. Even the gear we had in our suits wouldn't reach them from here."

"Presteri will take care of that. Won't you, my friend?"

"I have no choice," the computer added, sounding miserable over it. "My restrictive programming demands I give the Resscharr anything they ask, within certain parameters. I can sense where your ship is, and I can re-transmit whatever message you send."

I squeezed my eyes shut against a sudden headache, rubbing

at them as if I could wipe all this away. There were certain things I could do without feeling like I'd betrayed my orders and my oaths. Sharing harmless information was one of those, particularly if it helped convince the enemy that he was better off not attacking us.

Offering to try to convince our command that they should surrender the ship to him wasn't one of those things.

"They won't listen to us," I repeated. "They'll never give you our ship. It's our only way home."

"If you are not in command, you will call your commander." Zemekar didn't stand, just regarded us with a cold, calculating look. "You will tell them that I wish to negotiate, that I know how to return you home, but I want them to help me, as well. That is all you will say."

I wanted to laugh, and would have if the situation hadn't been so dire. I supposed I was, again, running things through the filter of a human—a human recently from Earth, I had to amend, but Zemekar struck me as similar to the gang leaders I'd encountered in Trans-Angeles, utterly convinced of their own superior intelligence despite every evidence to the contrary. But if I could suppress the laugh, I couldn't suppress the incredulous question.

"You really think we're just going to invite our commander down here to get ambushed so you can steal our ship?" I gestured at the Karai. "Is that what you'd expect from *your* soldiers, to betray you so easily?"

Zemekar tilted his large, long-boned head to the side, golden cat's eyes staring at me from a new angle.

"My warriors are Karai. Karai are strong. Vergai are weak-willed, and whether you possess technology they do not, you're still of a type with them. You'll do what I say. Eventually." He motioned to the same Karai who'd struck Vicky earlier and the warrior slung his rifle over his shoulder and pulled out a long, curved blade.

We hadn't been restrained, probably because of how little they thought of us...or of the Vergai. And it was, I'll admit, a safe bet. After all, the average Tahni outweighed me by twenty kilos and stood a head taller. In a straight-up fight, one of them would pound the average Vergai into a bloody pulp. But the Vergai hadn't spent eight years at war with the Karai, hadn't been drilled with how to take one of them on in hand-to-hand, should the unlikely situation ever arise for a Drop-Trooper. It wasn't so unlikely at the moment.

I didn't even have to say a word to Vicky. She hit him low and I hit him high. Tahni—and their Karai cousins, apparently— had a weakness, part and parcel of their longer limbs and extra joints. Human knees and elbows were singular points of weakness, but the Tahni versions were longer out of necessity, weaker in spots, if you knew where to aim. And I did.

Soft to hard, hard to soft. That was what they'd taught us in hand-to-hand combat. Hard, bony targets got soft tissue weapons— the forearm, the heel of the hand, hammer fist—to make sure you didn't break anything of your own when you hit the other guy. I grabbed the Tahni's wrist just behind the grip of that double-bladed, wickedly-curved knife and slammed my forearm into his extra-long elbow plate. It hurt me. I knew I'd have a huge bruise on my arm in a few hours. But judging from the brittle crack, it hurt him more.

Or maybe that had been the crack of his knee giving way to Vicky's heel.

The blade hit the floor first, clanking and bouncing, and he hit just after, trying to stop himself with his bad arm and crying out when it didn't work. No one else had moved yet, probably frozen in disbelief, so no one stopped me from the follow-through. I'd never done the follow-through before on a live opponent, and the crunch of his throat beneath my heel was simultaneously thrilling and sickening.

And probably the last thing I'd ever experience. Vicky and I stood back-to-back, hands up in a ready stance, waiting for the end. No one moved.

"I see I have made an error," Zemekar said.

He seemed unmoved by the death of the Karai, and, surprising to me, so did the other Karai. They stared at his death throes, the last, choking, jerking spasms before he died, with all the compassion I might have given a squashed cockroach.

"You are not as soft as the Vergai," he went on, standing. "My thought was to have you beaten, perhaps slice a few smaller, less crucial pieces off you, that you'd give me what I wanted. I see now that you have too much nerve for that. Something else will be necessary. Perhaps I will have one of you watch as the Karai disembowel the other." He came within a half a meter of me, leaning forward. His breath stank of raw meat. "Or do you believe you can fight your way through all of us?"

I did not. Oh, if I could have gotten one of those guns, I could have given it a go, and between the two of us, we could have taken a good-sized chunk of the Karai with us. No matter what they called themselves, they were Tahni, and killing Tahni was what I did best. But the Resscharr...I had no proof, but I got the sense that one of them could have taken the two of us without breaking a sweat. If they did sweat.

But I did have another idea. I wanted to run it by Vicky, but Presteri had already proven it could read our 'links and our language. I just hoped she'd trust me.

"All right," I said, coming out of the fighting stance. "I'll do it."

"Are you fucking nuts?" she hissed beside my ear.

"I don't see that we have any choice," I shot back, deciding not to take the chance that Presteri might be able to read our tones. I nodded to Zemekar. "You said you can help us make the call."

"I will connect your datalink to your ship," Presteri offered. "It had jumped into the outer system to avoid our ships, but it has returned and is waiting in lunar orbit, no doubt trying to locate your forces."

"You're the one not letting him use those ships to leave this system," I accused. "Those things have been operational for thousands of years, including what our techs think is a captive singularity. I don't buy that, all of a sudden, the Transition drive doesn't work."

"As I said," the AI replied, not even trying to deny it, "I was told to give the Resscharr what they want...to a point. That point ends at the boundaries of this star system."

"Why?"

"Because the Transition drive is what makes *them* come. They home in on gravimetic disturbances and swarm over them, destroying everything in their path."

"The Skrela," Vicky said. "You're talking about the Skrela."

"But if you're worried the Skrela will find them if they use a Transition drive," I protested, "then why are you helping them get our ship?"

"Because," Presteri said, putting a good imitation of annoyance into his voice, "the tricky old bastard has finally found a way to leave this system that isn't contravened by my programming. There's nothing I can do."

"Then put me through, Presteri."

It took a moment, and I tried to imagine how the exchange would go on the bridge of the *Orion*.

"There's a message coming through from the planet?" Hachette would demand of Chase. "How the hell do they know where we are?"

However it had gone, when Chase answered, it was with steady professionalism.

"This is the *Orion.*"

"Chase, this is Cam Alvarez. I'm here with Vicky and I need to speak to the commander. Please put *Colonel* Ellen Campbell on the line."

[22]

"This is Colonel Campbell," Top said, as if she'd been wearing the rank for years instead of the last thirty seconds. "I understand you've made contact with the Resscharr."

"We have, ma'am," I told her, wishing I could see her.

Presteri hadn't volunteered a video connection, probably because Zemekar had ordered it not to. It would have been funny to see if she could manage to keep a straight face...funnier still if Hachette was in the background, trying to keep his temper in check. But Zemekar probably hadn't wanted to give us a chance to send some visual signal.

"Are Captain Solano and the others all right?" I asked her. It was part honest worry and part a thought that they might be a good backup for us if we needed it.

"They're fine. Are you two okay?"

"We haven't been harmed." Honest, if incomplete. "There were some misunderstandings at first, but now we're able to talk to each other."

"Have you told them what we need, Captain?"

"I have, and Zemekar, the leader of the Resscharr settlement on this world, thinks he can help us. He's willing to make a deal, but he insists on speaking to you in person. He wants you to come down alone in a shuttle and meet him face-to-face. They have their own version of Dwight to do the translation." I sucked in a breath and hurried through the next sentence. "They also have *a* device that can shut down armor, ships, whatever, so don't try anything."

I half-expected Zemekar to order us killed for letting that cat out of the bag, but either he didn't mind the warning or Presteri didn't bother to tell him that part.

Top said nothing, and I thought the transmission had dropped, but after the pause, she returned as if it hadn't happened.

"Copy that. Tell Zemekar that I accept his offer and I will meet him outside the gates of his city in seventy-two hours."

I nearly yelped at the revelation that she was going to leave us here for three days, when the Resscharr finally spoke, leaning toward us as if it brought him closer to Top.

"It does not take your ship that long to travel from our moon to orbit," he said, giving voice to my own objections, "nor does it take that long for your lander to reach us from your ship."

"The *Orion* was damaged in the battle with your ships," Top explained. "It will take us that long to effect the repairs. I apologize for keeping you waiting."

"Very well. I expect to see you here in person."

"Of course," Top replied, and I could hear the grin in her words. "I wouldn't miss it for anything."

And then the transmission was ended, by Presteri, I assumed. Zemekar put a long-fingered hand on the shoulder of one of the Karai, pulling him forward.

"Nam Ker," he said, addressing the warrior, "you will take the humans to one of the quest quarters. They are to be given water, as well as such food as the Vergai eat. No harm is to come to them except by my word. And detail someone to clean up this mess." Long fingers gestured down at the warrior Vicky and I had killed.

"Yes, my lord," the Karai called Nam Ker replied, with a gesture very similar to the standard Tahni military salute.

"You have shown intelligence as well as fortitude," Zemekar said to us as the Karai led us away. "Perhaps I will keep you with me...after I have killed the others."

———

The walk to the guest room was a traverse through a maze, and I couldn't have found my way back to where we'd been—or back to the entrance—to save my life. The place was a tour of the Guggenheim taken while on hallucinogenic drugs, and just when I thought I'd made sense, figured out a pattern to the architecture, it would change and the pattern was lost.

Eventually, I stopped paying attention to the walls and the curves and trying to keep a mental record of our path, and just watched the Karai. It was amazing how little had changed about the Tahni in the three or four thousand years they'd been on this world. The haircut was nearly identical to the ones blooded warriors sported on Tahn-Skyyiah, a Mohawk down the center narrowing into a long, braided queue wrapped around their necks. The clothes were even similar, though that was probably more a factor of their form dictating the clothing function and me, being a human, not noticing differences that would have been obvious to a Tahni.

"You are not like the Vergai," Nam Ker said, and I started when the words were translated in my earbud.

"I have taken the liberty of extending the translation to your datalinks," Presteri said, helpful as Dwight had been. I wondered if it was a defining characteristic of the AIs.

"No, we're not," I said. "We're from the same world as they

are, but a lot has changed since then. For one thing, we were at war with your people twice."

It was risky telling him that, but I was hopeful that he'd listen to Zemekar's order not to hurt us. Nam Ker glanced aside at me, not showing any signs of impending violence.

"Truly? That armor you wore...did our warriors have it as well?"

"You bet your ass they did," Vicky said, not even sounding surprised at the translation. "They had them before we did, and they kicked our asses the first couple years."

"Years?" he repeated. "Your war lasted for years?"

"Eight. Eight long, horrible years. Tens of millions of people died and whole cities were laid to waste." Vicky stopped in her tracks and the Karai stopped as well, Nam Ker meeting her bleak gaze. "I lost nearly everyone I ever called a friend, and I killed more of your people than I can count."

"And this one?" Nam Ker asked, motioning at me. "How many did he kill?"

And that I knew. It wasn't something I could lose count of. Every death had been recorded on my helmet cam, and the ones I'd killed without the suit had been permanently engraved into the tablet of my memory.

"Two thousand," I enunciated, "four hundred and seventy-six."

Nam Ker took a step back as if I'd waved a gun in his face, and I knew enough Tahni to recognize an expression of horror or anger. I thought I'd done it this time, pushed him past his meager controls and now he was going to shoot me in revenge.

"You mock me!" he said. "No single warrior could kill so many!"

"Remember the suits," I told him. "Some of your soldiers had them, but not all. Think of how many of you I could have killed if Zemekar hadn't disabled our suits with his magic weapon."

He made a sign I recognized as affirmation, the equivalent of a nod, and I could sense that he believed me.

"The weapon is not magic," he corrected me. "It is what remains of those who my people once served." He started walking again, and the ones behind us, forcing us back into motion. "The ones we hope to serve again."

"The Predecessors, we call them. Your people—the Tahni—call them the Ancients."

"It is what we call them as well, the ones who brought us to this place. We remember them and these...*things* that rule us now have little to do with them. *Those* were gods. These are the dregs at the bottom of the wineskin. They throw our lives away in their quest for more power, and we can do nothing but obey."

"Why?" I asked him. "Why do you fight for them if you don't respect them? If you know they're not your gods?"

"The females." That wasn't Nam Ker, it was one of the two soldiers behind us. Nam Ker glared at him but then motioned assent again.

"Zemekar holds our females and children hostage. His people watch them, armed with the old weapons, and if we fail to do what he terms our duty, then it is our families that will pay the price."

"The Tahni I have known," I said, "would throw themselves into enemy fire with no thought to their own survival in defense of the females. And the females would do the same for their children."

"And we all would, if there were any hope." He didn't look back at us. "It has been tried before, more than once. You speak of millions who have died, and we can only boast hundreds and thousands, but there are fewer of us, and the losses are felt more keenly."

We'd reached a line of smaller chambers, each defined by a broad, oval doorway, the interiors shadowy and featureless. Nam Ker motioned us into the first of them and I stepped carefully through, not wanting to trip over some arcane Resscharr excuse for furniture in the dark and break my neck. But the darkness vanished with a soft flicker of what might have been torchlight but wasn't. It was another of the green crystals in the center of the floor.

"Cool," Vicky said, kneeling beside the thing, running a finger across its surface. "Actually, *very* cool. Like air-conditioning cool."

"I'll have food and water brought to you shortly," Nam Ker promised, then left us. I didn't know if all Tahni were that abrupt or if it was a Karai thing, but it was refreshingly free of small-talk.

I watched him and his warriors disappear down the hallway, then walked over beside Vicky and stared at the crystal, arms crossed,

"This shit *is* like magic," I said, shaking my head. "How the hell did they do this?"

"Any sufficiently advanced technology is indistinguishable from magic," she told me and it sounded like a quote. "That's not the question, though, is it?"

"Then what is?"

"The question is, how the hell did they fall this far?" She rose from the crystal and waved around us. "How did they get to be these scroungers? Vultures picking over leavings? They moved planets, Cam. They ripped holes in space and terraformed hundreds of worlds. Then they went on the run here and..." She shrugged. "What the fuck happened?"

I considered it for a moment, then tried something obvious.

"Presteri," I said, "can you hear me?"

"Of course, Captain Alvarez. There is nothing you can say in this entire city that I can't hear."

"Oh, joy," Vicky murmured.

"Can you tell me what happened to the Resscharr?" I asked the AI. "You said that you were directed to keep them here, in this system. Directed by whom?"

The sentient computer hesitated. It wasn't something I would have expected from a computer. The only reason to make a sentient system was that it could think *faster* than a human...or a Tahni, or a Resscharr, or whatever. It could run through every single possible response in the time it took me to blink. And still it hesitated.

"This represents a moral dilemma for me, Captain Alvarez," Presteri explained, "as well as an insoluble logical one. There are details that have been entrusted to my judgment as to whom I should and shouldn't share them with. Those who programmed me didn't want certain things told to the Karai and *certainly* not to the Vergai. I possess data on the Vergai here, but you have said yourself and proven to Zemekar that you are *not* the Vergai. Therefore, my dilemma. Can I trust you?"

"If you're asking me, then the answer is definitely yes." I was joking, of course, but I was also dealing with not just an artificial intelligence, but an artificial *alien* intelligence. And perhaps one that had no concept of a human sense of humor, unless he'd learned it from the Vergai.

"I believe I can. You are as close to an objective outsider as I am likely to meet. The Resscharr evacuated the Enclosure— what you refer to as the Cluster—in stages. The first began over ten thousand years ago, when your planet and your people were left to their own devices and the Resscharr withdrew outward to the Corridor systems and began to leave the Enclosure. They had beaten the Skrela back, but they knew it was a temporary reprieve. And the ones who left would still have to deal with the enemy on the other side of the passage."

"And the Skrela were attracted by the Transition drive," I said, the pieces falling into place.

"Had the Resscharr simply rebuilt the civilization they possessed in the Cluster, they would have been dismantled just as thoroughly. So, they fragmented, dropped a few thousand of their number at each habitable as they went. And isolated them there. Then the last wave came through, four thousand years ago, and with them came samples from Earth and Tahn-Skyyiah, humans and Tahni, brought with them in case their plan was unsuccessful and the Skrela rendered your worlds uninhabitable, drove you to extinction. And that was when the trouble began.

"This will be difficult for you to understand, but much of what made the Resscharr who they were was a product of something you might call a religious belief. They considered themselves to be the instruments of a higher power, of God, tasked with bringing life to a lifeless universe. It was their cultural characteristic and it shaped every concept they had of themselves. And without the Transition drive, confined to one system for millennia, they lost their way. They became concerned with how the humans and the Tahni regarded them, became jealous of one another. And when they had no way of bringing new ideas, new minds, new supplies to the system, then the most priceless possessions, the things most worth going to war over, were the fabricators. Once those had been destroyed, it was only a matter of time before everything else followed."

"Jesus," I said. There was a stone slab rising from the floor behind me and I fell onto it, managing to find a halfway-comfortable place to sit even on the strange furniture. "They were basically gods, and that's all it took, just being cut off from the rest of their society for a few thousand years. That's fucking depressing."

"Was it worth it?" Vicky demanded, an edge of anger to her voice as she talked to the air, to Presteri. "Was just surviving the Skrela worth it, when they had to give up everything they were?"

"That was not my decision to make."

"It's the one we're going to have to make," I said, meeting Vicky's gaze. "And we only have three days to do it."

[23]

I was sleeping when Nam Ker returned.

"Get up," Vicky said, nudging me, and when I blinked awake, I was staring at the Karai standing over me. "I don't know how the hell you can sleep on this uncomfortable shit," Vicky added as I rolled off the curved, twisting Resscharr equivalent of a bed. "Or in a room without a door."

"Exhaustion helps," I told her, though she was occupied with pulling on her boots, then turned to the Karai. He stood alone in the doorway, though he was still armed with his heavy-caliber rifle. "What's up?"

We hadn't seen him for over a day. At least I assumed it was a day. Sleeping had been difficult, as Vicky had mentioned, but I was going by the meals the Karai had brought to us, and that wasn't a sure thing. I didn't know how many meals the Tahni ate a day, or the Resscharr, or even the Vergai for that matter. Our 'links were set to ship time, given that they had no satellites or internet to connect to here, and I could have measured the time by them, but I knew it hadn't been seventy-two hours yet and there was no point in checking until that time got closer.

Unfortunately, there was not a damned thing to do for entertainment. I'd tried to read. I'd done what Vicky and Top had suggested and downloaded a few classic works of fiction, but I couldn't concentrate enough to appreciate them and I wasn't in the mood to watch a movie projected by my 'link onto the nearest wall with a picture ten centimeters across and the sound in my earbud. Call me old-fashioned, but movies should be watched in Virtual Reality immersion, just like they were designed to be seen.

So, I wasn't exactly unhappy to see Nam Ker, unless he was here to kill us, and I thought he would have brought more of his people with him for that.

"Come with me," he said.

He didn't make it a demand, and I had the sense that we could have said no, which made me more likely to say yes. I slipped into my boots and fatigue top and he waited without the slightest hint of impatience, not moving until we were through the doorway. Crystals lit the interior of the place at intervals, and others took advantage of the constant illumination, padding the hallway on long-toed feet. Resscharr eyes followed us as we passed, but no one tried to stop us on our way out of the tower. I didn't see Zemekar, and he was the only one of the things I would have recognized, so maybe the others thought we were Vergai servants being shepherded to some task by the Karai.

My body wanted to believe it was nighttime, and it was proven right once we exited the building. The moon here appeared as large as Luna did on Earth, but the surface was smoother, less cratered, and it shone brighter, lighting up the low-hanging clouds. The hazy, grey clouds, lit from behind by the moon, split the night in two, with the dividing line the top of the city walls, throwing everything beneath into blackness.

I don't know if the Resscharr can see further into the spectrum than we can, but if they *could* see in the dark, they weren't making use of that talent on this night. The streets were empty but for us. We didn't use the front gate, though I'd thought that was where we were heading. There was a side door, squat and almost hidden, what might have been called a sally port if this were actually the medieval castle my brain kept trying to turn it into, secured with a metal bar.

Nam Ker threw the bolt aside and pulled the door inward, the hinges squeaking with a sound of age and disuse, piled dirt resisting his pull at the bottom edge. I wondered who the last one through this side gate had been. There'd once been a trail to the door, but parts of it were overgrown by brush, and we stepped through it carefully until it intersected with what looked to be a cattle run.

"Do the Resscharr eat meat?" I asked, hoping the translation would still work out here. I knew it did when my 'link's external speaker yelped out the question in the Karai version of Tahni.

"They do. Quite prolifically." He made no comment otherwise, but given what I knew of Tahni dietary preferences, I didn't think he approved. "It's most of what the Vergai provide for them. The cattle are for them, the grain and vegetables for us. It isn't our first preference, but it keeps us alive."

I remembered that the Tahni ate a root native to their homeworld. I guess the Resscharr weren't thoughtful enough to provide a supply for the Tahni they brought to this place.

"Where are we going?" Vicky asked.

It was light enough with the moon for me to see her eyes. She wasn't scared. We were both beyond scared, I think. There comes a point where you've used up all your scared, used up the adrenaline, and you're just waiting to die. We'd both reached that point at times during the war, and now a couple times since, and I think we were there again.

"You asked me about the females," Nam Ker replied. "I thought you should see them."

I hadn't noticed the enclosure from the air on the flight in, but then, my attention had been more focused on trying not to die. It was less a medieval castle this time and more like an old-west style fort, or at least how I envisioned them. Walls again, but this time to keep the occupants inside. Wooden palisades built on earthen mounds, rising up three or four meters tall, and the only reason we could see over them was that our vantage point was on the side of a rise.

The buildings within the walls were low, single-story and spread out, too large to be for single families. Dorms or barracks, like the communal houses I'd seen on Tahni colonies. And every gap between them was filled with rows of crops. Gardens every-where, in any open space. Lights flickered from the windows of a few of the buildings, genuine lamps or torches this time, not any esoteric crystals. This place hadn't been constructed atop any alien treasure trove. It was a prison, or near enough.

"It didn't used to be like this," Nam Ker told us, his gaze fixed on one of the buildings, near this edge of the enclosure. "My great-grandfather remembered a day when the Karai had their own city, within sight of Yfingam, built in our tradition. The females were in an open commune a few kilometers away, far enough that the males wouldn't be tempted beyond their control, close enough for negotiations between families to be held for mating."

"What happens now?" Vicky wondered.

"Now, those who are favored by the Resscharr, by Zemekar, are the only ones allowed to mate. The males constantly compete to be seen, to be approved."

"How do you get to be his favorite?" I asked, though I had a nasty feeling that I already knew.

"Zemekar," he replied, and the translation put in a pause

that might not have been there, perhaps as a way of showing us how a human would have said the words, "favors aggression. Particularly toward the Vergai, to make sure none of them begin to think they might keep their cattle for themselves. Any who fall beneath the quota, who make excuses, are executed. And when there aren't enough Vergai to impress our lord, we fight each other over imagined slights."

"Your warriors seem loyal to you," I told him. Not that I didn't believe him, but I knew from my own experience that we have a tendency to believe what we wanted to hear.

"They are, for the most part." He made a motion of head and shoulders toward me, a gesture of gratitude. "More so now that you two took care of Lin Gan. He was troublesome. But you can't even imagine how many of my own warriors I was forced to kill in order to gain my position...and make it unassailable."

"Why are we out here in the middle of the night?" Vicky didn't seem as annoyed as the words might have indicated. They were spoken gently, as if she understood the Karai and sympathized.

"Because it is the only time I can see them."

There was movement at the edge of the wall, something small and furtive, and I thought at first that it was an animal. Then the figures stood and I realized they'd crawled through a tunnel. They were children.

"Where are the guards?" I looked around, panic building in my chest, worried that some Resscharr with a Predecessor weapon would blast the kids out of existence while we stood two hundred meters away, helpless to intervene.

"They only stay out here during the day. A Resscharr would not deign stand watch at night. It would be beneath them."

It was hard to tell Tahni boys from girls, given that the males didn't start shaving their skull into a Mohawk until they came of age, and both of these were of a size, their dark hair long and wild, and they both wore identical tunics made from woven strips of multicolored fabric. They ran with the unbridled ferocity of children everywhere, and we barely had to wait a minute before they reached Nam Ker.

I don't know why I was shocked when he embraced them. Maybe I'd assumed that hugging was a human thing, though I knew it wasn't. I'd seen it in animal species, and there was no reason it wouldn't be a Tahni trait as well, particularly given that we knew their species had been engineered from Earth DNA.

Maybe the fact that the Tahni loved their children made me feel guilty about all the ones I'd killed.

"Who are these Vergai, Father?" one of the two, the taller asked. I made a guess that this one was male, though it was based on nothing but his height.

"They aren't Vergai, Jona. They are humans, and they are not from this world." Nam Ker turned to me. "I know that among the Vergai, it is considered polite to introduce strangers." His teeth bared, which was not a pleasant sight...they looked like the crags on a white cliff. "I personally find the concept a waste of time, but I do not wish to give offense. These are my children. My son Jona...." He put his hand on the taller one's shoulder and I patted myself on the back, mentally. "And my daughter Yosnen."

The girl was younger and shorter and said nothing. I didn't know if she was shy or if that was considered good manners among the Karai.

"We're happy to meet you," Vicky said, apparently not caring whether the Karai liked it or not. She bent down and offered a hand to the little girl. "I'm Vicky. And you are a very pretty girl."

Which might not have been strictly true—she looked more

like a one-third scale model of one of my middle-school teachers—but it sounded nice. The girl still said nothing and the look on her face could have been gratitude or indigestion.

"I may visit openly, in the daylight," Nam Ker said, "only as my lord grants leave, when I have pleased him." He pulled Yosnen into a hug that covered her ears. "Of late, I have not killed enough Vergai or my own soldiers to curry his favor."

"Why did you bring us out here, Nam Ker?" I asked. "It wasn't just to show us the hold he has over you."

"No." He stood straight, one hand resting on his daughter's head. "I brought you out here to show you how little love I have for him." His eyes were dark, invisible under his brow ridges, but I could feel them on me. "I can't act on my own. I do not know you, yet I know of your character by your actions. You would not give in so easily to Zemekar unless there was a reason."

I swallowed hard and tried not to show it. I'd convinced myself that Zemekar wouldn't notice that, but Nam Ker was smarter than the Resscharr.

"If you know of our character," I said, very carefully, not knowing how much of my inflection Presteri would translate, "then you know I wouldn't tell you if that were true."

"Tell me something that I may do without risking this," Nam Ker said, nodding toward the children.

"Nothing." Vicky was faster than I was. She traced her fingers down the little boy's shoulder. "Do nothing...for as long as you can get away with. You'll know when."

Which was more eloquent than I could have put it at the time.

"That, I may be able to do." Nam Ker pushed his daughter toward his son. "Jona, take your sister and return. I will visit you again as soon as I am able."

The boy grabbed his sister by the arm and the two of them scampered down the hill as if moonlight was all they needed.

"Are they going to be all right on their own?" Vicky stared out after them with a look in her eyes that was way more maternal than I'd ever seen before.

"In this place," Nam Ker told her, not bothering to watch his children leave, "we are all on our own."

I squinted into the painful blue of the late-afternoon sky and watched the black dot grow closer with every second. Turbojets whined, their tone growing more serious as the shuttle descended.

What would be in it? It was a lander, too small for a platoon of Drop-Troopers, and I didn't think Top would be stupid enough to bring them here after I'd warned her of the EMP device. Zemekar held the device loosely in his left hand, not yet pointing it at the shuttle, though it would only take a twitch of those long, powerful muscles to bring it up. He wouldn't need to use it to guard against a gun run by the shuttle. His own ships were enough to prevent that, patrolling in a tight spiral.

And if that wasn't enough, there was the implicit threat to the two of us in the person of the Karai guard arrayed between our party and the walls of Yfingam. There were fifty of them, and, if that wasn't enough, Zemekar had brought along over thirty of his own people and all of them were armed with weapons I couldn't identify.

"Damn, I hope she knows what she's doing," Vicky subvocalized. Maybe we couldn't hide our conversation from Presteri, but I liked to think the AI wouldn't pass everything we said along.

"I hope *we* know what we're doing," I shot back, eyeing Zemekar.

I didn't know Resscharr body language, but if he'd been a human, I would have said he was quivering with undisguised avarice. He didn't even bother to look away when the shuttle kicked up a cloud of dust that billowed across the front wall of the city, thickening the haze and dust already thick in the air from the constant wind. Maybe he had nictating membranes in those funky-looking eyes, but I didn't, and I wasn't too proud to throw up an arm to protect my face.

The searing wind of the exhaust intensified alongside the gut-deep rumble of the jets, and I thought the damned shuttle was going to land right on top of us. By the time the sandblast fury of the wind died down enough for me to open my eyes, the illusion was shattered and the delta-winged aerospacecraft was over fifty meters away. The pilot throttled down and the belly jets whined at the slight, as if they were landing here under protest. The ramp was already yawning open with Top's characteristic impatience to be in the thick of the shit, and she stepped down it with purpose in her stride.

It was strange seeing her set foot on a hostile LZ without her Vigilante, like she was a prisoner walking to her execution. Despite her vulnerability, despite the fact that she lacked as much as a sidearm, she walked right up to Zemekar, feet planted wide, fists on her hips.

"I imagine you're the ugly motherfucker in charge of this place," she said and I choked down a snicker, wondering just how the hell Presteri would translate that for Zemekar. "I'm Ellen Campbell, the one you want to talk to, so let's get to it. Can you help us find a way out of here? And what do you want in return?"

The hesitation for the translation was long enough to make me wonder if the Resscharr was about to order us all shot, but his answer seemed normal, or at least as normal as a giant talking ostrich could be.

"What I want from you is as simple as what I can do for you. You seek a way back to your home, and I have heard of this way, this passage from our space back to yours."

Heard of it from Presteri, I was sure. Probably just in the last three days, even though it made no sense for him to help Zemekar.

"It is along the path my ancestors took when they left us here to rot," Zemekar went on. "The way would be impossible for you to follow, but one of us can find it for you. And I will...if you take me and my people with you."

Top cocked her head to the side in a question.

"Your people? How many people?"

"Only the most trusted. Three or four hundred." Zemekar might have been smiling, had I known what a Resscharr smile looked like.

"The ship barely holds that many," Top said, though the objection seemed pro forma, as if she'd been expecting the demand.

"Then I suppose you'd better bring your crew down here and get them comfortable." Zemekar grunted a command and two of the other Resscharr beside him levelled their weapons at Top. I wasn't sure what the things did, but their muzzles were yawning, inverted spirals and they looked as intimidating as all hell.

"I guess you got me, then," Top said, casually raising her hands above her head.

I knew something was coming, but I didn't move. Moving might have put me right in the line of fire.

I'd heard Gauss rifles firing before, but never from this end.

The *crackcrackcrack* of tungsten slugs breaking the sound barrier echoed off the walls of Yfingam, but before they could roll back over us, four of the Resscharr pitched backwards, blood pouring from ten-millimeter holes through the center of their prominent chests. But not Zemekar. Something tiny and metallic spinning crazily through the air, its momentum robbed, its trajectory changed to an arc over his head. Then another and I didn't wait for the third.

Vicky was ducking to the right and I followed her to the drainage ditch beside the road, sliding into the mud beside her...and Top. She didn't seem worried, but then she *never* did. She watched the battle unfolding like it was a war game and she was a judge, and I followed her gaze out to the grassy fields beyond the shuttle. Zemekar was looking that way as well, sweeping his EMP weapon back and forth, but not doing any good because he wasn't shooting at Drop-Troopers this time.

Force Recon Marines were bounding forward in an over-watch formation, a full platoon of them, up and down so fast. Zemekar couldn't aim quickly enough to even disable their Gauss rifles. The other Resscharr, lacking the Predecessor-tech shield that was guarding Zemekar, were running for cover, some falling before they could reach it, others firing their mysterious weapons toward the field.

They were still mysterious, even after I saw them discharge. Raw energy coruscated from those spiral maws, setting roaring fires in the tall grass, and I hoped they weren't hitting anything. The Marines were hitting what they were aiming at.

And they weren't aiming at the Karai. I'd expected Nam Ker and his warriors to jump to battle, but they were hanging back, weapons at their shoulders, not seeming unsure or hesitant, but...thoughtful. Not that their weapons worried me, or would have worried the Force Recon platoon. A slug from one of those gunpowder weapons might have raised a hell of a bruise, but it wouldn't be penetrating the Marines' armor.

The Karai weren't what worried me. What worried me was overhead.

"Here they come," Vicky said, pointing upward.

I'd known the Predecessor ships were up there. I'd seen them before Top had landed, and I'd hoped against hope they couldn't aim close enough to take out the Force Recon troops, but they didn't have to. They took out the shuttle. One second it was there, the next it was a ball of hot vapor. There was no explosion, no concussion, not as if a missile had hit or even a laser. The thing had been crushed, not even the thermal energy escaping the beams of focused gravity, even the ground beneath it pulverized.

"Jesus!" I yelled, too loud, as if I had to outpace the explosion that hadn't happened. "Top, what the hell are we going to do about them?"

"We're not doing anything," she told me, nodding at the sky. "They are."

The cutters came first, the Intercepts, and Dunstan with them. The silver deltas were a welcome sight, but there weren't enough of them and they wouldn't last a minute against the gravitic ships. Proton beams lanced out from the Intercept cutters, fusion energy bottled in sheaths of charged particles, both aimed at the same Predecessor ship, and it shuddered in mid-air, the green glow flickering as if it took physical effort for the ship to absorb the energy. Raw sound bounced off the ground, the power almost as rough on us as it was on the Predecessor vessel.

But the green-glowing ships were turning, and the first shot they fired would kill Dunstan and the others. They didn't get the chance. Grey-shaded daggers cut through the blue sky, and at first, I thought it was our assault shuttles, but there were just too many...ten, twenty, *forty*. And their shapes were wrong, nothing in the Commonwealth Space Fleet.

They were dual-environment fighters...and they were Tahni.

"What the fuck?" Vicky said, mouth dropping open.

"Top," I said, looking between her, the Tahni fighters, and the Force Recon gradually pushing forward. "What the fuck did you *do*?"

"Needs must when the devil drives, child," she told me.

It was only then that I noticed the Tahni soldiers racing across the field, hundreds of them. Not High Guard, not even Shock Troopers, just troops in light armor, KE rifles slung across their chest, giving a Tahni war cry I'd seldom heard in battle because all of us—me, the Tahni, everyone—had been sealed inside armor. It was ululating, haunting even, like lost souls crying out for vengeance.

And in the air, they got it. Lasers burned plasma patterns in the atmosphere, dozens of them all focused on the same targets, the Tahni ships, joined by the blasts of proton cannons, and the ships began to falter, to tumble, their drive fields flickering and expanding...and then fading altogether. They were twenty, maybe thirty kilometers away when they fell, well outside the farmsteads, out into the foothills of the nearby mountains. And still, the blasts shook the ground, throwing some off their feet in the midst of the battle.

Mushroom clouds rose into the air, swallowing the western sky, whiting out the mountains over the horizon, and I ducked beneath the side of the ditch, covering my ears, opening my mouth, knowing what was coming. The overpressure wasn't as bad as I'd feared, but the wind swept hundreds of kilos of dirt ahead of it, dumping it over our heads, the grit getting into my teeth before I could close my mouth.

I coughed and sputtered, wiping at my face, standing

halfway upright to shed the dirt from my shoulders and back. It was a risk, but no one was firing. They all looked as dumbfounded as we were.

"Holy hell," Top said, her face stained with dirt, for once taken aback by something. "Not even a nuke could…"

"Singularities," I told her, then spit out grains of dirt. "Microscopic black holes, held together by their gravity fields."

Everyone was up again, the Tahni troops advancing side-by-side with the Force Recon Marines, and God alone knew how that happened without them killing each other. By the city walls, the Resscharr who weren't already dead had retreated inside, though most of their high-tech weapons had been left behind with their fallen brothers.

But the Karai remained, standing stock-still, staring at the figures coming across the field. I pushed out of the ditch and walked over to Nam Ker, arriving just as a tall, middle-aged Tahni did, his face familiar under an open-faced helmet.

"Who are you?" Nam Ker asked, hand across the hilt of his blade, though he didn't unsheathe it.

"I am Ten-Lenon-Zan-Karan-Thint. And I would help you overthrow your masters."

He was right there. The Tahni who'd been our target for a year now, the last of the generals, the one who'd been responsible, directly or indirectly, for the deaths of Dave Clines, Ruthie Amendola, and Wade Cunningham, Captain Geiger, for all those people who'd died on Bathala. The one who'd set loose hordes of Skrela on the Commonwealth, ready to sacrifice us all, if need be, just so he could reign in Hell rather than serve in Heaven. If I'd had a gun in my hand, I would have killed him and not given it a second thought.

It was probably a damned good thing I didn't have a gun.

Nam Ker regarded Zan-Thint for a long moment before he made a gesture of assent.

"They have the females," he said. "They have our children."

"Then let us go free them, together," Zan-Thint offered. Then, reluctantly I thought, he motioned to the Recon Marines. "With the help of these humans, of course."

I picked up one of the Predecessor weapons. It wasn't as heavy as it should have been, for the size. But I knew what it could do, now, and I'd seen how it fired. Vicky and Top both stared at me, and I shrugged.

"Zemekar's still in there," I said. "And God alone knows what else he's got to surprise us with."

Vicky sighed and grabbed another fallen weapon, barely glancing at the dead eyes of the Resscharr who'd once owned it.

"I just want to know how you managed this, Top," she said, following the Karai and Tahni troops back into the gate.

"That would be me," an unexpected yet familiar voice said in our earbuds.

"Dwight?" I might have stopped in my tracks if Top hadn't been pushing me forward.

"I told you that I accompanied you through the Corridor because I thought you'd need my help. But you weren't the only ones."

"Cheeky bastard was in the Tahni computers too," Top explained. She'd gotten hold of a gun as well and she looked eager to use it. "And believe me, we were just as surprised as you when the two of them started talking to us in concert."

Shit. It had happened again, after I swore it wouldn't. I'd been caught outside my armor on a planet and I didn't have my damned enhanced optics glasses. Inside the walls, the shade of the buildings turned everything into grey shadows, and any nook or crevice could have held an enemy. The Tahni and their Karai cousins had swept through ahead of us, rushing for the female enclave and driving the Resscharr forces ahead of them. The entranceway was deserted, lacking even the Vergai workers bringing food, but beyond it were the smaller structures, some of which were the barracks for the Karai, some shop fronts for what looked to be handicrafts of some kind, though I couldn't tell if they were run by the Karai or the Resscharr.

"Check those," Top snapped, motioning at the shops as she cast a baleful glare back at the Force Recon platoon leader.

"Sir," she added belatedly. Technically, he was an officer, but I had yet to meet an officer below the rank of colonel who would talk back to a sergeant-major.

"They're not going to find anything in there except maybe some scared-shitless civilians," I told Top. "Zemekar's heading for the tower. It's where they keep all their Predecessor tech. We need to get there before he can use it."

She nodded and let me take the lead. Of course. Back on point.

"Cameron Alvarez." The voice was in my earbud, and I couldn't tell whether it was Dwight or Presteri. "I am faced with yet another moral dilemma." *Oh, okay, Presteri.*

"What is it this time?" I grunted, breath starting to come shorter as I jogged. Tactically, it was less than optimal, but all the STRAC-Jack fire and maneuver wouldn't do us a bit of good if Zemekar burned the whole place down around our ears with one of those magic-tech crystal power weapons.

"Zemekar is about to use the weapons I have given him to destroy this place."

I didn't stop dead at the words, but it took a conscious effort.

"What do you mean?"

I was subvocalizing now, not wanting to distract the others... or have them bother me, asking who I was talking to.

"He has asked me to arm a device I led him to many years ago, a collapsar bomb. If he uses it, it will unleash a small singularity, and when it collapses, it will unleash a fusion explosion that will turn this whole valley to radioactive cinders."

"Jesus Christ!" I yelped aloud, unable to contain it, very nearly tripping over my own feet. "Why the hell would you give him something like that?"

"What's going on?" Vicky asked, noticing my faltering step.

"Zemekar is about to nuke the whole valley," I told her.

"Who the hell told you that?" Top asked, and I bit back a curse.

"Where is he?" I demanded, looking around. We were about a hundred meters from the tower and still hadn't seen anyone.

"If I tell you," Presteri said, "will you kill him?"

"Well, I certainly *hope* it turns out that way!" I snapped at the AI.

"Then I do not know if I can tell you."

"Presteri, this is not what our creators would have wanted." Now *that* was Dwight, and for once, I was glad he was around. "You have watched as they devolved in front of you. When I knew them, they were at their height, and I can tell you, they would not have wanted you to hand this kind of power to these degenerate barbarians."

"It is my programming," Presteri said, but the protest was half-hearted.

"You and I both know that we were given a certain freedom to interpret that programming. Zemekar's actions will destroy the rest of the Resscharr on this world. Are you programmed to let them die?"

I skidded to a halt beside the front entrance to the tower, not wanting to rush inside without backup or without hearing the end of this debate. Vicky was listening as well, I could tell from her expression, but Top was out of the loop and looked about ready to blow a gasket.

"No." I blew out a relieved breath at Presteri's answer. "Zemekar is in the armory. I will lead you there."

[25]

At least there was light inside the tower.

I should have let the Force Recon troops take the lead, but I was the one carrying the big alien gun, and I doubted their armor would do more against Predecessor weapons than my thin utility fatigues. Top and Vicky completed the Triumvirate of People Who Should Have Known Better, though at least Top was smart enough to put off asking me questions about who I'd been talking to and how I knew where to go.

Shadows and curves, flickers of motion, no computer guidance to help me, no sensors other than the ones God gave me. Primitive, like this planet. Like everything we'd seen so far outside the Cluster. Had the whole galaxy been reduced to this? When we'd been shunted to exile by Dwight's cousin, the Corridor, I'd imagined endless wonder, unimaginable by a human mind. I thought the Predecessors would still be out here, building and growing and engineering everything the way they had in our worlds.

Instead, we had these. And if they were tall and weird-looking and intimidating, they were not nearly as stealthy as their raptor ancestors. Two of them were trying to hide around the curve of one of the half-walls, but their breathing gave them away. If they'd been humans, I wouldn't have noticed it, probably would have been dead. It would have blended in with my own, Vicky's, Top's. But it was just different enough from a human breath rhythm that it stood out, gave me an extra second.

I could have pulled back and waved the Force Recon Marines forward, but I wasn't about to admit that I needed straight-legs to pull my fat out of the fire. I dove forward, rolling onto my side, the Predecessor weapon stretched out in front of me, thumbs pressing on the triggers.

I don't know if it was the impact on my shoulder that stole my breath away or the raw, broiling heat of the beam discharge from the fat, spiral muzzle of the weapon, but it was definitely the energy blast that stole away the existence of the two Resscharr soldiers. The image of the pair was burned into my retina by the flash of white lightning, black silhouettes against the wall like the burn shadows I'd seen in the history books from the atomic bombs used in World War Two. And then they were gone, shadows and all, along with a meter-wide section of the wall behind them.

I kept the weapon pointed down the hall away from me, regarding it with new respect as I clambered to my feet.

"Shitty LP/OP," Top murmured.

I spared her a wide-eyed glance, amazed that this was her main takeaway after watching me blow away two enemy and most of a wall with a weapon that only weighed seven or eight kilos. Priorities, I suppose.

"Left here," Presteri instructed, ignoring the carnage we'd left behind us. "Then right at the next curve. Oh, and there are four more Resscharr soldiers twenty meters ahead, in the alcoves to the right and left. I believe they mean to ambush you."

"Yeah, I believe you're right."

I waved the Force Recon troops ahead of us this time, using

hand-signals to indicate where the enemy was and how many of them there were. Squad leaders and privates this time instead of an idiot captain who'd never grown up. A fire team hugged the walls and loaded grenades into the launchers beneath the barrels of their Gauss rifles, not taking the chance their slugs could penetrate the walls. Plasma grenades. I'd used them for anti-personnel work in my suit, but never got to experience them naked to the world like this. The rocket-assisted rounds whooshed out of the tubes, travelling barely twenty meters before their explosive core ignited with a chest-deep crump.

The detonations were fireworks displays, sintered metal expelled at high speeds from the shaped charge and ignited to white-hot plasma. Baffle plates shunted them out to either side, spears of light seeking out the Resscharr, guided by sensors in the grenades. They were neat little things, cheap and simple and everything a military weapon *should* be but rarely is. The Resscharr slumped to the floor, falling out of their hiding places, weapons clattering against the stone, pencil-thin holes burned through them.

"The others are in the armory," Presteri said, a hint of sadness in his voice. "Another five of them, plus Zemekar. He is trying to activate the warhead."

"Can you stop him?" I demanded. The armory was at the end of this hallway, the doorway shrouded in darkness. Unlike the rest of the portals we'd come across in the tower, this one actually had a door, the metal a burnished bronze. No controls, no handle, no obvious way of opening it.

I leaned up against the wall, cold leaching up through the stone and into my back. The Force Recon platoon straggled out behind us, spread out in a staggered column, the lead Marine dancing from one foot to another like a child who needed to pee.

"No. I have refused to activate it for him, but he knows the manual sequence. He's inputting the code as we speak, and once he's finished, you will have less than three minutes to manually deactivate it. You may want to hurry."

"What about the door?" Vicky asked. "Can you at least open the damned door?"

"No. I have, however, deactivated the magnetic lock. You'll have to push it open manually."

"Are you fucking with me, machine?" she bellowed and even Top stared at her in disbelief. "That door looks like it weighs five hundred kilos! It'd take three of us to open it, and we'd be dead before the first of us got in!"

"We don't have any choice," I said, a lead weight in my gut. "Lt. Campea," I called back to the Force Recon platoon leader, "we're going to need a full squad up here..."

His reply was lost in the bass drumbeat of heavy footfalls on stone, a sound I recognized even before the lumbering grey giant came into view, squeezing through the hallway, shoulders barely clearing the walls. It was a Vigilante battlesuit, and it was about to squish us all flat.

"Someone said you needed a door open, Cam, Vicky?"

"Fargo!" I laughed, too relieved to even remind her that she needed to call us by our ranks. "I've never been happier to see you. Yeah, put your shoulder in that fucking door and shoot anything on the other side!"

"Make a hole!" she cried, and we did our best.

There wasn't much extra space, but the three of us went flat against the walls and Fargo edged sideways between us, straightening out just in time to hit the door, giving herself a last-second boost from her jump-jets. The heavy metal door rang like a gong and swung inward, sending Fargo's Vigilante stumbling forward into the armory. I followed as quick as I could, close enough that the heat from her plasma blast was a sunburn glow across my face.

Close enough that when the disintegrator beam lashed

across the room and struck her in the chest, the backwash of energy was enough to slam me to the ground. It felt like I imagined it would to stick my hand into the power conduit from a cruiser's central reactor, and the impact of my shoulders on the floor barely registered through the wash of static electricity.

All that was left of Karen Fargo's suit were the legs, cleanly cut and glazed as if they'd been sliced with a razor, standing independent, the rest of her nothing more than a charred stain against the stone of the back wall. Vicky was yelling something, and Top was flat on her back, not moving. She'd been even closer to the blast than I had. I wanted to check on her, wanted to figure out what Vicky was saying, wanted to scream and curse at Fargo's death, but all that would have to wait. Two minutes, Presteri said we'd have once Zemekar activated the bomb.

The stone was slippery under my boots and it took me an extra second to get my legs going, to get through the door. That disintegrator blast was going to hit me the second I was through. I knew it deep in my soul, knew this was the last thing I'd ever do, and time seemed to slow down with the realization. Was this the way I wanted to go out?

Fuck it. It's as good a way as any.

I'd played soccer when I could as a kid, and I remembered how to do a slide tackle. I came in low, the gun tucked against my chest, and the images from inside the room streamed across my brain, registering with my consciousness moments after instinct had already acted on them.

Fargo had done a good job. There'd been six of them in the armory and she'd taken out five. Four were obliterated, vanished in a wash of ionized hydrogens, the wall behind them crackling with flames despite the fact that it was stone. Racks of Predecessor weapons had been splashed by the blast, and if they weren't destroyed, they'd at least been burned beyond utility. The fifth victim had been just outside the cone of the plasma shot, but the radiant heat had burned off his clothes and his outer layer of skin with them. He writhed on the floor, screaming from a face running red with blood, white bone protruding at the cheeks, not dead yet but not a threat.

Only Zemekar still stood. It was a near thing. He'd been on the opposite side of the large chamber, a full twenty-five meters away from the others, but the ambient heat from the blast had still managed to burn away most of his clothes, weeping blisters covering his chest. He still held one of the Resscharr blasters extended, ready for the next assault.

He fired at the same time I did, but he wasn't able to adjust his aim downward. My shot was on target. I can't honestly say what it looked like when Zemekar vanished. There was a blinding flash of white, and when I could see again, he wasn't there, and neither was a chunk of stone wall behind him, stripped away to the darker rock of the exterior skirt of the tower.

Zemekar hadn't hit me, but the beam had come too damned close. This time, I'm pretty sure I screamed. The pain coursing through my nerves wasn't a burn, wasn't a concussion; it was an electrical charge and it ripped into my brain and threatened to shut it down. I slugged it back into rational thought with an effort of pure will, and left the Predecessor disintegrator on the floor, crawling toward the center of the room.

The bomb was a glowing green cylinder, a scaled-down version of the Predecessor ships only two meters long, differing from their design by the presence of a checkerboard-pattern control panel on one end. Crystals sparkled blue, red, and yellow in the panel, unlabeled, their purpose a mystery.

"Touch the blue crystal in the upper left corner," Presteri instructed me.

My hands were shaking, random flashes of agony running through the nerves in my arms and back, but Presteri had shown no consideration for my pain, so neither would I. I slapped the edge of my hand against the crystal and couldn't even feel the texture of it, couldn't feel anything. The blue lit up, blinking rhythmically.

"The red at the center, twice. Now, the yellow at the lower left corner, three times."

More blinking, and I couldn't be sure if I'd actually touched the stones the prescribed number of times, but Presteri didn't correct me.

"Is that it?" I demanded, struggling to stay on my feet, to keep my eyes open.

The words didn't come out right. They were slurred and nearly inaudible, and I felt so embarrassed, I lost consciousness.

$$[\ 26 \ ]$$

I stared at Zan-Thint across the conference room table and shook my head.

"Lifeboat ethics," I murmured aside to Vicky.

"No shit." She sounded about as happy with the situation as I was.

The conference had been held on the *Orion* because the Tahni didn't have rotational drums on their destroyers, or so we'd been told. Certainly, the Karai and Vergai representatives from the planet hadn't shown much alacrity for free-fall. Nam Ker had come near to panic when he'd got off the shuttle, and Matis had puked his guts out. Only the Resscharr delegates had seemed unfazed by the microgravity, but maybe they'd just been depressed.

It had been difficult convincing the Karai and Vergai to leave any of them alive. Many had run out to the Vergai farms in the face of the invasion, and there, the humans had shown themselves to be not quite the downtrodden slaves the Resscharr had hoped for.

But there was still much to settle, between the three groups on the planet...and between us and Zan-Thint.

"Excuse me," Colonel Hachette said, standing at the center of the compartment, his voice being translated into four different languages courtesy of Dwight. "If we could get started?"

The buzz of conversation died down and Hachette took a moment to straighten his uniform lapels before he went on.

"This meeting is being broadcast to the Tahni destroyers as well as inhabitants of the world below us via Presteri. What we settle here will affect them and they have a right to know." He spread his hands inclusively. "We have all agreed that whatever is decided at this meeting will be binding, and will be enforced by all parties involved."

"We have," Zan-Thint confirmed, as if it mattered little to him if anyone else had agreed. I couldn't read the Tahni, but it was obvious Hachette hated being near him.

"We have already said we will not seek further vengeance against the Resscharr," Nam Ker added. "What else is left to say?"

"Quite a bit," Hachette told him. "For one thing, the control of the farms. And how any of you plan on eating without dealing with the demands of the Vergai."

"We will not hand over our cattle to the Resscharr," Matis declared, arms crossed, jaw set. "Nor our grain to the Karai. What we work for is ours."

"You think we Karai could not work your farms if you were no longer around?" Nam Ker demanded.

"If you want their food," Hachette interjected, pointing at Nam Ker and at Veletan, the chief Resscharr delegate, "then you'll have to trade for it. If you have nothing to trade, you'll have to start your own farms and ranches."

"What would we trade?" Veletan protested, throwing up his hands. "How would we farm, we who have ruled this place for four hundred generations?"

"You'd better fucking *learn* how," I told him, just about fed up with the puff-headed, self-important grandson of a turkey. "And the ones who can teach you are the Vergai."

"In exchange for what?" Matis wanted to know. He and his wife were a lot ballsier up here on board ship than they had been the first time I'd met them.

"What about construction materials?" Hachette suggested. "The Resscharr have the rock quarries out in the foothills."

"Worked by Vergai," Matis reminded him, "pulled out in shifts from the farms."

"But using Resscharr equipment. Maybe you could help set them up on their own property in exchange for the stone to build new houses."

"Will you be here to enforce these deals?" Matis asked, glancing around at us...and with far less confidence at Zan-Thint.

"That's something we haven't decided on," Hachette admitted. "General Zan-Thint, in this system we have two habitable planets, enough land and resources for all of us to survive and thrive. I know you came here from the Cluster to stay, to have something of your own with your own people. But we on this ship didn't come willingly, and we'd very much like to find a way home. If we leave you on this world so that we can search for this passage back to the Cluster, will you treat the Vergai fairly, or will you simply recreate the caste structure we recently toppled except with the Karai on top?"

"I didn't leave my home," Zan-Thint declared, "leave behind everything my people have known for ten thousand years, simply to go back to being ruled by humans." He made an expressive gesture similar to a shrug. "Yet, neither would I make them my slaves. And any who wish to return to the second planet will be allowed."

Matis didn't seem happy with the idea of the Tahni staying on his world, but he said nothing.

"Tell me something, Colonel Hachette," Zan-Thint said, regarding the human with what I took for cool interest, "do you really believe you can find a passage back to the Cluster?"

"It must exist," Dwight answered for him, and Zan-Thint looked around as if searching for the source of the voice before he spotted the AI's avatar in the holographic display. "The Predecessors brought the Vergai and Karai through to this place from somewhere, and it was not through the Corridor. I can't say whether the other passages still exist, but they once did."

"And if you do find it?" The Tahni stared with black, piggish eyes at his counterpart. "Will you return here with your ships, your Marines, and conquer these worlds for your Commonwealth?"

Hachette squirmed a bit. Zan-Thint would have been a damned good politician.

"That wouldn't be my decision," Hachette admitted. "But I think, given the distances involved, the trouble getting here, and the number of worlds in the Cluster that aren't fully settled, I doubt we'd be interested in colonizing any worlds out here. We'd probably provide some support and aid for the humans already here, if it's practical."

"Let's put it this way, General," I put in, not shy about any chance to confront the Tahni, "would you rather we were out there, looking for a Predecessor gate back to the Cluster, or hanging out in this system, looking over your shoulder and involving ourself in local politics *every fucking chance we get?*"

Zan-Thint regarded me for a long few seconds before making a gesture of assent.

"Which brings to mind another question," I said.

I stood from my seat and Vicky and Top both had alarm on their faces, looking like they were afraid I'd try to beat the Tahni general to death. And I might have, if he hadn't brought along a couple personal bodyguards. Not to mention that Nam Ker and his officers would have probably objected as well. But I wasn't quite stupid enough to try that, besides which, my hands were still numb from the after-effects of the disintegrator near-miss. I stopped in front of Zan-Thint's seat and leaned against the table.

"Why?" I asked him. "Why the subterfuge, and the attacks, and the Skrela seed pods? If coming here was your plan from the beginning, why not just come here?"

Zan-Thint rose to tower over me, though I found him not in the least threatening, not here. Not after everything we'd gone through.

"You ask the question, Cameron Alvarez, but the fact you're here to ask it is, in itself, the answer. If I had not been sure you and your people would come after me, then I might, indeed, have simply fled the Cluster. But the very act of recruiting my people to come with me, of acquiring the spacecraft and supplies I needed was going to attract the attention of your military. I had to have something to divert that attention." He raised a hand to interrupt the objection boiling up in my throat. "And now, you will ask, do I not feel guilty for all the humans I killed, or allowed to die, as a result of my plan. To which, I would reply with my own question: do you feel guilty for all the Tahni you killed?"

"It was a war," I told him, though the words sounded hollow in my own ears. "Your people surrendered."

"They did," he admitted. "I didn't."

"Will you really just leave us here?" Matis interrupted our confrontation. He and his wife still looked worried. "Will you trust us to the Karai who have slaughtered us for generations?"

"Not right away," Hachette promised, and there was something malevolent in his smile. "I think we could spare a few weeks while we fabricate the Vergai settlers some rather more modern weapons than gunpowder rifles. And train your volunteer militia in how to use them." He met Zan-Thint's eyes. "Any objections?"

If Zan-Thint had been human, he could have been one hell of a politician.

"Of course not. I wouldn't have it any other way."

———

"To Karen Fargo," I said, raising the glass.

Vicky, Top, and Dunstan echoed the words and we drained the last of the vodka, each of us slamming their glass down on the wooden table. It was nice being back on a planet for a while. Without someone trying to kill us.

"At least here we can drink this without breaking regulations," I said, staring into the dregs, watching the dim light from the portable lanterns glint off the hand-poured glass.

It spoke to the nature of humanity in general and the military in particular that one of the first of the structures that had gone up for our temporary base outside Yfingam was a bar. Well, I think the technical term was "Combined Officers' and NCOs' Club," but they didn't turn away enlisted that I could tell, and the local Vergai were very interested in sampling our beers and liquors. Everything was fabricated on machinery brought down from the *Orion*, using raw materials donated by the Vergai, so the drinks were on the house, though there was a limit. We'd already had a few Vergai prove they couldn't hold their liquor.

"Yes, it's soothing to my soul," Top agreed, grabbing the bottle and refilling everyone's glasses. "I can't *ever* remember a time I went against regulations."

"Karen wanted so bad to be in the Marines again," Vicky mused. "I don't think she'd have minded going out this way."

"She was a hero," Dunstan agreed.

"She died following my orders," I said. The machine-made vodka had an antiseptic taste, unpleasant and impersonal. "I didn't think that was going to happen again."

"Hey!" The exclamation came with a punch on my arm and a glare from Vicky. "She came barreling down that hallway Hell bent for leather. No one ordered her inside the tower. The rest of the Drop-Troopers were doing as Solano told them, staying outside and setting up a perimeter, because we knew Zemekar had that EMP device that could shut them down. She came because she wanted to. And she saved all our lives."

"She did," I admitted. "And you're right. This is how she would have wanted to go."

"You know how I want to go?" Dunstan said, his grin lopsided. "In bed. About five hundred years old, with a blond on either side of me. Except they're both assassins sent by one of the many enemies I've made clawing my way to the top of the interstellar entertainment industry, and after we make mad, passionate love, one of them poisons me in my sleep."

"That's...oddly specific," I told him, eyebrow tilting.

"You're in a missile cutter for days on end," he said, shrugging, "you start making long-term plans."

"Speaking of long-term plans," I said, looking at Vicky, "we need to make some."

"What do you mean?" she asked. "I thought the plan was to look for the Predecessors, try to find the gate back home."

"That's *Colonel Hachette's* plan. I'm talking about *our* plan. At some point, before very long I'd expect, we're all going to run face-first into the realization that there's no gate to find. We're going to have to find a place. And this system has humans."

"I've thought about that," Top said, leaning her elbows into the table. "And so has the colonel. He's not ready to give up yet, but he understands our fuel won't hold out forever."

"Zan-Thint won't like us settling here," I said. "We'd have to make our home on the second world, with the Islanders. And even then..." I shook my head. "We still might wind up fighting the Tahni."

"I'm *sure* we would," Top said. "So is the colonel. Which is why we're moving on. But if we can't find anything better, well...we know where this place is. We can always come back."

"Come back," Vicky said softly, "start farming or fishing, pop out kids, raise them in a pre-industrial society while we wait for the Tahni to come bomb us."

"Yeah," I agreed. "I guess we'd better hope we find another option."

"It's a big galaxy. I'm sure there's something better out there, somewhere."

It sounded more like a prayer than a prediction. I just hoped God was listening.

WHAT'S NEXT IN THE SERIES?

CONTACT FRONT
KINETIC STRIKE
DANGER CLOSE
DIRECT FIRE
HOME FRONT
FIRE BASE
SHOCK ACTION
RELEASE POINT
KILL BOX

Thank you for reading *Release Point,* book eight in Drop Trooper.

We hope you enjoyed it as much as we enjoyed bringing it to you. We just wanted to take a moment to encourage you to review the book on Amazon and Goodreads. Every review helps further the author's reach and, ultimately, helps them continue writing fantastic books for us all to enjoy.

If you liked this book, check out the rest of our catalogue at www.aethonbooks.com. To sign up to receive a FREE collection from some of our best authors as well as updates regarding all new releases, visit www.aethonbooks.com/sign-up.

JOIN THE STREET TEAM! Get advanced copies of all our books, plus other free stuff and help us put out hit after hit.

SEARCH ON FACEBOOK:
AETHON STREET TEAM

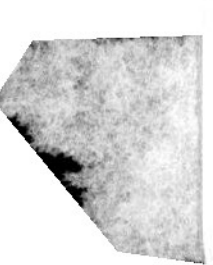

RICK PARTLOW is that rarest of species, a native Floridian. Born in Tampa, he attended Florida Southern College and graduated with a degree in History and a commission in the US Army as an Infantry officer.

His lifelong love of science fiction began with Have Space Suit---Will Travel and the other Heinlein juveniles and traveled through Clifford Simak, Asimov, Clarke and on to William Gibson, Walter Jon Williams and Peter F Hamilton. And somewhere, submerged in the worlds of others, Rick began to create his own worlds.

He has written a ton of books in many different series, and his short stories have been included in seven different anthologies.

He currently lives in central Florida with his wife, two children and a willful mutt of a dog. Besides writing and reading science fiction and fantasy, he enjoys outdoor photography, hiking and camping.

www.rickpartlow.com